Rosemary Rowe is the maiden name of author Rosemary Aitken, who was born in Cornwall during the Second World War. She is a highly qualified academic, and has written more than a dozen best-selling textbooks on English language and communication. She has written fiction for many years under her married name. Rosemary has two children and also two grandchildren living in New Zealand, where she herself lived for twenty years. She now divides her time between Gloucestershire and Cornwall.

Acclaim for Rosemary Rowe's Libertus series:

'The story is agreeably written, gets on briskly with its plot, and ends with a highly satisfactory double-take solution' Gerald Kaufman, *Scotsman*

'Libertus is a thinking man's hero . . . a delightful whodunnit which is fascinating in the detail of its research and the charm of its detective team' *Huddersfield Daily Examiner*

'The character of Libertus springs to life. A must for anyone interested in Roman Britain' Paul Doherty

'The characters are believable, the action well paced and the twists and turns of the plot keep the reader on his/her toes' *Historical Novels Review*

'Rowe has had the clever idea of making her detective-figure a mosaicist, and, therefore, an expert in puzzles and patterns. Into the bargain, he is a freed Celtic slave, and thus an outsider to the brutalities of the conquerors, and a character with whom the reader can sympathise' *Independent*

'Superb characterisation and evocation of Roman Britain. It transports you back to those times. An entirely compelling historical mystery' Michael Jecks

'Cunningly drawn and the very devil to fathom until the final pages' *Coventry Evening Telegra*

D1462720

ENEMIES OF THE EMPIRE

Rosemary Rowe

headline

First published in 2005
by HEADLINE BOOK PUBLISHING

First published in paperback in 2005
by HEADLINE BOOK PUBLISHING

10 9 8 7 6 5 4 3 2

ISBN 0 7553 0519 1

Typeset in Plantin by Avon DataSet Ltd,
Bidford-on-Avon, Warwickshire

Printed and bound in Great Britain by
Mackays of Chatham plc, Chatham, Kent

Headline's policy is to use papers that are natural, renewable and
recyclable products and made from wood grown in sustainable forests.
The logging and manufacturing processes are expected to conform to the
environmental regulations of the country of origin.

HEADLINE BOOK PUBLISHING
A division of Hodder Headline
338 Euston Road
London NW1 3BH

www.headline.co.uk
www.hodderheadline.com

To John and Linda – with much love.

Foreword

Enemies of the Empire is set in the early weeks of AD 188, at a time when most of Britain was a Roman province, administered by a single governorship answerable directly to Rome, where the increasingly unbalanced Emperor Commodus still wore the imperial purple and ruled the Empire with an autocratic and capricious hand.

Interestingly, at this period the outgoing governor, Pertinax, had recently been promoted to the more prestigious North African provinces, from where he would shortly rise to become Prefect of Rome (second only in importance to Commodus himself) and ultimately – and briefly – Emperor. Since there is no reliable evidence to show the precise date of his departure from Britannia or, strangely, the name of his successor, this novel, like its predecessor, postulates that Pertinax continued to maintain nominal control over both provinces at once, using local appointees until a new governor could be installed. (This is entirely speculative, of course, and probably unlikely, but such an arrangement is not impossible and there are historical precedents elsewhere.)

The province over which he ruled was the northernmost outpost of the Roman Empire, occupied by Roman legions, criss-crossed by Roman roads, and subject to Roman laws and taxes. Most of the quarrelsome local tribes had settled into an uneasy peace, but there were still sporadic clashes in the border areas to the north and – as in this narrative – the west, where there was a long history of opposition to Roman rule.

It had been the policy, when an area was first colonised, for Rome to seek alliances with tribal chiefs, who were then often installed as local 'kings' or given high posts and honours in the new administration. It was an effective practice, and was successfully followed in Britannia, as elsewhere. Tribes which persisted in revolt, or continued to resist the new regime even after they had been offered terms, were summarily dealt with – as massacres such as that at Maiden Castle testify.

But there were those who continued to rebel. The best-known revolt, by an alliance of tribes in the south-east led by the Icenian Queen Boudicca, had some success at first – killing large numbers of the occupying troops and burning half of the new Roman capital (Londinium) – but was afterwards ruthlessly suppressed.

Some fifteen years before Boudicca, and far off to the west, the so-called 'king' Caractacus, supported by the red-haired Silurian tribe and the wild and warlike Ordovices slightly to the north, held out against the might of Rome for almost two years before he was captured and led in chains to Rome. The spirit of rebellion did not die with him and throughout the second century the western borders were a byword for unrest.

There is no evidence of trouble during the period covered by the novel, but there is mention only a few years earlier of continued skirmishing and ambushes on military supply trains in the area. Indeed, it was so troublesome that the Romans made special arrangements to deal with it. Apart from the permanent garrisons along the fortified frontier ('Offa's Dyke' is almost certainly built on a Roman wall) they brought in the system of so-called 'marching-camps', where legionary and auxiliary forces were maintained in tented camps, ready to move quickly in support in case of insurrection or disturbance. Many of these camps were disbanded after the Iceni revolt and the troops were moved to serve elsewhere, but a few remained throughout our period, and one is mentioned in the narrative – though there probably was no camp so near to Venta (Caerwent) at this time.

Caerwent is now a smallish settlement, but in AD 188 it was a thriving town, straddling the main road from Glevum (modern Gloucester) to the border garrison at Isca (Caerleon). It was the tribal capital, or 'civitas', of the Silurians and the centre for local administration of the area. Many of the ruined buildings have been disinterred and are visible today, and it is clear that the town was Roman in design, with a forum, basilica, mansio, and bath-house roughly in the positions suggested in the text. There is also what may have been a fuller-dyer's shop, and perhaps a butcher's too, but I have taken liberties with the locations of these. (There is no indication of a lupinarium, although most large towns had at least one licensed brothel somewhere within the walls.)

There is no evidence at all that the town was divided into opposing factions, as suggested in the narrative, although a letter from first-century Judaea hints at the kind of 'protection racket' mentioned in the tale, proving that it was not unknown within the Empire. Certainly key members of local families who had historically supported Rome were likely to be Roman citizens by now, with all the legal privileges that implied, and have positions of civic responsibility; other free-born men were not so fortunate and no doubt harboured grudges and ambitions of their own, even if they had acquired wealth as many traders did.

Of course, not all freemen were wealthy. Many were simple shopkeepers and craftsmen in the town, or farmers in the local area. Some might be peasants scratching a bare living from unforgiving land, or working long hours in stinking fuller's shops and other industries. Some were known to sell themselves into slavery to survive. For of course, as in the rest of the Roman Empire, the real economy of Venta depended on the slaves, who had no rights of any kind and were the mere 'living tools' of their owners. Many had harsh masters and wretched lives but there are instances of genuine affection, such as Libertus exhibits towards his Junio.

Although Venta was on the outskirts of the Roman world, inscriptions and records suggest that most people probably spoke Latin, for trade and administration purposes at least, even if Celtic dialects survived at home. The presence of a Roman temple suggests that the Roman deities were worshipped, while a Celtic temple just outside the walls implies that older gods were not ignored. (The Romans were generally tolerant of local deities, and often subsumed them under Roman ones – Mars, for instance, was equated with a good many native gods.) Christianity was not at this time a forbidden religion, although the refusal of its adherents to sacrifice to the imperial gods could lead to persecution if the culprit was denounced. Only Druidism was a capital offence, perhaps because it was equated with human sacrifice and the cult of severed heads: there are several terrifying descriptions of the sacred groves.

The Romano-British background to this book is derived from exhibitions, excavations, interviews with experts and a

picto... ...y of (sometimes contradictory) written an...
although I... This is, however, a work of fiction and
there is no claim ... my best to create an accurate picture,

Relata refero. Ne lupt... academic authenticity.
you what I heard. Jove himse... *m omnibus placet.* (I only tell
...'t please everybody.)

Chapter One

'A civic banquet in your honour, Excellence? Here in Venta? Tonight?' I stared at my wealthy patron in dismay.

I had never wanted to come to this remote tribal civitas in the first place. Two days of jogging and jolting in a heavy carriage along military roads is a punishing experience for ageing bones (and at fifty my bones are already far more aged than most) even when every hoofbeat does not take you nearer to the wild, forested outskirts of the Empire, where not only are there the usual hazards of brigands, wolves and bears, but there is always the entertaining possibility of a rebel ambush and a disaffected Silurian sword through your vitals.

Besides, I had left a wife and slaves at home, to say nothing of a new and lucrative commission for a memorial pavement for a fountain at the baths, bequeathed in his own honour under the will of a recently departed wealthy local citizen and councillor. But when His Excellence Marcus Aurelius Septimus – personal representative of the absent governor and my personal patron and protector – invites you to attend him on an official visit to the border legion at Isca, on the western frontier of the province, to say 'I'm sorry, I'd prefer to stay at home' is really not a possibility.

So here I was, draped in a wilting toga, travel-stained and sore. And we had not reached our destination yet, only a

1

mansio – a military inn and staging post – at Venta Silurum, the local capital, with the prospect of another day's travelling in view. 'Tonight?' I said again.

The last thing I wanted now was a wretched civic feast, where I would be expected to eat too much rich Roman food, drink too much Roman wine and endure not only eulogies about my host, but endless tributes to my patron too. And there would be tributes. Marcus is rumoured to be related to the Emperor and, until the new imperial governor arrives, is ruling this part of Britannia by depute. No dinner host would dare omit some appropriately fulsome homage as part of the after-dinner entertainment. It could go on for hours.

Marcus misinterpreted my anxiety. 'I'm sorry, Libertus, my old friend, but I'm afraid the invitation was for me alone. I've been asked to accompany the chief magistrate and open the local assizes in the morning, too. It's a bore, but it is an honour, naturally – lictors and processions, and all that sort of thing. Still, I'm not really expected to preside at any trials. There are no serious cases to be heard – nothing the local *civitas* authorities can't handle perfectly. We should be able to set off again by noon. Till then, I'll have to leave you at the mansio – no doubt our friend the *optio* here will take care of you.'

He nodded towards the youthful officer who was currently commanding this establishment: newly promoted by the look of him. His armour was so burnished it half dazzled you, and his dark hair was so severely cropped it looked like stubble corn. He was bristling with self-importance and eagerness to impress and was so overawed by my patron's presence here that he had come in person to bring us the dinner invitation from the messenger, and was now waiting by the door for some reply, his round face screwed into an earnest frown.

At Marcus's word he leapt towards us, almost tripping over his sandal-straps in his desire to help, 'Of course, Excellence. I'll have my cook prepare some food for this citizen at once . . .'

I flashed him my most ingratiating smile. 'Just bread and cheese would please me very well,' I said. I have eaten in a mansio before. There is always cold food for passing messengers, in a hurry to deliver the imperial post, and I wanted to avoid the stodgy bean and oatmeal stew on which the ordinary Roman army seems to march.

I need not have worried. The optio gave me a suspicious look and said, 'There is also some roast pork with fennel that you can have. We were preparing for His Excellence's coming.'

I nodded. A legionary soldier on the move has to prepare his own food, by and large, but in a mansio a common kitchen is the rule. No doubt the duty cook had done his best, expecting the arrival of the great, and I would be the one to profit by this effort at producing an exotic dish. I only hoped the cook was adequate. 'That would be delightful,' I replied, and was rewarded by a frosty smile.

'In that case,' Marcus said, rising to his feet and addressing the optio, 'you may tell the messenger that I accept. I shall retire to the bath-house and prepare. You can send two of my personal slaves to attend me there.' The young officer hurried off, and my patron turned to me. 'Libertus, my old friend, I shall leave you to your meal.' He extended a ringed hand for me to kiss. 'It is unfortunate, but there it is. One must do one's civic duty, after all.'

'Of course, Excellence,' I murmured, making a deep

3

obeisance and trying not to smile. Marcus is a much younger man than I am, and born and bred to Roman ways. Given the choice between a mansio meal, however carefully prepared, and being guest of honour at a lavish feast with good wine and slaves and perfumed dancing girls, I knew where his preference would lie. The prospect of an official procession, with cheering spectators and all the pomp of office, would not displease him, either. However, I did have a little sympathy. I knew, better than he did perhaps, what it was like to be obliged to go where one would prefer not to be. 'Don't worry about me, Excellence. It's been a tiring day.'

He patted my shoulder as he left the room. 'And you'll be glad to rest. I'll see you tomorrow, then. Goodnight.'

It was not quite the truth, I thought, as I struggled to my feet when he had gone. Now that I had an hour or two of daylight to myself, I had perversely decided on a little expedition of my own. Silurian gold and silver is famous everywhere – beautiful beaten work in sinous Celtic shapes – and it occurred to me that this was a perfect opportunity to acquire a silver cloak clasp for my poor abandoned wife. I knew that she had always wanted one. She had been unhappy at my leaving on this trip, although she understood the need as well as anyone and had tried to hide her feelings with a smile.

'Well, you will have to go, since Marcus wants you to, but I shall count the nights till you return again. It is such an inconvenient moment too, with that big commission for the fountain at the baths, and poor Junio with poison in his foot. I don't like you travelling without a slave.'

Junio, my workshop apprentice-cum-personal slave, had stepped upon a piece of jagged glass: his foot had swollen very nastily and although he was improving rapidly, it was obvious that I would have to leave him at home. 'Better if Junio stays here to mind the shop. He can produce some preliminary sketches for the memorial pavement, perhaps.' I have been teaching Junio the trade, and he has a talent for it. 'That way we can contrive to keep the contract for the job, and you can continue to treat his foot with herbs. If he recovers, get word to me and I will send for him. In the meantime, no doubt Marcus will provide me with a slave.'

And so he had. The lad was waiting for me in the ante-room, right now, with all the rest of Marcus's retinue: Promptillius, a dough-faced fellow with a foolish smile, who doubtless did his best and spoke when spoken to, but a poor substitute for my own impudent Junio, who often seemed to know what I required even before I'd thought of it myself, and whose comments and sharp understanding were a joy.

I thought of sending for my borrowed servant when the optio returned, which he did a moment afterwards, but my doughy-faced attendant was already at his heels. However, being Promptillius, he offered no remark but simply stationed himself politely at my back – which I have always found an inconvenient place for slaves, since one has to twist round to talk to them. I had mentioned this fact to him several times, but to no avail. Promptillius had been trained since birth in Marcus's house, and he invariably forgot.

I ignored him, and addressed myself to the optio, who was enquiring briskly when I wished to have my meal. Having expected to entertain the most important man in all of this part of Britannia, it had clearly injured his pride to find himself playing host to me instead – a mere pavement-maker, albeit one who had become a Roman citizen. Marcus had made no secret of my humble origins, or the fact that I had been captured as a slave and bequeathed my status on my master's death, even while boasting of his cleverness in finding me and using me to help him solve some intractable crimes. He did not add that I'd saved him more than once from political embarrassment, or that I'd been asked to Isca now because the commander there had expressed an interest in meeting me, after I'd solved the murder of his predecessor.

As far as the optio was concerned I was obviously just an upstart tradesman, with a wealthy patron but no influence, whom it was his unpleasant duty to feed and entertain. If I wanted his co-operation in my plans, a little flattery was clearly needed here.

I gave him a conspiratorial smile. 'I will eat a little later on, I think,' I said, choosing my words carefully. 'It will give your cook a little longer to prepare, and I had a trivial shopping trip in mind. Not something I could bother Marcus with, but I was wondering if you could give me some advice?' It was a gamble, making such an overt appeal to his self-importance, but I saw him preen. I hurried on. 'I was hoping to buy a silver dress-clasp for my wife. Perhaps you would care to join me in a glass of something, and tell me where I can find the best quality and at the lowest price?' I indicated the stool opposite, the one on which Marcus had been sitting earlier. 'A man like you, I'm sure you know the town.'

I saw him hesitate and then make up his mind. He thrust out his chest like a pigeon, took the stool, and shouted for the guard outside the door, who was soon dispatched to fetch two goblets and a jug of not-so-watered wine. Every mansio has a stock of such delights, available at a reasonable charge for the benefit of passing officers, and the optio's collaboration more than merited this small expenditure.

'Forum's the best place if you want a bargain,' he said confidentially, emptying his goblet at a gulp. 'I could give you a guard to go with you if you like, but it might be better if you find your way alone.'

'Better not to wear my toga, either, I suppose?' As a citizen – particularly a citizen in Marcus's retinue – I should have worn my formal garment in public at all times, according to the strict letter of the law, but for one thing it was travel-stained by now, and for another I hate wearing the cumbersome thing. 'Gives the wrong impression, do you think?'

He laughed. 'Any trader who sees you wearing that will immediately assume that you are rich, and raise his asking price accordingly,' he said. 'Same thing if they see you with a slave – especially one in a fancy uniform like that.'

I could see exactly what he meant. Traditionally only Celtic *noblemen* had slaves – usually from rival tribes taken as prisoners of war – and then only to do the hard work on the land, not to dance attendance on their personal whims. Marcus's servants, on the other hand, were always handsomely attired, in scarlet tunics embroidered with gold, in case anyone should miss the fact that the owner had considerable wealth. 'The Silurians don't care for private pages, then?'

The optio grunted. 'Here in Venta, in particular, where Romans are never very welcome anyway. Still think they're heirs to old Caractacus, some of them.'

I nodded. Caractacus was the legendary chief who held this area and led a spirited resistance to Roman rule for years. He had been defeated a century ago, but it is well known throughout Britannia that there are still Silurians who have never wholly accepted the occupying force. There were rumours of occasional frontier skirmishes even now. 'Still trouble?'

'More than we admit.' My new friend was getting expansive now. 'And not just beyond the border, as people seem to think. Sometimes you see captured Roman helmets openly on sale here in the marketplace, and there are places in the town where it's not wholly safe for us to go, especially after dark. One of my soldiers disobeyed my orders once, went to a tavern on the wrong side of town and was attacked. Stripped of everything he had, even his weapon, and was lucky to get out of it alive. We had to hush it up. Even the town watch patrols in groups. Though it's not only us – the most violent incidents occur between the rival tribes themselves, though we try to ignore them when we can. No point in making a tense situation worse.' He sighed. 'But that's not your concern. You go in your cloak and under-tunic, and you should be all right. You may not have red hair like the locals but you are fairly obviously a Celt, even if you're from another tribe. Say you are a freeman-trader come from Glevum, which is true. Just don't tell them you're a Roman citizen. They'll make a point of cheating you, if they think you're one of us.'

I nodded slowly, as if considering this, though I had come to much the same conclusion for myself. 'As long as Marcus never hears of it. I am a member of his party and his official guest. He might think my wandering around the marketplace, incorrectly dressed, was insulting to his personal dignity.'

The optio dropped one eye in a wink. 'No one but you and I need know that you have gone – and the man on duty at the gate, of course. I'll tell him to let you in again. It shouldn't take you long. Take your attendant to keep an eye on you, but keep him at a distance if you can. You don't want to advertise your wealth. Go straight to the forum: you'll find good silver there and in the first street just past it on your right. Though you should hurry. It will be dusk soon and the silver stalls will close up for the night.'

I thanked him fulsomely, and – seeing that the wine jug was quite empty now – took his advice and hurried off, through the front gate, past the guard and out into the street, with Promptillius lurking at my heels. Venta is a local tribal capital, and – despite what the optio had said about unrest – was clearly built on the Roman model, though on a modest scale. It was not hard to see which paved road led into the centre of the town, and I passed along a grid of criss-crossed streets and into the little forum with its large basilica. The colonnaded market square was busy, even in the late hours of the afternoon, and I had to fight my way through thronging townsfolk, carrying their dinners and shouting their wares, and pedlars spreading their offerings on the pavement fronts. Already, as a stranger, I was drawing curious looks.

There was a silver stall, as the optio had said, but I could not find exactly what I wanted there, and the stall-holder's eyes kept drifting to my slave. My own attendant, Junio, in circumstances like these would have melded with the crowd, but Promptillius succeeded in looking so conspicuous that in the end I lost patience with him. 'You see that corner by the pastry shop? Stand there and wait till I come back, otherwise my clasp will cost me twice the price. Don't move until I tell you, do you hear?'

He nodded, glumly, and took up his post – looking like a sentry at a gate – while I went off to find the street of silversmiths, dressed in a modest under-tunic and cloak and without the encumbrance of an attendant slave. The best way to find a bargain, I was sure.

So there I was, in Venta, in the growing dusk, examining the silver dress-clasps on a stall and haggling happily with the vendor over the price, when I looked up and saw a dead man walking down the street.

Chapter Two

Not merely a dead man, but the very one I was commissioned to create a memorial pavement for.

In any other circumstances, I might have thought I was mistaken and made no more of it. Gaius Flaminius Plautus was a common enough type: short, stocky and muscular with greying reddish hair and a round and equally reddish face. Scores of men look very much like that, especially in this tribal area, and this individual was dressed in a cloak and tunic of a dingy browny-green – the commonest and cheapest of all dyes. But Plautus had one identifying mark, a jagged, livid scar across his face, the result of some childhood accident. The face I saw now was disfigured by the selfsame scar.

Besides, it was clear that the man had recognised me too, and was as shocked as I was at the encounter. I have never seen such a picture of dismay. He turned deathly pale, then quickly pulled up his hood as if to hide his face and, averting that identifying scar, turned on his heel and scurried off into an alleyway nearby.

I stood for a moment, debating what to do. I almost wondered for an instant if I had seen a ghost. For how could there be doubt that Plautus had been dead? I had attended his funeral myself.

I had seen him buried – or what was left of him after he

was cremated on a pyre – in an elaborate marble house-tomb prominently positioned by the road outside the North Gate of Glevum. I had personally admired his funeral chest (marble and intricately carved) and the piles of grave goods which were incinerated with his bones. It was all done properly, as befitted a rich man who had made a fortune importing olive oil – no question of omitting any ritual, so that the soul was restless afterwards. I watched as one of his fingers was chopped off and buried separately (making the token burial in the earth); listened to his eldest son Maximus give an impassioned speech; comforted his widow as she sobbed becomingly behind her veil; and even tipped the sorrowing slaves who had accompanied the funeral litter to the pyre. There had been a splendid feast, provided by his will, together with a day of commemorative games. The whole town talked about it for a week. It was the kind of send-off any Roman citizen would want.

And Plautus was very much a Roman citizen – it was the thing about him I remembered most. Not that he was born that way, of course: like me, he was a Celt who had come to that distinction late in life. But he'd embraced things Roman with a greedy glee. Indeed, it was a joke among the forum wits that Plautus was more Roman than most visitors from Rome, all of whom, when possible, he sought out and entertained.

I thought about the man I had known. The very picture of respectability. So socially conventional that he was slightly dull. He cultivated Roman habits, ate only Roman dishes and drank Roman wine, spoke Latin with more polish than any other Celt I ever met, and dressed in a formal toga at all times.

So ostentatiously Roman were his habits that he'd been

something of a legend in the town. Indeed, the man seated next to me at that elaborate funeral feast was full of little witticisms at the dead man's expense: how he very seldom laughed, unless the joke was patiently explained; and how Plautus's town-house was exactly like his wife – built on the Roman pattern, tall, substantial, over-ornamented and expensive to maintain.

'Of course, our Plautus gained his citizenship the expensive way, by honourable service to the Empire,' I remembered my informant saying, with a laugh – meaning that our dead host had used a portion of his wealth either to grant favours to the Emperor direct, or to grease some consul's greedy senatorial palm. 'The same way he got himself elected to the *ordo* afterwards. Well, I hope he enjoyed the honour while he lived. He paid enough for it. Now, where's that slave-boy? I want a bit more of that splendid wine.'

There'd been some justice in that, I thought, remembering his words. Plautus had made a reputation for himself on the municipal council by saying very little and spending quite a lot – a vote-winning combination, since every councillor is expected to fund public works out of his private purse. Plautus had funded a good many public works.

He must have had considerable wealth. Even after his unfortunate demise – or what had seemed at the time to be his demise – crushed by falling masonry while inspecting the progress of his own new colonnade, he had still left a substantial sum, both to his widow and to the town. The words 'A much-mourned benefactor of Glevum' had been inscribed upon his monument at his own expense, and there was even talk of the wine-importers setting up a statue in his memory. A life of boredom and unexceptional success.

Not at all the sort of man you would expect to find

scuttling down alleyways in Venta, dressed in a shabby tunic – even when alive.

I must have imagined it, I told myself. It had been a long day and I was tired. It was impossible that Plautus should be here. It is said that vengeful spirits return to walk the earth, so perhaps they do, but I could see no reason why his shade should come to haunt me, in particular. He owed me no ill-will. Of course, I had done some work for him before, a little pavement in his country house, but he had been very pleased with that – so pleased that his family had chosen me to design that memorial mosaic at the baths. I shook my head. Too much of the mansio's watered wine, perhaps, although I had been careful not to over-indulge.

I looked back to the silver stall, resolving to conclude my purchase and then collect Promptillius and go back to the inn – but, as I turned, there was Plautus again, peeping at me round the corner of a wall. He drew back sharply, but I had seen his face. There could be no doubt now. No phantom has to turn and scuttle off like that. This was Plautus and he was very much alive.

I should have known better. I am getting old and I have run into enough difficulties in the past, investigating matters at my patron's instigation, without setting myself unnecessary problems of my own. But I can never resist a puzzle and anyway, I told myself, this was a matter of professional concern. I could not build a memorial pavement for a man who wasn't dead.

I dropped the dress-clasp that I'd been haggling for – leaving the stall-holder gaping like a fish – and set off across the forum in pursuit. I skirted nimbly round the stalls and down the street, until I reached the alleyway where I'd seen Plautus go.

Even then, I might have left it there. The alley was a very long and narrow one and my quarry had already vanished out of sight. But then there was a movement in a doorway halfway down and there was the man again, or at least his head. Then, obviously realising that he had been seen, he dashed out of the aperture and down towards a narrow opening at the far end of the alley.

I set off after him again, with a growing feeling of having been misused. If Plautus was not dead, what was he doing here? And – it suddenly occurred to me – if he was alive, whom had we been so mournfully burying at his funeral? Of course, the corpse was wrapped from head to foot, in deference to that crushing accident, but somebody had been the centre of all those rituals. I knew that from the cremation pyre if nothing else. Burning human flesh has a distinctive smell.

With all this in my mind, I hurried after him, down to the opening which I'd observed before, and was just in time to see him hastening along it, almost at the other end by now. 'Plautus?' I shouted. 'Wait! I want to talk to you.'

He did not look back, just pulled his cloak about him and began to run even faster.

From what I had seen of Venta Silurum to this point, even the main streets are barely wide enough to take a laden cart. So you can imagine that the alleyways were small. The one along which Plautus had now disappeared was so very narrow that it was difficult to get down it at all – it seemed to be merely a gutter for the eavesdrip from the overhanging roofs, and a rubbish dump for kitchen waste from premises nearby.

From the smell, I guessed that rainwater was not the only thing that ran along the drain. Even in fine cities like Glevum households and businesses often use adjoining alleyways to empty piss-pots in, so it was not really a surprise to find that the same thing happened here in Venta too. This alley was particularly odorous, perhaps because it ran alongside what was obviously a fuller's shop, where clothes were cleaned and dyed. Such businesses use human urine in their trade, for treatment of the cloth, and will sometimes set up collection pots in public places for the purpose, or have a contract with larger householders. This fuller, by the smell of it, was doing very well. Never mind, I told myself, the shop would be a landmark later on, when I wanted to retrace my steps.

I picked my way along the path – if I can call it that – and found myself in a narrow street of shops, set in small blocks of two or three, with several floors of wooden dwelling-space above. Much town building in Britannia is on this kind of plan, but here the blocks (or *insulae*) were smaller and more crowded than I was accustomed to, and the upper floors proportionately meaner and more crammed. Even from where I was standing on the corner of the lane, I could see slaves beating mats and shaking dusting cloths from windows in the favoured first floor apartments; while on the upper storeys, where the poorer people lived, scraps of ragged clothing dangled from openings to dry, and black, curling, acrid smoke spoke of hazardous cooking on open braziers in little airless rooms. People swarmed at the doorways that opened to the street, and on the narrow staircases that I could glimpse within. Most of them looked suspiciously at me. Obviously strangers didn't often come this way.

The shops were clearly busy, though. It was almost evening now, but tradesmen still sat behind their counters and their barriers, selling everything from pots and pans to wine. Buckets of live eels squirmed outside the fishmonger's, a butcher in a bloodstained apron further up the street hacked pieces from a carcass hanging from a hook – skin, tail, lolling head and all – while other vendors offered salt, carved bone, sandals made to measure on the spot, eye ointments, or memorial monuments. Pie sellers went by with trays of greasy wares, and plodding donkeys carried panniers of turnips, wood, or wool. There was a stall directly opposite piled high with armour, as the optio had said – not only Roman helmets, but dented shields, leather jerkins, cheek-pieces, even entire mailed tunics and protective greaves – some of them of foreign, strange design. One decorative, flat-backed arm-piece had a Celtic look – an exquisite serpent swallowing its tail – while others I recognised as work from Gaul.

The stall-holder saw me looking and came out to stare at me. He was a small, hunched, shrewd-faced man with a decided leer and such a cunning, conspiratorial air that I half expected him to come sidling up and begin hissing in my ear, 'You seeking something special, friend? A dagger? Javelin? Sword? You got money – you come round the back. There's lots more things inside.'

But he said nothing and when I made no move he spat contemptuously on the pavement and went back into the living quarters at the rear, obviously deciding that I was not a customer. I wondered if he really did have weapons hidden somewhere in the shop, and, if so, who his clientele might be. It is still a capital offence for civilians like myself to carry arms in public places. Yet there was another stall of battered armour further up the street. It was disquieting. You could buy almost anything in this part of Venta, by the look of it, if you knew where to go and whom to ask.

Of Plautus, however, there was by now no sign.

Chapter Three

'Citizen?' A voice behind me made me whirl round. There was a woman standing at my elbow – a woman with a pock-marked face and hennaed hair, dressed in a showy tunic which displayed her legs, and giving off an overpowering scent of onions, sweat and cheap perfume. One of the other things that you could buy here, evidently. She was smiling at me with discoloured teeth.

I breathed a sigh of undisguised relief. From her greeting I had feared that I'd been recognised, or at least that my Roman status had, and that – as I'd been warned – was dangerous. But women like this were likely to call everybody 'citizen', in the hope that flattery would earn them a slightly higher fee.

'Looking for a companion, citizen?' she persisted, coming very close and breathing onions and violets all over me. She spoke Latin in what I'd begun to recognise as the local style, fluent but strongly accented, with a lilt which was intended to entice. 'Very cheap. Very clean. Black girls if you want them. Exotic dancing girls. Virgins for a fee – or, if you are really prepared to pay, I've got a girl who can . . .' She leaned forward and whispered something in my ear so astonishingly lewd that it made my jaw drop open and my eyes pop out. She grinned with satisfaction at my shocked surprise. 'Two of them together, if you like.'

So she was not (as I'd supposed) a common prostitute, looking to earn a few coins on her own account, but manager of the local *lupinarium* with a whole bevy of licensed girls in her control, and hawking for business like the proprietor of any other establishment. I tried to drag my mind away from the astounding images her words had conjured up and was about to politely decline her services when a sudden thought occurred to me.

'I am looking for somebody,' I said. 'Not, alas, one of your girls tonight. I saw a friend of mine come down this way just now, but I've lost sight of him. I wonder if you saw which way he went? A man of middle age, about my height, in a green tunic, with reddish hair going grey.'

She interrupted with a scornful laugh. 'You look around you, traveller' – now that I was no longer a potential customer the courtesy title had swiftly disappeared – 'I don't know where you come from, but you'll find that many people look like that round here.'

She was right, of course. The Silures are famously stocky and red-haired, and green is one of the commonest of dyes. There must have been a dozen traders at the counters opposite who would have fitted my description perfectly.

'This one has a jagged scar across his face,' I said.

This time there was the faintest pause before she laughed again. 'You think that I have time to examine everyone? Stranger, I've got customers to find. And so, if you'll excuse me . . .' She would have turned away, but I prevented her. There was something in her manner which made me persist – a sort of triumph at having found an answer to my words.

I moved in front of her. 'However, not so many people come down this alleyway. Perhaps, since you were standing there, you saw which way he went?'

She shook her head. 'I've got other things to do besides watch out for passers-by.'

'On the contrary,' I persisted. 'That is exactly what you do. You watch out for passers-by, and when you see a possible client you accost him and tout for trade. Strictly speaking, it's against the law,' I added, in the hope of sparking a response, 'but that is what you were doing all the same. Why else did you decide to speak to me?'

She was sulky now. 'Only because you are a stranger to the town.'

'How do you know that?'

She shrugged. 'I've not seen you before. Most people who come down this way, I recognise. Either they're regulars, or they've got a stall, or else they live round here. And anyway—'

I cut her off. 'Then the man in the green tunic was somebody you knew? Somebody who lives here in the town?'

Her face turned scarlet. 'That wasn't what I said. I don't know him, in particular. It's just that I vaguely recognised his face – while yours is one I haven't seen before.'

'So,' I said, making the obvious deduction from all this. 'You do know which man I was speaking of?'

She realised then that she'd betrayed herself. All vestige of pretended courtesy deserted her and her voice was thin and bitter as she said, 'You think you're very clever, I suppose. Well, I wouldn't tell you now which way he went, even supposing that I knew.' She seemed to recollect herself, and went on in a less aggressive tone, 'Which actually I don't. There must have been scores of people passing along here today, with green tunics on, and some of them have scars – there's been a lot of fighting in these parts. How am I supposed to work out which one is your friend, let alone remember where he went?'

I made no answer for a moment, but I looked at her. Despite her protestations, or perhaps because of them, I was fairly sure by this time that not only did she know exactly who I'd been following, but she could easily have told me the direction he'd gone in. Why was she choosing to obstruct me in this way? I wondered if she somehow knew I was a Roman citizen. According to my friend the optio, Silurians were often deliberately unhelpful to anyone associated with their conquerors.

But, I asked myself, how could she know anything of the kind? I was to all outward appearances simply a humble Celtic traveller, with the traces of a cauterised slave-brand on my back. Was it the presence of Promptillius, perhaps? He had made himself conspicuous in the marketplace. But I had come directly from there: surely there was no time for gossip to have got here first?

She must have interpreted my bewildered pause to mean that I'd accepted what she said, because the persuasive smile appeared again and her distinctive odour wafted over me as she leaned close and murmured, in what she doubtless hoped was a seductive tone, 'You are the only stranger hereabouts. We don't get many handsome visitors in this part of town. Obviously I'm interested in you, and whether you want to come and see my girls.'

Flattery now! With my grizzled grey hair and weathered cheeks I'm no youthful Hercules! Whatever did she hope to gain by it? Perhaps she wanted money to tell me what she knew. As soon as I had thought of that, I wondered why it had not occurred to me before. 'How much do you want?' I said.

She misinterpreted again. 'Depends on what you have. Three *sesterces* for a basic girl – virgins are extra . . .' The smile was broader now and she began to count off the price-list on her fingertips.

I interrupted her. 'To tell me where Plautus went, and how I get to him.'

'Plautus?' She sounded mystified. 'Who's Plautus?' And then, 'He's not—' She stopped abruptly. 'You mean your friend. The man in the green tunic you were speaking of?'

This was getting more baffling by the moment. 'That's right,' I said. 'Gaius Flaminius Plautus. At least, he was called Plautus when I saw him last. Do you know him by some other name?'

She had turned pink again. 'Of course not, traveller. I don't know him by any name at all. In fact, I told you, I've no idea what man you're speaking of.' She paused. 'So you're not even tempted by what we're offering? Most passing traders are. If it isn't armour that they're looking for, it's girls. Well, that's your affair. If you don't want my girls, I'll go and find somebody who does. But you don't know what you're missing. I've got the best girls in Venta. You ask anyone.' She turned and began to walk away.

Suddenly I was loath to let her go. A man whom I had thought dead and buried was walking round this town alive, and I was sure that this woman knew more about him than she was telling me. 'Wait!' I called after her.

She turned.

'What is your name?' I asked. 'And where can I find you?' Then, realising that she was unlikely to answer that, I added feebly, 'In case I change my mind. About your services.'

She looked unconvinced. For a moment she seemed to hesitate, as if she was weighing caution against commerce. Commerce won. 'My name is Lyra,' she confessed at last. 'You'll find me in the street of the oil-lamp sellers, at the further end. Ask anyone, or just walk down until you see the sign.'

I nodded. I knew what the sign would be. A crudely carved phallus etched into the paving of the road – many towns had something similar.

'Ask for me by name, and I'll see that you get a special rate,' she said. And having offered that final inducement, she walked off down the street. She must have been twenty-five at least, well past her prime, but she still moved with that special and provocative wiggle of the hips which ladies of her profession always seem to learn. That, perhaps, is why I watched her until she was out of sight.

Or almost out of sight. Just before she turned the corner opposite and vanished from my view, I saw her stoop and mutter a few words to a ragged child who was squatting on the street outside a butcher's shop. She paused so briefly before straightening up and walking on again that if I had not been following her so closely with my eyes, I might not have noticed that she'd stopped at all.

The child waited for a moment till she'd gone. Then he glanced in my direction, scrambled to his feet and disappeared round the counter into the interior of the butcher's stall. A moment later, he was back, sitting exactly where he'd been before and looking anywhere except at me, with an expression of bored disinterest on his face. Shortly afterwards two older boys came out into the street.

They were good. I had to give them that. So good that, if I had not been already on my guard, I should never have suspected them at all. Certainly I had no qualms at first. They behaved like any other boys, tumbling and chattering and arguing about a cup-ball on a string. The larger of the two, a tallish youth with gangling limbs and a mop of auburn curls, gave the smaller one a playful push and ran away, still dangling the cup-ball in his hand, and making derisive gestures as he went.

His companion – smaller and leaner but otherwise very similar – shrugged with pretended unconcern and turned away, to go and lean against a wall not very far from me – the very embodiment of sulking youth. It was only when I turned and met his eyes that I realised, from the startled speed with which he glanced away, that he had positioned himself there on purpose, and was watching me.

It was disquieting.

I tested my theory by the simple method of walking a little further down the street, and stopping to admire the armour on the stall. Sure enough, when I glanced round, the boy was there again, apparently engrossed in shying small stones at a lame dog that was limping down the street.

I declined the offer of a dagger with a dented blade, 'dragged from a dying Roman soldier in the field, not very far away', for twice the price that a new one would have cost in Glevum any day and sauntered a little further. I was tempted to cross the roadway and follow Lyra round the corner to my left, but a moment's consideration suggested something else. If this lad – who was still hovering at my heels – was really following me, it was possible that his gangly companion, who'd gone running off like that, had also been no idle bystander. The most likely explanation was that he'd been sent to take Lyra's news as fast as possible to someone else, and I could think of only one person in this town to whom such a message could possibly be sent. Plautus, the dead man who was no longer dead.

Of course the 'messenger', if that was what he was, had long since disappeared, but I had seen him go and that gave me at least a direction I could take towards some explanation of this mystery. Accordingly, I set off the way I knew he'd gone, though I dawdled at many of the stalls and took good care not to glance behind. If I was correct in my suspicions, I did not want my little follower to realise that I knew that he was there. We must have presented a merry spectacle, both pretending to be absorbed in something else and each affecting to be unconcerned about the other's presence. I took a side-street, then another one, still feigning to examine all the wares displayed. But when I hovered beside a busy copper stall, and picked up a cooking-pot as if to buy, I could see the boy, not very far behind, reflected in the burnished surface of the pan.

We had reached the limit of the shops by now, and the street had dwindled to a murky lane of taverns, wine stores and *thermopolia* – the hot-food stalls which serve cheap drink and questionable soup. It was beginning to get dark, besides, and some of the stall-holders were folding up. Taverns were lighting lamps or setting flaming torches in the holders at their doors. I hovered at the counter of one thermopolium, as if contemplating the purchase of some soup, then hurried round the corner into another of Venta's very narrow alleyways.

It was darker there, as I'd expected, and I stood back hard against the wall, hoping to be lost among the shadows. A moment afterwards, the boy appeared and, with an air of innocence, stood at the corner and glanced down the lane. I hoped that he would venture after me, but he did not – simply stood at the entrance peering down into the dark, evidently bemused at losing sight of me – so, after waiting for what seemed an age, I stepped forward briskly, seized his arm and dragged him into the alley after me.

'Now,' I said, shaking him none too gently. 'What's all this about? Why are you following me?'

He began to protest that he was doing nothing of the kind, but that was so evidently absurd that the words died on his lips and he lapsed into silence once again.

'Well?' I prompted, with another shake.

He shook his head. 'You can't frighten me. I won't tell you anything. Even if you torture me it won't do any good.' He raised his head and added with a certain pride, 'I took an oath.'

The answer was so absurdly innocent that I almost smiled. I have seen the Roman torturers and the torments they inflict, and I knew what their instruments could do to tender flesh. It was obvious the boy had no idea. I wondered how long he would endure before he broke down in abject tears and told everything he knew, begging for the agony to cease.

I asked, 'How old are you?'

It was clearly not the question he had been expecting, and he blurted, 'Eight summers,' in a startled voice, before he thought better of it and added, 'Though that won't help you. I haven't given anything away.'

I had the measure of my captive now. The boy was terrified, though trying to be brave, and it was easy to startle information out of him. I was eager to exploit this fact as much as possible. 'Oh, don't worry about that,' I said. 'I know who you and your brother are working for. I saw him in the alleyway today, before your friend Lyra delayed me in my tracks. I know she sent that child to fetch you from the shop.'

The boy had gone so rigid in my grasp that I knew I was right, even before he muttered, in a strangled voice, 'Who told you that? It wasn't me.'

'I know a great deal more than you suppose,' I said. 'You

are Rufinus, aren't you?' I picked the name at random, but not without some thought. It means 'red-headed one' and is a common appellation amongst the Silures. Since this lad and his brother both had auburn curls, 'Rufinus' seemed a fairly likely guess.

I was lucky 'Well, you're wrong,' the lad said hotly. 'Rufinus is my brother. I'm Paulinus.'

I nodded judiciousy. 'Then it seems that I was slightly misinformed. I wonder what other errors have been made? You are the sons of the man who owns that fresh-meat and offal stall I saw you coming from . . .' I paused expectantly.

'I'm not saying anything,' Paulinus said, thereby confirming what I'd merely guessed.

'And you and Lyra share the same concerns,' I went on. The boy said nothing, so I tried again. 'I think you work for Plautus' – no reaction there – 'or at any rate run messages for him.'

'Plautus?' There it was again, that note of genuine bewilderment with which Lyra had repeated the name. 'I've never heard of any Plautus. Who is he?'

He was so clearly puzzled that I paused to think, and in doing so must have somehow dropped my guard, and momentarily loosened my grip upon his arm. I was still considering what tactic to use next when Paulinus twisted round, tore himself free and made a dash for it. By the time I had recovered enough to lumber to the corner after him, he had nipped past the thermopolium and was halfway down the street where deepening shadows swallowed him at once

A moment later the only trace of him was the sound of running sandals on the paving stones, ringing like mocking laughter in the dark.

Chapter Four

'Well, stranger, are you planning to buy some soup, or not?'
The owner of the thermopolium, a bearded giant of a man
with shoulders like a bull and an expression of no great
intelligence or pleasure on his face, had shambled from the
shadows of the stall and was standing in front of me, his
heavy ladle in his hand.

Nothing had been further from my mind, but one glance
at this hairy colossus was enough to convince me of where
wisdom lay, and I reached into my tunic for my purse. 'A
small helping, please.' And then, since he was watching, I
was obliged to force it down – a greasy broth of cabbage
leaves and what looked like bits of goat: eyeballs, hoof-
parts, ears and other things I didn't even try to recognise.

Still, it was warm, and after money had changed hands
the monster with the ladle seemed more amicably inclined,
though he still wore an expression of distrust. 'You a stranger
in this part of town?' he said, scooping a floating piece of
turnip-end from the cooking-vat and adding it tenderly to
my plate as though he were offering me a special treat. 'We
don't get many visitors down here. Not unless they are
looking for something particular.'

It was a question really, and something about his manner
suggested that it would be imprudent not to offer a reply.
For a moment I almost contemplated telling him the truth,

that I was following a man I thought was dead, and how Paulinus had been tracking me, but – looking at those brawny shoulders and distrustful eyes – I was suddenly aware of how unlikely that would sound. I searched my mind for some more plausible account.

I found it. 'I was given an address. The street of the oil-lamp sellers.' I paused. He was still looking suspiciously at me and I took the final plunge. 'A woman named Lyra keeps a house there, I believe.'

The mistrustful manner vanished, and a leering smile spread across his face. 'Ah!' he said. 'Is that it! I wondered what you looked so furtive about. Well, don't worry, friend. You're in Venta now. No one will think the less of you for having human urges – quite the contrary. At least the men won't.' He glanced behind him, and then moved closer before adding confidentially, 'Have you got a wife?'

I nodded. I was about to say 'In Glevum', but before the words were out, he was already rushing on.

'I thought as much. My wife is just the same! Picked up with this peculiar new cult – you know, the one whose god was crucified, if you ever heard anything so ridiculous – and now she seems to think my simplest pleasures are wicked and depraved. She prays all over me if I have too much to drink, let alone visit Lyra and her girls.' He poured out two battered beakers of cheap over-watered wine from an amphora leaning on the wall, and pushed one in my direction. 'She won't even make sacrifices to the Emperor on public holidays. She'll get herself in trouble over it one day – and me too, I shouldn't be surprised. I've had to forbid her to go to meetings and lock her up indoors.' He downed his drink in one gigantic gulp. 'Women! Who needs them, eh? Except in the way you're looking for, of course.'

He gave me a nudge which almost spilt my drink.

I wouldn't have minded: it was horrible – rough and sharp, despite the fact that it was two-thirds water. Even as it was he reached across and wanted to fill up my cup again. I shook my head.

'It's getting late,' I said. 'I must go, or I'll find the doors are closed.'

He laughed. 'I don't know where you come from, my friend, but round here the brothel doors are never closed. Always some young lady willing to oblige. Here, I tell you . . .'

I shook my head. I hadn't meant the brothel doors, of course. I was thinking of the mansio, suddenly, and an unpleasant notion had occurred to me. Once the town gates are closed, the door of the military staging post is barred and a guard is posted outside on the street, so although nocturnal stragglers can gain admission afterwards, it does involve a challenge by the person at the gate, and – dressed as I was – there would be a lot of explaining to be done. My friend the optio would be off duty by this time, and I was not anxious for my exploits to reach Marcus's ears next day. And almost certainly, I was already late.

Besides, I remembered, with a guilty start, I had left Promptillius outside the pastry shop, and I could not return till I'd collected him. Promptillius was the sort of slave who, if I'd been captured or carried off by thieves, would never think to institute a search but would wait exactly where he'd been told to wait until he died of cold and hunger – and feel he'd done his duty perfectly.

I pushed away my half-finished wine. 'Can you tell me how to get back to the forum?' I began, but once again the hot-soup seller interrupted me. My apparent interest in the house of prostitutes had evidently made an ally out of him, and now he was advising me as though we were old friends.

'Don't go to Lyra, brother. She gets all the trade and charges double if she gets the chance. And the town watch are given special terms, so they ignore it, even when her ladies break the law. She's had unlicensed women there – slaves, widows, runaways, all sorts of thing – and several men have had their purses slit. And will the courts do anything when you complain? Of course they won't. They're all the same, these old Silurian families. Look after their own and never mind the rest of us.'

This was sufficiently interesting to make me forget Promptillius and pause to ask, 'Lyra is connected to senior people in the town?' That seemed to be the gist of what he had said.

He shrugged. 'Connected to half of Venta as far as I can see. Mind you, it's not unusual round here. You know what these border families are like. Everyone who is not a cousin is married to your aunt, or was your father's brother's husband's uncle's wife. You know the kind of thing.'

I did. There were tribes much like that when I was a boy: whole villages linked by ties of blood and marriage. 'But Venta is a civitas,' I said. 'Surely the whole tribal capital can't be linked by blood like that.'

He drained his third beakerful of wine and gloomily filled it again. 'Don't you believe it, friend. There are two or three main families who run everything. Hold all the important civil offices and, naturally, own half the buildings too. Everyone pays rent to one of them. Depends which part of town you're in. They're always feuding, too, amongst themselves – a lot of nonsense about who supported Rome, and who was responsible for which atrocities. All years and years ago, of course. Most of it is legend by this time, in any case, but they can't forget. Or won't, more like. I sometimes think Silurians actually like to have something to keep quarrelling about. It's the same with these constant little uprisings and forays against the Roman fortresses. They never let it go. Asking for trouble, if you ask me. Can't accept that we've lost the border war and the imperial legions are here to stay.'

I remembered those dented helmets on the stalls and the tales of marauding ambush parties who still stalked the roads. What would they make of a Roman citizen like me, I wondered, someone accompanying a high-level delegation to the nearby fort, if they found him wandering around the town without protection and without a slave? It was not a comfortable thought and I changed the subject hurriedly.

'And you?' I said. 'You're not Silurian, then?'

'Oh, there's plenty of us newcomers, of course, trying to ply a trade or earn an honest crust. I came here from Eboracum years ago. Figured that in a newish market town they needed soup, and since this was on the high road to the border, there would be lots of trade. Too much competition where I was. Had a scheme to take in travellers, too, at one time – there's a room we hardly use upstairs and I thought it might bring in a *sestertius* or two – but I thought better of it in the end. Too many fleas and pickpockets in your house – you never know who you might be taking in. You don't want to get caught up in one of these old feuds by accident, and anyway we're too far from the gates. Mind you, even the hot-soup stall hasn't worked out as well as I had hoped. It isn't easy here. By the time you've paid your taxes and your rent and your dues, there's no more than a bare living to be won.'

Taxes and rent I understood, but, 'Dues?' I said. 'You mean a payment for the fire-watch?' I paid a voluntary levy to a fire-watch where my workshop was, and it had once saved it from completely burning down, though it had to be extensively rebuilt. 'I can see that you might need one, in a trade like yours.'

He gave a scornful laugh. 'You can call it the fire-watch if you like,' he said. 'Certainly if you don't pay it there's a very good chance that your shop will catch alight. Or bowls and equipment will mysteriously break. And of course no clients will ever come your way.'

I stared at him. 'What do you mean?'

'I told you, there are two or three important families in the town. If they protect you, you will be all right. It costs, that's all. You pay one of their boys to keep a watch for fire, and there isn't any fire. Change your mind, and there is likely to be a conflagration soon. Of course, it's impossible to prove anything, and people keep it quiet, anyway. For one thing they're too afraid of what would happen if they complained to the authorities, and anyway what could the soldiers do? The garrison don't like that sort of thing – it suggests that there is too much local power and the soldiers are not wholly in control – though it goes on all the time behind their backs. It works, too, in a way. You don't have trouble if you pay your dues.'

'Who to, exactly?'

'Depends what part of town you live. We pay one lot, down this bath-end side of town – but if you're down at the amphitheatre end, you'll pay another group.' He stopped, and said abruptly, 'Now, I've already talked too much. If you want those girls I was telling you about, turn left at the next corner and go straight on till you reach the outer wall. You'll find another thermopolium there. They've got a place upstairs. There are illustrations on the wall of what the girls can do. You can't mistake it. Say Lupus sent you.' With that he stiffened, looked round, whisked his beaker out of sight and went on in a different tone, 'Now that's four goblets of wine you owe me for.'

I was about to protest, since I had not asked for mine and he himself had drunk the other three, but the appearance of a buxom woman from the inner door convinced me that I was in the presence of his wife. She had a home-made tallow taper in her hand and had obviously come to replace the one which was guttering feebly on the wall, having burned down almost to the fixing spike. I had not heard her coming, but Lupus's ears were evidently more attuned than mine, and he was so much bigger than I was that I did not argue. I pulled out a coin and paid him what he asked. After all, he'd given me a lot of information, free.

As I thanked him and went out to the street, I heard the woman's voice raised in rebuke. 'Giving him the address of sinful premises like that! Have you no care for your immortal soul? And don't tell me that you didn't because I heard every word you said. I wish I could persuade you that falsehood is a sin, even if you're only lying to your wife . . .'

I turned away and tiptoed off into the night, not following the directions he had given me, but the other way, where I hoped the forum and Promptillius were.

Chapter Five

It was getting extremely dark by now, and I could hear the creaking sounds of carts and shouts and movement in the more distant streets. Like any garrison town, Venta obviously did not permit wheeled traffic within the walls in daylight hours. Here, from what I was learning of the place, the free movement of legionary troops was even more important than it was elsewhere.

However, in the narrow lane of shuttered shops where I now found myself nothing stirred at all. No donkey carts or lurching wagons here. Even the apartments on the upper floors showed little light – only an occasional guttering candle at a window space or the dull glow of a cooking brazier within. There was an eerie quiet, and I felt uneasy, as if the street had eyes, and unseen spies were keeping watch on me. In fact, when I reached the corner where the dyer's was, and saw the tiny, shadowed alleyway-cum-drain that I had come through earlier, I baulked at walking down it on my own. Instead I decided to keep on along the slightly wider lane in the direction of the nearest sounds. I could hear raised voices, just a street or so away.

Even if that route did not take me to the forum, I told myself, at least there would be someone I could ask, and once I had collected Promptillius I could quickly make my way back to the mansio and bed. Of course, I had some qualms about the reception I might receive, both from the owners of the voices ahead and from the soldiers at the mansio gate, but anything was preferable to walking on alone down these dark, sinister and unfamiliar streets. A massive building loomed up to my right. I recognised the public baths I'd heard about, though they were now closed and shuttered for the night. It seemed a shell of hollow emptiness. The walls threw menacing shadows, patches of deeper blackness in the darkened street. I hurried past. I hardly dared admit, even to myself, how welcome the prospect of the military inn – light and warmth and a nice straw mattress safely under guard – had suddenly become.

I heard a noise behind me – a rustle, followed by a creak. I whirled round, but there was nothing there. In the end I hurried on, growing more uneasy with every step I took. Several times again I thought I heard a stealthy footfall at my back, but when I turned my head there was only the darkness and the shadowed street, though once I did catch a hasty scuttling sound and what sounded like the stealthy scrape of steel, as if someone nearby had drawn a sword.

This was more menacing than any visible pursuer would have been, and I found myself walking more quickly all the time until I was nearly at a run, but the footsteps seemed to be even closer now and I was almost completely out of breath. I was relieved to see a human form ahead – a trader with a burning torch, whipping and cursing at his donkey, which had stopped dead in the middle of the narrow street and was clearly disinclined to move, although it was blocking up the passageway. I halted, of necessity – and I heard the following footsteps falter too. Taking advantage of the momentary respite, I dodged past the swearing donkey man and his four-legged obstacle, and hurried round the corner out of sight.

I had turned into what was obviously a more major thoroughfare and I hid there in a shadowed doorway for what seemed an age, panting, leaning on the wall and listening to the thudding of my heart. I kept a sharp eye on the way I'd come as well. However, no one came down the alley after me and after a few moments I began to feel rather foolish for giving way to fear. For the first time I stepped into the roadway where I now found myself and began to look about me trying to take rational stock of my surroundings.

Everything seemed to be quite normal here. An ordinary street, paved and guttered, and grooved by passing wheels, fronted by shuttered workshops, town houses, flats and temple entrances, like any major street in any Roman town.

There were lights here too – oil lamps and tapers in the window spaces of the apartments overhead, and two great lighted torches flaming on the wall outside a tavern opposite, making two pools of brightness on the paving stones, and illuminating the faces of a group of youngish men who now lurched, laughing and arguing, from the door. Wealthy Silurians, from the look of them. They were drunk and noisy and belligerent, and I had no doubt that these were the authors of the shouts which I had heard from several blocks away.

Boisterous revellers bursting from a tavern are not companions I would generally choose, especially as three had clearly imbibed far too much cheap wine, but after the eerie silence of the streets tonight that torchlight drew me as it would a moth, and their rough oaths and guffaws were like sweet music, better than the plaint of any Roman lute.

I hurried in the direction of the light, intending to ask these noisy newcomers which way the forum lay. As I approached them it became clear what they were arguing about.

39

'And I tell you, that *myrmillo* was a fix. There's no way he could have dodged the net and trident for so long and then all at once gone over like a stone and dropped his dagger on the floor like that, so that his opponent had him pinned down helplessly. And the way the arena judges looked the other way, it was preposterous! Pity they weren't fighting to the death. I thought they might have done today, but no – only a flogging for the useless ones, as usual. I'd cheerfully have given the signal to have them cut his throat.' The speaker was a stout red-haired young man, and obviously well-to-do – even in this light I could see that he was dressed in an expensive woollen cloak secured with an elaborate jewelled clasp. He spoke with the careful diction of the drunk.

The smaller of his two companions laughed. He was a thin, pale, dark-haired youth with a fawning expression and what looked like a rash of spots round his mouth. Certainly there was no hint of beard – the boy might have been fifteen or so, at most, but he obviously hoped to sound like a sophisticate. He said in a tone of exaggerated boredom, 'Well, what do you expect? The whole contest was only got up at the last moment, in honour of that Roman magistrate. I can't imagine he was very thrilled. The preliminary show – the comic mock-fighters and the wooden sword brigade – were better entertainment than the troop itself. Then only four proper fights before the light got bad. And did you see the introductory parade? Pathetic costumes – scarcely a plume or precious stone in sight. And as for the heralds and the trumpeters! Wherever did the patron get these people from? I only hope that civic feast he's hosting now is better organised.'

The other two ignored him. 'Now listen here, Aurissimus,' said the stoutest member of the trio, seizing the young man who had spoken first and pushing him against the doorpost. 'Don't think you're going to get away with this. I know you and your wretched arguments and I'm not having it. We had a fair wager, and it stands, whatever you thought about the fight. You backed the confounded heavies and I backed the lights, and I've got more than a thousand witnesses that my net man won.'

His victim struggled, but with the obstinacy only to be found in wine, he was protesting still. 'Only because the fish-helmet fell down at his feet deliberately. I don't call that a contest, I call that a cursed sham. Be reasonable. I tell you what. Double or quits the next time. What do you say to that?'

'We had a bet, confound you. Pay up, or I'll have to beat it out of you.'

'How can I reach my purse, if you don't let me go?' the other muttered thickly, and then, as his companion grudgingly released him, 'They don't nickname you Cupidus, the grasping one, for nothing, do they?' He gave his neck a rueful rub.

'At least I don't earn my name for having flapping ears, listening to all the gossip in town,' Cupidus said, jeering in return. 'You owe me three *denarii*, Big-ears! Pay up, or we shall see if you are a better fighter than your fish man was!'

Aurissimus 'Big-ears' was still arguing. 'By rights I owe you nothing, except a hiding in the street.'

Cupidus clenched both his fists at this, and I was beginning to think that I was going to witness another contest of my own, when suddenly the third man noticed me. He tugged at his companions. All argument was forgotten instantly, and the three men turned as one to stare at me.

'Well, well,' said Cupidus, and with a sneering swagger he

took a step towards me. 'What have we got here? A stranger? Where have you sprung from? What are you doing here, alone and after dark?' His tone was mocking. 'Come to buy my friends and me a drink, have you?'

Nothing had been further from my thoughts but all at once it seemed a good idea. I did not fancy a dispute with three drunken men. Any one of them I might have tackled, even at my age, but combined and linking arms across the causeway as they now were, all at once they were formidable. They were all well dressed, well spoken and clearly affluent – the sort of people who can bribe town guards – and obviously they were looking for a fight.

That would have been alarming in itself. I had heard tales of bands of wealthy, drunken youths like this roaming city streets after dark, fighting, causing damage, and terrorising passing townspeople. It was a problem which had started long ago, in Rome – the Emperor Nero was said to have led such a gang himself – and though he and the fashion were both long dead by now, there were still corners of the Empire where such things survived. Perhaps Venta was one of them. But there was a still more worrying possibility. I remembered what I had already learned, that areas of the town were unofficially controlled by rival family groups, and I wondered if I'd encountered one of them.

Wisdom seemed to lie in a peaceable response. 'I saw that there was a tavern over here,' I said, as cheerfully and casually as I could, deciding that the presence of the inn afforded me a reasonable excuse for being in the vicinity. 'I should be more than happy to provide a mug of wine, if you will tell me which way the forum is.'

Big-ears looked stonily at me. 'The forum, eh? Now why would you want the forum at this time of night?'

These men were wealthy, but not citizens, at least not law-abiding toga-wearing ones. It was clear from their talk that they'd been at some form of public games – a gladiatorial contest thrown together in Marcus's honour, by the sound of it – held in some amphitheatre in the town. If I had been invited to accompany my patron tonight, no doubt I would have been required to endure that quintessentially Roman spectacle as well.

But if these youths were not invited guests (and their presence at the tavern suggested that they weren't) they must have bought tickets for the privilege. Not hostile to all things Roman, then. A moment's reflection suggested that my best hope was to give them some version of the truth.

I tried my most winning smile again, and said in the best Latin that I could produce, 'I left my slave outside the pastry shop there, with strict instructions that he was to wait for me. I'm a visitor from Glevum, just here for the day. I went off looking for silver cloak clasps for my wife, and now it seems that I have lost my way.'

If I was hoping to impress them, I had failed. Cupidus gave another scornful laugh. 'You left your slave behind? A likely tale! Whoever left a servant standing by and went walking after dark in a strange town without a bodyguard? Come on! You'll tell me next that you're a citizen and the town guard will worry if you're set upon.' He took a lurching step forward and thrust his flushed face close to mine. I could smell the cheap wine and vomit on his breath.

I didn't like the tone of this at all. 'I am a citizen, in fact,' I said. 'I understand that you've been at the games. In that case you'll have seen the visiting magistrate who was guest of honour there. His name is Marcus Aurelius Septimus and he comes from Glevum, over to the east. I'm a member of his

43

party. I came here with him and I'm staying at the mansio tonight.'

Cupidus put a heavy hand against my chest and pushed me roughly up against the wall. It seemed to be his favourite form of argument. 'You think I'm blind and stupid, Tunic-face? If you're a citizen, how come you're dressed like this? And why weren't you with him at the games as well? You just heard us gossiping and made this story up.' He gave me another brutal shove. 'You're a low-born nobody – that's what you are. A liar and probably a thief.'

'He's worse than that, Cupidus,' said the spotty boy. 'He's a spy. I saw where he came from, when I came out just now – just to relieve myself, that's all; it wasn't that I'd drunk too much and had to get some air – anyway, I saw him. He came down that alleyway and was hiding in that doorway over there. Straight from the baths quarter of town.'

Cupidus grabbed the neck of my tunic and forced my head and shoulders back against the wall. Drink had given him uncommon strength. 'Is that so, my friend? A con-founded bath-side spy, are we? Well, we know what to do with spies. The same thing as your ancestors once did to mine – may their spirits never sleep in peace.' He laughed. 'That makes you sweat with fear, does it? The thought of having your private parts cut off and stuffed into your mouth?'

It was enough to strike terror into my bones. Such things have been reported in the past – and these youths were so buoyed up with drink that any atrocity was possible. But I have had dealings with would-be torturers before, and I knew that often those who talk most act least, and that to show panic was to play into their hands.

Somehow I forced myself to say, as calmly as I could, 'I

doubt my ancestors did anything to yours. I have no connection with this area. I came from Glevum, as I told you earlier, but I was born a freeman and a Celtic chief, hundreds of miles from here, far off in the south. I was captured and sold as a slave, and on my master's death was freed and bequeathed the rank of citizen. I told you, I came here with the Roman magistrate. I am no part of any local feud. Look at me. Do I even look like one of you?'

Spotty-face had plucked up courage now, and he joined in the taunts. 'What's that supposed to prove? I haven't got red hair either, nor the stocky build. My mother was from another tribe.' He turned to Cupidus. 'Of course the man's a spy. Why else would he be setting out to hide?'

Cupidus sneered at me. 'We'll see if you tell another story when we get you back and let the tribal elders question you. They fought alongside the Romans and they've learned a trick or two. They know how to make a man confess the truth.'

'And so do I!' Spotty-face had drawn a wicked-looking dagger from underneath his cloak. Carrying such arms in the street is a capital offence, even in more peaceful areas: here, with all the local problems I had heard about, the law was likely be ferociously enforced, but this boy did not look as if he cared. This was clearly an ancient weapon – and a deadly one, judging by the nicks along the glittering blade, and the fine carved sheath which he'd revealed at his belt, its writhing serpent clearly visible in the flickering red glow of the tavern torch. It was a tribal dagger, to be reckoned with. He handled it as if he were not at ease with it himself, though he brandished the blade with relish, right before my eyes, carving elaborate patterns in the air.

I flinched, despite myself – such novices are more

dangerous than practised criminals, who at least have some idea of what they're doing.

'Come on,' Spotty-face said eagerly. 'We'll question him ourselves.' He turned to me. 'Let's have the truth from you, before I make you disappear the way my uncle did.'

I was about to protest weakly that what I had told them was the truth, when Big-ears suddenly spoke up. 'Drop it, Laxus. Don't let's be hasty here. He might be right. I did hear that the Roman magistrate put in at the mansio and left a number of his party there. I suppose it is just possible that this man is one of them. Certainly he isn't local, from his voice. I've never set eyes on him before.' Spotty-face looked at him contemptuously, but he hurried on. 'Suppose he is what he says he is, and the important Roman is his patron? Do you want to bring the wrath of the authorities down on your head? After all the money that your father spent on seeking civil office and trying to attract the attention of the provincial imperial power – even packed your seven brothers off to join the legions, just so that they'd all earn citizenship at the end. What do you suppose he would say, if you threw all that away and offended an important magistrate? Do you no good to be your mother's favourite then – he'd cut off your *peculium* and leave you penniless. You'd be lucky to escape from army life yourself. And me, as well, since I consort with you. So, you do what you like. I want no part of it.'

Cupidus had not let go of me. 'The man's a spy,' he said. 'You heard what Laxus said. He came from down the bath-house way and lurked – you know what those barbarians are like. Spies everywhere. Just look at him. Does he look like a Roman citizen to you?' He banged my head against the wall to emphasise the point. 'What do you propose? We let him go? Our families would be delighted about that! They'd cut off more than your peculium then!' His voice was slurred but he was in control enough to give me another sharp tap against the wall.

A little more of this treatment and I would be as fuddled as they were, though Big-ears, at least, seemed to be capable of sober thought. I said – as clearly as I could with Cupidus leaning heavily on my chest and crushing me against the stonework – 'Well, there's one easy way to check. Take me to the forum and we'll find my slave.'

There was a pause. You could almost hear the workings of their minds. Then, very slowly, Cupidus let me go. 'Very well,' he said. 'But no tricks, you understand. You lead the way and we'll be right behind. And if you're lying, Jove have mercy on you . . .'

' 'Cause we won't,' both the others chorused, as if this was some kind of motto between the three of them.

I was still a little shaken from events, but I did have the wit to point out that I still did not know which way the forum lay – that this was, after all, what I had asked them in the first place.

'Round that corner to the left and then straight on,' Big-ears said, gesturing impatiently. 'The pastry shop is on the outside of the forum buildings, to the left again – let's hope that slave of yours is waiting there.'

So I had virtually been round the market in a square, I thought. I set off, as slowly as I dared, trying to buy a little time and think through the evening's extraordinary events, though I was uncomfortably aware of the still drunken trio at my heels.

Venta was a town of many secrets, it appeared. First Plautus had appeared, although he was supposed to be dead and buried. Then Lyra, apparently, had set spies on me, and Lupus from the thermopolium had told me that, under the outward appearance of Roman civic rule, the town was virtually in the grip of rival local gangs. One, clearly, was the so-called 'bath-side' group, and – in trying to escape from them – I had stumbled into the hands of my inebriated friends, who evidently regarded the latter as mortal enemies.

Perhaps I could use that fact to my advantage here. 'You might be interested to know that I think one of your bath-side friends was following me earlier,' I said, slackening my pace to speak to them. 'That's why I was hiding in the door, to try to throw him off. I wonder why they were on my tail. Thought that I was an associate of yours, perhaps.'

Cupidus was clearly unimpressed. He gave me an unfriendly shove. 'Keep walking, friend.' He was still flushed with drink and his face was wreathed in an unlovely leer.

I had no choice but to comply. We were back in the commercial quarter now, and here and there men ran about with flaming links while small ox carts unloaded charcoal, wood and oil into half-shuttered shops, but at a prod from Laxus's dagger I edged past without a word. I gave up all thought of reasoning with my captors and walked in silence, while they whispered taunts and jeers, until the dark bulk of the forum loomed up in front of us. It was deserted now. The colonnaded buildings which enclosed the forum square, and the massive outline of the basilica at the further end, were mere dark silhouettes against the sky.

I stood there blinking stupidly, almost unable to believe my eyes. I hardly needed Cupidus to come up behind and murmur unpleasantly into my ear: 'There's your pastry shop. Where's this famous slave?'

Chapter Six

I found myself gazing pointlessly up and down the empty street. I would have wagered a great deal that Promptillius had the kind of dogged and dutiful stupidity which would have kept him remaining obediently in a burning shop, if someone had not ordered him to move. But there was not the slightest sign of him.

Matters were looking distinctly menacing. Spotty Laxus still had his dagger at my back, and for a moment I thought that Cupidus was going to urge him on, but at that instant a grubby boy came out of the pastry shop. He was thin, half starved and wispy, perhaps seven or eight years old, and he was carrying a board, on which was piled what looked like the wood-ash of a fire. I guessed he was a slave-boy, set to work to clean the ovens out ready for the next day's cookery: it is not unusual for tradesmen, even humble ones, to have young slaves like this, especially when they sell necessities. There is always some family more wretched than their own which has not the wherewithal to pay its bills and is happy to offer an unwanted child instead, reducing the number of hungry mouths to feed.

There was an oil lamp still burning in the shop, judging by the glow that filled the door, and the child stood a moment on the threshold, blinking in the dark. When he saw us he stiffened. 'What are you doing here again? My master has already paid his dues this month.' He was trembling so much that he spilt some of his ash, and he looked as if he would have bolted back inside if he had dared.

Cupidus came up behind me and seized me by the neck. He said, unpleasantly, 'It's not you we're after . . . this time. We're looking for a non-existent slave. This lying wretch,' he gave me such a shake that my teeth rattled, 'declares he left one waiting here. You get on with what you're doing, and be quick or I'll tell your master you were standing gossiping.'

The lad's eyes were wide with fright: the whites shone in the moonlight. He knelt to scrape up as much as possible of what he'd spilt, and, failing, scuttled round the corner to the passageway where obviously the household's midden was.

As he was disappearing, I called after him. 'I don't suppose, since you were working here, that you happened to see anyone yourself?' I guessed that he was not often spoken to without a curse or a blow, and I deliberately used a courteous form of words and tried to make my tone as kind as possible.

It worked. He stopped and looked at me, then volunteered, 'A plumpish fellow with a big round lumpy face?'

I nodded. 'Exactly like a loaf of unbaked bread.'

That made him smile. 'I saw him. Wearing a scarlet tunic you could hardly miss. He was standing over there.' He nodded towards the pavement opposite.

Big-ears turned to Cupidus. 'There you are, you see. It's just as well I didn't let you two go rushing into things. It seems there really was a slave.' He was clearly the most nervous of the three, which was probably why he had been the voice, throughout, of caution and restraint.

Cupidus gave his nasty grin again. 'And how do we know that? We've only got his word for it – his and this wretched slave's. They probably arranged all this between themselves. Amazing what people will agree to say, if you promise to pay them a sestertius or two.'

The child was shaking his head nervously. 'He was there for simply ages. You ask anyone. You couldn't help but notice him: he was dressed in such a fancy tunic, like a uniform, and he seemed to be in everybody's way. I wondered what he was doing there.'

I nodded. That sounded like Promptillius to me. 'When did he give up waiting?'

The child shrugged, cascading another little pile of ash. 'I'm sorry, sir, but I can't answer that. He was here last time I looked, that's all I know.'

'And how long ago was that? An hour? Or more?' Aurissimus snapped out.

The boy had found confidence from somewhere, because he answered back. 'I don't know. How am I supposed to tell? No water clocks in our house.' Aurissimus took a threatening step towards him, and he added hastily, 'Just before sundown. I came out to get more logs and charcoal for the fire, and I noticed he was still hanging around then.' He frowned. 'Talking to somebody, I think, now I look back on it.'

'What sort of somebody?' Surprise and anxiety made me sound as sharp as my companions had, and I saw the poor lad flinch instinctively. I softened my voice, and added, 'Can you remember that?'

He was terrified, you could see it in his face, but he shook his head. 'I wasn't paying much attention at the time. My master beats me if I take too long. He'll beat me now, when I get in again.'

'Nothing to what we'll do, if you can't tell us more than that.' Cupidus was scornful. 'Show him your dagger, Laxus.'

51

Laxus waved it, dangerously close. 'Does that refresh your memory at all?'

The poor lad was almost blubbering by now, and the board slipped entirely from his hands and clattered to the ground. 'A boy, I think. A big boy – that's right – he had a cup and ball. That's all I know. I remember looking at it and wishing that I had one like that.'

'Huh! Not good enough . . .' Cupidus began, and motioned Laxus forward with his blade. What would have happened to the little lad I cannot guess, but my startled exclamation interrupted them.

'Rufinus! Lyra's messenger!' I said. 'You're sure about the toy?' I turned towards the child-slave, who had dropped to his knees and was trying feverishly to scoop up the scattered ashes with pathetic, trembling hands. He glanced up at me with a tearstained face.

'I didn't really look at anything but that,' he managed, between sobs. 'I'm sorry, sirs. I didn't think it mattered. It's all I can remember – honestly. I swear by all the gods . . .' He went back to scrabbling at his hopeless task again. It was clear that he feared a thrashing from his master over it.

His plight touched me, so that for a moment I forgot my own potential danger and, ignoring Laxus and his knife, went over and squatted on my haunches next to him. 'Of course you were looking at the cup and ball. Because you longed to have one of your own?'

The child looked up at me. 'I never had a toy. I had a sort of cart-thing once my father carved for me, but when he sold me to the pastry-cook . . .'

My turn to nod. I too had been a slave, but only as an adult. My childhood had been a very happy one, full of dogs and horses and gambols on the cliffs and in the streams, with playthings and playfellows aplenty. What this child's miserable existence must have been, I could only half imagine.

'He was amazing,' the boy added, with tearful eagerness, as if sharing a special confidence. 'He kept the ball up all the time and never dropped it once. I got a thrashing when I got inside for watching him so long. I'm sorry if I should have noticed more.'

'You did very well,' I said, and he looked so grateful that it touched my heart. Praise was as rare as toys in his young life. 'Here.' I put a hand into my purse and pressed a sestertius into his hand. He looked incredulous. It would be taken from him, like as not, but I felt that some reward was due. 'Tell your master you have been delayed by helping a Roman citizen to find a missing slave, and that I will be here in the morning to buy some honey cakes. Tell him to put half a dozen on one side for me. Here's half a denarius to pay for them.' With any luck, I reasoned, a lucrative order from a customer would be enough to soothe his master's wrath.

He flashed me an uncertain smile, and hurried round the corner with the coins and what little ash he'd succeeded in collecting up again. The others made no move to stop him going.

'Very pretty,' Cupidus jeered. 'And you expect us to believe that the boy is not in your employ? Or in the pay of your bath-side friends? Well, let me tell you, this is my father's area. He won't take kindly to your bribing servants here to tell their confounded little lies for you.' He shouldered up to me, more belligerent than ever, and made to seize me by the neck again.

Aurissimus restrained him. 'Cupidus, don't be more stupid than you have to be. All right, you can't recognise a cheating net man when you see one, but can't you take in what's right before your eyes?' He turned to me. 'You said the youth who came was Lyra's messenger. Who's Lyra?'

I was about to protest that surely he must know who Lyra was, and then of course I realised that he did and he was testing me. I remembered the reaction to her name from the keeper of the thermopolium, and I said hastily, 'I was in the town, looking for a silver cloak clasp for my wife. Lyra approached me and offered me her girls. She gave me an address – the street of the oil-lamp sellers – although I didn't go there at the time.' If the spy system in this part of town was half as good as that in the bath-house area, I knew that my movements could easily be checked. I didn't mention Plautus. I was certain that part of the story would never be believed.

Big-ears was looking at me with amused contempt. 'But you went there later, did you? After dark.'

I was reluctant to say anything which might be proved false. I compromised. 'I never found it,' I said truthfully.

He laughed. 'So you got lost and wandered round the bath-house area? Lyra's wolf-house isn't over there – it's on this side of Venta, where all the soldiers go. No wonder you were followed. A thief, most likely, hoping for your purse. It's a marvel someone didn't cut your throat. They don't like strangers in that part of town.' He turned to his companions. 'I don't believe the man's a spy at all. He's just an idiot who can't control what hangs between his legs. That's why he wasn't present at the games. Made some excuse and sneaked off in the dark, looking for the wolf-house. It all makes sense. That's why the poor fool left his slave behind. I'll bet he's got a wife at home, as well, and didn't want her finding out where he had been.' He gave another hoot of mocking mirth. 'And then he didn't find it after all. It's true. He can't have done. He gave money to that slave. Lyra wouldn't leave a customer with silver in his purse. If he didn't spend it willingly, the girls would get it from his clothes while he was occupied with something else.'

'But surely she can't steal from them?' I was startled into speech. 'The penalties . . .'

He swept my words aside. 'You may come from a big city, stranger, but you're strangely innocent. Of course she'd have your purse. It often happens. Very few complain – not when they've been busy with one of Lyra's specialists. If it came to court, they'd be a laughing-stock.'

I resisted the temptation to retort that he clearly knew all about the brothel and its ways. It was obvious that Big-ears was the self-appointed thinker of the group and saw himself as the voice of reason. I suspected that this was less the product of intelligence than the result of his being the most nervous of the three, but since he was arguing for my release I held my tongue. Neither did I voice the sudden thought which I had almost blurted out a moment earlier: why had Lyra sent Rufinus to find my slave? How had she known that I possessed one, come to that? I'd assumed the boy had been sent to warn Plautus, but it seemed that I was wrong.

In fact, it was a mystery which I found troubling. I had parted company with Promptillius long before I spotted Plautus and went after him, so when Lyra had approached me it was in an altogether different part of town. So how had anyone identified Promptillius as mine? And what was the message that Rufinus passed on to him?

For there had been some sort of message, I was sure of that, and probably ostensibly from me. It was the only thing I could imagine that would have persuaded the stolid Promptillius to desert his post. I said quickly, before Big-ears had time to think this through himself, 'Well, if you gentlemen are satisfied, I should be getting back. My party will be concerned for me by now, and sending out a search, I shouldn't be surprised.'

Cupidus was lurching into thought. 'So, where's your slave gone now?'

It was a question I had asked myself and failed to find a convincing answer for, but I said – with what I hoped was confidence – 'Gone back to the mansio, I should think. Do you want to come there with me and see? You can check out my story with the guard.'

I half hoped they would give up at this, and let me go, but to my surprise they all three seized on it, and a moment later we were walking, single file, in the direction of the military inn. Laxus walked behind me, uncomfortably close, and I was aware of the dagger which he still held unsheathed, but hidden now beneath his cloak, presumably in case the guard should notice it. I wondered what would happen if I denounced him to the sentry on the gate, but it was not an experiment I cared to make. Spotty-face was clearly anxious to prove himself a man, fearless and ready with a knife. I didn't wish to provide him with the opportunity.

As we approached, the soldier on guard duty came out to block our way. 'Who is it, and what's your business here?'

Laxus urged me forward with his blade. I took a step into the ring of light which blazed from the torches hanging on the wall. The burly guard drew his sword and looked me up and down. 'What are you doing here? And who are these?' He examined my companions, his armour glittering in the torchlight with a hundred little reflected flames. 'I know you three. Get off home, or I'll report you to your fathers. I am surprised at you, old man, cavorting with these rogues. You've no idea the trouble they cause.'

'Not cavorting,' I said firmly. 'I asked them the way, that's all. And perhaps you could resolve a little disagreement we had. I say that Marcus Aurelius Septimus brought a citizen-client of his here today, before he went to the games. Can you confirm that?'

The soldier seemed to think a moment before answering. 'A bet, is it? Well, what you say is true. I can't see why I shouldn't tell you that. It's no secret that His Excellence was here. But his client is not here at the moment, if that's who you want. He went off shopping in the market with a slave, and he's not yet returned. The slave came back alone a little while ago.'

That reassured me. Promptillius was safe. When I got inside I'd talk to him and try to piece together what exactly had gone on, and who had sent him the order to go home. I turned to Cupidus. 'You see? It is all exactly as I said. I was telling you the truth.'

They seemed to realise the force of this. The effect upon all three of them was startling. I have seen something of the kind before, when people have discovered suddenly that I'm a Roman citizen and under the protection of the law – and these three had more to fear from that than most. Not only were they possibly guilty of *injuria* – infraction of my dignity – they'd actually laid violent hands on me. And I knew about that dagger, too.

Laxus had turned sallower than ever in the torchlight. 'I never touched you,' he protested fervently. 'It was them. They urged me on. They thought you were a spy.'

Cupidus was vigorous in self-defence. 'Well, you can't altogether blame us, citizen. You come lurking round the tavern in the dark, dressed like a nobody, and start hiding in doorways and sidling up to us. What are we going to think? It's just the sort of nasty trick those bath-siders would use – sending a stranger round to spy on us, pretending he had come to ask the way.' His voice was shriller now and he was talking fast. 'We've had this sort of thing before, and the next day or week or month, you can depend on it, there is an ambush somewhere off the beaten track and some member of our family is attacked or disappears. No wonder we treat outsiders with distrust. Why, if I get hold of one of them I'll . . .'

Aurissimus took him gently by the arm. 'Come on, Cupidus, that's enough. You've made your point. We've had too much to drink. Let's go, before this citizen decides to lay a charge.' And, rather reluctantly, Cupidus allowed himself to be led away, with Laxus trailing after them.

I stood and watched them till they were out of sight. Only then did I start to feel secure.

The guard must have read my feelings in my face. 'You look relieved to see the back of them. If they've been harassing you, you should have told me so. I'd have had them in for questioning and pleased to do it too.' He winked. 'We've had a lot of trouble with young men like that – writing on buildings, fighting in the street, pawing women and frightening the elderly. But of course, I know those three – all sons of wealthy fathers hereabouts. Their families have got influence, and no one local dares to bring a charge.' He sighed. 'I don't know what's come over young people nowadays. No respect for proper authority, that's what. It's all down to drink. Too much money and not enough to do.'

He was obviously inclined to chat and I was glad to hear a friendly voice. I was in no danger here. 'They do come from important families, then?' I said. 'I rather guessed as much.'

His teeth gleamed in the torchlight as he grinned. 'Not as important as they'd like to be. Those three cousins in particular. You know what it's like. When we got here – the army, that is – and took over in the area, we laid out the town and appointed a few of the most loyal local chiefs to help us run it – made them citizens and put them on the council, all that sort of thing.'

I frowned. 'Their fathers are on the ordo?' If those youths were citizens as well, that put a different complexion on the thing.

My informant laughed. 'Nothing so exalted. But they would like to be. Set themselves up as patrons of the town, at considerable expense, and run the local suburb where they live – they're on every council and committee which doesn't actually require you to be a citizen – and try to court favour with the authorities, but at the same time they resent us, because we didn't select them as councillors in the first place.' He sighed. 'Perhaps we should have done. They fought beside us too. But nothing is ever simple round here. The tribes are always quarrelling among themselves, and it's hard to work out who are the natural chiefs.' Like many soldiers he talked of the Roman Empire as 'we', as if imperial decisions were his personal concern.

'I understand there's quite a lot of tension in the town. Rival groups have power in different parts of it.'

His face closed like a door. 'Not as far as we're concerned, they don't. The civil administration works, that's all that worries us. If these people want to carry on old feuds behind locked doors, that's up to them. As long as they don't interfere with the free passage of supplies and troops, they can murder one another till there's no one left, as far as I'm concerned. Just provided they don't start bringing cases to the courts, and that's not very likely. Now – you've kept me gossiping too long. Move on.'

Obviously I had touched a nerve. I flashed a smile. 'I will,' I said. 'Thank you for being so helpful. I'll see that His Excellence hears of it. Goodnight.' I started to walk past him into the mansio.

The sword flashed down across the entrance like lightning, forming a gleaming barrier. 'And what do you think you're up to? You can't go in there.'

Chapter Seven

For a moment I thought he was jesting, but one glance at his swarthy face convinced me he was not. All trace of the earlier friendliness had vanished suddenly, and he was looking very menacing indeed.

In vain I argued that I was the citizen he had talked about. He clearly did not believe a word of it. 'My name is Libertus,' I said urgently. 'I am that client of His Excellency, and I am staying at the inn. Surely you must have been expecting me?'

He looked at me coldly. 'I'm not expecting anyone tonight, not even a mounted messenger with the imperial post. Anyway, as you would have discovered if you had made proper enquiries, Libertus may be a tradesman, but he is a Roman citizen, not a scruffy traveller like yourself.' He looked at my cloak and tunic with contempt. I remembered the optio's promise not to disclose the fact that I had gone out without my proper dress. Obviously the officer had kept his word. The first man on duty at the gate had seen me go, of course, but there had been a change of guard since then.

'Send for the optio,' I said. 'He'll vouch for me.'

'The optio is off duty by this time, as you would have realised, if you had ever been inside an inn like this. And his instructions were to bar the gate.'

I cursed myself. It had not been specifically referred to, naturally, but what I knew of such establishments should have forewarned me that this would be the case. Some subordinate would be on duty in there now, one who had never seen me. I tried another tack. 'Well, what about the slave – Promptillius? He'll know who I am.'

'And how am I to call him? Leave the door, so you can slip inside? I wasn't born last moon. In any case, he isn't here – as you would have known, if you were the person that you claim to be.'

'But I'm the citizen Libertus . . .' I began again.

He interrupted me. 'Now don't start that again. Of course you're not. Promptillius has gone to join his master at the feast. He had the most precise instructions from the man himself. Written orders, too. I saw the wax tablet they were scratched onto myself. I made him show me when I let him in, as proof of his identity. So it's no use you pretending otherwise.'

'Promptillius has gone to Marcus?' I was bewildered now.

'He's gone to join his master! This Libertus fellow. You heard what I said. Don't look at me like that. I saw the note. The slave was to come here and tell us that there'd been a change of plan: Libertus the pavement-maker was to dine with his patron after all, and attend the assizes in the morning as a spectator. He wanted his slave to take fresh clothes and go to him at once, so that he could bathe and change and make ready for the feast. Now, I don't know what you're playing at, my friend, but it won't work with me. Some trick of those young scoundrels, I suppose. One of their stupid wagers, was it, that you could get inside the mansio? You should have more sense, at your age. Well, it didn't work. I'm not as stupid as they take me for. So, are you going to move along, or shall I lock you up, for trying to impersonate a citizen?'

He had his sword-blade to my throat by now. I moved along.

His threat was not an idle one. Impersonating a citizen can, at worst, mean death – although it did occur to me, as I slunk off into the shadows, that since I really was a citizen, the charge would be difficult to prove. In fact – although it would mean a beating, chains and an uncomfortable bed of stinking straw – at least inside the military cells I would be safe. I would have a roof above my head and be protected from the other harassments, half-glimpsed and wholly unexplained, which had dogged me ever since I got to town. In the morning I would be brought before the optio, who would quickly have me freed – and what would happen to the pompous sentry then! I almost considered going back and defying him to carry out his threat, but I had thought of another, less drastic solution to my plight – one which did not involve a thrashing!

There is one place, at least, where a man can find a bed, behind a curtain and in privacy, at almost any time of night without too many questions being asked. Of course, there were the other occupants to think about – the girls with interesting specialities – but such females are paid to please their clients. I reasoned that if a customer required them to simply let him sleep while they kept watch, presumably they could be persuaded to do so, at a price.

I would not go to Lyra's brothel, naturally. I was certain that she'd set Paulinus onto me, and probably my unseen follower as well, and in any case I remembered what Aurissimus Big-ears had said about the dangers to one's purse in her establishment. However, the owner of the thermopolium had spoken of that other wolf-house with the girls upstairs, whose doors were always open day and night.

The premises were not far from his own and the area was not controlled by Lyra and her friends. If I could find my way there, that seemed the safest place.

Even so, the plan involved some risk. It was getting very late by now, and I would have to retrace my steps back to the bath-house sector of the town where I had been followed so disturbingly before. My sole directions were from the hot-soup stall, so my only course was to go back and find the place from there – though Lupus's thermopolium itself would be long shut by now. Such establishments stay open only as long as there are customers or until the stock of soup runs out.

Going back again through those deserted streets was not an inviting prospect, but I could not stay where I was, and by now it was threatening to rain. The first drops were already bouncing off the paving stones. I thought wildly of finding shelter underneath an arch, but that was less inviting still: such places are often frequented by vagabonds and thieves and – since murder is the safest form of robbery, as it leaves no witnesses to bring a case – I knew that if I attempted such a thing I would be lucky to survive the night. If I'd had the slightest notion of where my patron was feasting, I might have dared his anger and burst in on him, but I had no idea who his host was, far less how to find him in this unfamiliar town. The wolf-house seemed to be my only hope.

Cautiously I made my way along the shadowed streets, trying to recall my earlier movements and retrace my steps. I expected at every turn to hear footfalls behind me and know that someone was trailing me again, and once I did pause – thinking I heard a muffled, rhythmic thump – but it was only my own heart pounding in my ears.

I went up the alleyway where I'd followed Plautus earlier,

and came to the narrow passage by the fuller's shop. If I wished to find my hot-soup stall with certainty, there was little choice but to go where I had gone before, and edge up there in the dark and wet. I almost baulked at the prospect, but then I remembered the dining knife I carried at my belt. Marcus had given it to me quite recently, and I'd had it newly sharpened for this trip. I took it out, wishing that I'd recalled it earlier: it was not much protection but it made me feel a good deal more confident. Thus armed, I made my way gingerly up the sinister and oppressive little passageway, but encountered nothing worse than stench, the slippery blackness and the now relentless rain.

I reached the corner where the armour stall had been. Still nothing. The stalls were closed up long ago, the piles of wares all taken in and locked away from thieves. Lacking these landmarks, it was hard to find my way – the street seemed longer and wider than before and ominously empty.

I moved to the very centre of the road, between the carriage ruts, telling myself that there I was less likely to be surprised by anyone lurking in a doorway, or watching from a window space above. My sandals seemed to make a startling slapping noise on the wet paving stones, and I was getting drenched, but nobody threw open window shutters to shout down at me, and the one couple I passed (slaves, by their tunics, underneath an arch) were too busy with each other to pay much heed to me. Or so, at least, I hoped.

Then, on the distant corner of the street, I recognised the thermopolium. To my surprise I saw the glow of torches from within and the door stood wide ajar. The soup stall was still open, seemingly – certainly there were people in the shop. Quite a group of people – some of them women, by the look of it. I could see their shadows on the wall as I approached.

Suddenly I felt a flare of hope. I remembered how Lupus, the owner of the shop, had said to me that he'd thought of letting out a room. Of course, his wife had voiced objections to the plan, and he'd done nothing further, but it did occur to me that there might be sufficient space upstairs for me to sleep somewhere. It was just possible that his wife could be persuaded to agree. I would be prepared to pay them very well – the whole contents of my purse, if necessary – and I remembered that the woman was a Christian. I don't have much dealing, in the normal way, with followers of that extraordinary cult but they have the reputation of being honest folk, even if their beliefs are rather odd. An appeal to her religion might well do the trick and save me tramping further through the wet.

Well, there was only one way to find out. I took a deep breath and tiptoed down the street towards the open door, still keeping circumspectly to the far side of the road. I saw that the females were not the wolf-house girls, as I had half expected at this hour, but a group of ageing, stoutish matrons in sturdy Celtic plaid. The men – by their fish-scale armour, brawny arms and leather tunics – looked like members of the town watch. All solid townspeople. No sign of Plautus or his youthful spies. Reassured, I crossed the road and made towards the doorway of the shop.

And then I saw what was lying on the floor – something which had been hidden from my view till now by the presence of the crowd of onlookers.

Lupus was sprawled against the counter, quite obviously dead. His tunic had been ripped aside and somebody had not only slit his throat, but savagely slashed that giant form from throat to stomach. There was more of Lupus oozing out onto the tiles than was good for anybody's health. One of the watch was standing over him, holding the lighted taper in his hand.

Lupus's wife was standing, shaking, in another woman's arms, convulsed with silent sobbing, while the others looked on, silent and appalled. It was like a dumb-show at the theatre, representing death.

I suppressed the cry of horror which had risen to my lips, but before I could even think of slipping off again, Lupus's wife glanced up and saw my face. Her eyes bulged with astonishment. She shrugged herself free from the arm that sought to comfort her and raised an accusing finger at me as she found her voice.

'That's him. That's the man. The one I was telling you about. He came in and was drinking with Lupus here tonight. I saw them together with my own two eyes. See, he is still carrying a knife! Seize him, guards. I accuse him of this killing. You are all witnesses to that.'

Before I had the chance to think, let alone make any move at all, I found myself – for the second time that night – flung up against the wall. The town-watch guards were rougher than my drunken friends had been, and more efficient too. The knife was knocked flying from my hand, and I was bound – none too gently – at the wrists. At the same time a filthy rag was stuffed in my mouth and I was jerked painfully upright again by the remnants of my already thinning hair.

It was of no use to struggle and I was powerless to protest – the woman had made a formal accusation, in front of witnesses, and the only escape now was through the courts. A man can only be prosecuted, of course, if he is captured and delivered by his accuser to the authorities, but I had saved the watch the trouble and expense of catching me by walking straight into their arms.

The senior guard insisted on the usual formula. 'Before Jupiter, and in the name of Rome, you accuse this man of crime?'

She nodded. 'Didn't I just say so? Who else could it have been? He was here with Lupus just before he died. When I came out, he scuttled off – I thought he looked suspicious at the time. There was no one else about. I went into the back room – just to rinse the dirty cups in a bowl of water which I keep out there – and the moment I was gone he must have slipped back here and cut my husband's throat. There was no time for anybody else to get into the shop. I was gone an instant, no more, when I heard the thump. When I came back I found poor Lupus, lying there – like this. And he hadn't even been baptised.' She burst out again in helpless sobs.

The smaller guard nodded sagely. 'Anything missing, that you know about?'

She looked down at the body on the floor. 'He still has the arm-purse that he was wearing,' she said, with some surprise. 'I probably disturbed the villain before he had a chance to cut it free. The money chest from underneath the counter's gone.'

I was amazed. Christians in general avoid the law – their refusal to swear upon the Roman gods, particularly the Emperor himself, often leads to their being executed for treason themselves. And here was this woman making baseless charges against me! I tried to make a protest, but the gag prevented it. I managed only a muffled 'Mwmm!' before a sharp jerk brought my head up painfully and almost pulled my hair out by the roots, reminding me that speech was not allowed.

'You mind your manners,' the guard said nastily. 'You're coming to the jail with us. We'll soon see then what you've got to say.'

I nodded dumbly. This was not what I'd imagined earlier. I could have endured a night locked up in a military cell, inside the mansio. But this would take me to the public jail. I only hoped that I would have a chance to speak before they gave me to the torturers. If matters proceeded according to the letter the law, I would have a brief chance to state my case before a magistrate – and so reach Marcus, possibly – but I was not even confident of that. The evening had gone from terrible to worse. However, there was little help for it. I submitted to what was, in any case, inevitable now, and did not struggle as they looped a second rope round my neck and led me ignominiously away.

At least, I told myself, shivering with damp and tiredness and cold, this solved the problem of where I would spend the night.

Chapter Eight

The evening when they dragged me to the town jail in Venta is not one I wish to dwell upon and certainly not one I'm anxious to repeat. First I was hustled through the rainy streets, almost more quickly than my legs and heart would stand. One of the guards was holding the halter round my neck, and he kept jerking it and dragging me along so I was half choked to death and scrabbling like a stray dog on a leash. Nor was this a private spectacle. The clop of hobnailed sandals and the clank of armour must have alerted the sleeping townspeople, because doorways and window spaces which had been empty when I passed before were suddenly alive with curious onlookers. As we passed the closed-up bath-house, there were even jeers.

We halted at the prison, a dismal building in a courtyard. The stone walls were as thick as tree trunks and, judging from the steep steps leading downwards from the door, much of the accommodation was underground. A bleary warder with a torch came out to squint at us.

'This one's accused of murdering a hot-soup seller down the bath-house end of town, and stealing all his gold. Claims he isn't guilty, but don't they all? We found him with a knife. Stick him in a dungeon overnight, and tomorrow we'll see what the inquisitors can do,' my captor said, shoving me forward into the jail.

My mouth was still tightly bound so I could not protest, and they pushed me without ceremony down the flight of stairs to where a leering guard unlocked a heavy door.

There was very little light or air down there, but by the taper that the warder carried I could make out a sort of stinking cellar of a dungeon, where three wretched prisoners were already chained up. Not only were they tethered to the wall, but their hands and feet were linked by chains to a collar round the neck, so that the unfortunates could not sit or stand, and were compelled to grovel on their knees, like dogs, to lap for slops of food. It is a method often used by dealers when transporting slaves, so I know how uncomfortable it is.

The atmosphere was damp and foul, besides, and so cold that it struck instant chill into my bones. I shivered. I was already soaked through by the rain and a night in here would be the end of me, I thought – and even if I did survive, there would no doubt be torturers awaiting me at dawn, unless I could reach Marcus first. Something must be done.

I was almost at the limit of my strength after the progress through the town, but I gathered what effort I could still command and as one the guards undid the gag and pushed me down onto the filthy floor, I raised my head and managed to croak out the magic formula.

'I am a Roman citizen. I appeal to the provincial governor.'

It was a desperate gamble, even then. Since the official governor, Pertinax, had left the country to take up his new African command there was a danger that, after this appeal, I would stay locked up until his successor was installed. However, since Marcus was opening the local court tomorrow, I hoped that they would call on him to deal with me – quickly, while he was still in town. It was likely that they would: since he was Pertinax's representative and the senior magistrate for miles around, it would have been an insult to his dignity to do otherwise.

Of course, it was possible that he would decline to hear the case, I was aware of that. He could not know that I was in the dock. No one, so far, had even asked my name. It was clear that my captors would not risk his wrath by interfering with the feast to carry any messages from me, and since he was not returning to the mansio that night, he was quite unaware that I was not tucked up safely in my bed.

'I appeal to the imperial courts,' I said again.

One of my escorts gave a scornful laugh and aimed a kick at me, and for a moment I thought they would dismiss the whole idea, just as the soldier at the mansio had done. But the warden, in particular, was looking doubtful now.

'Here, look out,' he said. 'Suppose he's right? The penalties for mistreating a citizen are severe. And why would he claim to be one if he's not? That's a capital offence.'

The town guard who had dragged me by the neck looked contemptuous. 'Him, a citizen? Then what was he doing down the bath-house end of town at night? You don't have to be a sibyl to know that's not very safe.' One of the prisoners made a snorting sound at this, and the guard repaid him with a savage blow.

All the same, the warder seemed to feel that Roman authority had been called into question by the guard's remark. 'We are the representatives of Roman law round here, and we have things under control. It's just that it isn't sensible to go where you're not welcome after dark. But if he is a stranger to the town – and I for one have not set eyes on him before – it is just possible he didn't know.'

He gestured to the others to join him at the door. There

was a hurried consultation in which I strained to catch the words 'can't be too careful . . . what have we to lose? . . . it will be the worse for him tomorrow, if it proves a lie'.

I was fortunate. The two members of the town watch still looked sceptical, but the warden's wariness prevailed.

My escorts looked at each other and then, exchanging nods, came over to where I was still sprawling helpless on the floor. 'We'll give you the benefit of the doubt, my friend, but woe betide you if you're telling lies,' the younger man muttered as he yanked me to my feet. That was as much of an apology as I was going to get.

'If you are a citizen, why didn't you tell us earlier?' The other guard, who had pushed me over, was suddenly concerned to dust my tunic down, where it was stained by contact with the soiled muck on the floor. He sounded mildly aggrieved. 'How were we supposed to know that you were anyone?'

I attempted to point out that I'd not had the chance to tell them anything, since they'd forced that wretched rag between my teeth. One of the pathetic creatures chained against the wall let out a feeble murmur of encouragement at this, and was promptly beaten for his pains.

The warder was anxious to cut short my complaint. 'A most unfortunate mistake, but it is over now. And I had no part in it. I hope you will remember that, if you turn out to be telling the truth and there's any official complaint. Now, we'll take you somewhere a little more appropriate. If you will come with us . . . ?'

He hurried forward with his torch and keys to push back the heavy door, and I found myself being propelled upstairs again almost as quickly as I'd been hustled down. Bound and still haltered as I was, I slipped and stumbled, but the two guards took my arms and half supported me, until we came to a small room halfway up the stairs.

It was still a prison cell, there was no doubt of that, but it was a good deal better than the wretched hole downstairs. Here there was a pile of cleanish straw, a proper cup and drinking jug (though both were chained to the wall), and – best of all – a little window-opening high up overhead, through which night air was blowing, wet and cold and carrying the tang of horse dung from the street, but blessedly fresh and pure compared to the atmosphere I'd breathed below.

One of my erstwhile escorts slipped the rope noose from my neck, while the other slashed the knot that bound my hands. With my arms free it was possible to rub the spot where my makeshift halter had been chafing me, and by the glow of the torch – with which the warder was now lighting a small taper on the wall (another concession to the status I claimed) – I could see the raw lines on my wrists where the tight bonds had been. Roman-trained guards know how to tie a knot.

The warder was still all concern for me. He seemed to be a decent sort, according to his lights. 'I could bring you a bit of ointment, if you can pay for it,' he said. 'And a woollen cloth of sorts. Might make a kind of blanket for you overnight. And in the morning, you can see the governor of the jail, and tell him who you are. You let him know that I looked after you. There's water in the jug, and I think there might be a bit of bread upstairs. Anything else, you can send out for when it's light – supposing that you possess a purse? Otherwise there might be a moneylender who could see you through, if you can sign the right assurances.'

I shook my head. 'I know what kind of interest those

feneratores demand, especially if they know you're desperate.' I didn't add the obvious, that few men are more desperate than a prisoner in a cell. They force you to pledge everything you own for the most basic of commodities, and the contract is binding under law, so that even if the wretched prisoner is found guilty of his crime and executed, the debt is still enforceable and his surviving family has to pay. I would not subject my beloved wife to that.

The warder looked at me. 'I can't bring you anything unless you pay.'

'The moneylenders won't be necessary. Fortunately, I have some money of my own.' I touched the drawstring pouch which was still hanging at my belt. 'Although it appears that I have lost my knife somewhere. It is quite a valuable thing – I might have traded it for goods.'

If I hoped that the remark would disconcert the guards into returning my knife to me, I hoped in vain. The larger one laughed.

'Oh no you don't, my friend. That knife is evidence. Even if you prove that you're a citizen, you had an illegal weapon in your hand. And we are witnesses. You can't get out of that.'

I realised with a shiver that my knife had not simply been appropriated, as the belongings of accused men sometimes are. It would be produced against me at my trial, as proof that I was carrying a blade. That in itself was a capital offence, whether I was a citizen or not. Especially in this rebellious capital, no doubt, despite the stalls of armour in the streets and the dagger which Laxus had been wielding earlier.

As if in answer to my thoughts, the warder said, 'That is a bit unfortunate. The town authorities here are even more than usually concerned about arresting people who walk about with arms. There are still folk here who think it's in their tribal interest to slip a knife between a pair of Roman ribs.'

Thank all the gods that Marcus himself had given me the knife, for dining purposes, though I began to wish I hadn't had it sharpened quite so well.

Well, there was nothing I could do about it now. I turned my attention back to present needs. I would have to pay in coin for anything I had, and even simple things were going to cost me dear. I made a bargain with the warder for a blanket now and a fresh oatcake in the morning – though I had no great confidence that I would ever see the goods. Certainly I'd never get the honey cakes I'd paid for earlier. However, I passed over most of the coinage I had and the three men withdrew. As the door closed behind them I heard the key grate in the lock, so I settled on my pile of straw as best I could, given that I ached in every limb, and tried to convince myself that my dismal situation might have advantages.

I was safer in a cell than I might have been outside, that was one benefit. It appeared that in Venta I was actually at risk – though whether that was just me, or whether it would apply to any traveller, I could not quite be sure. I suspected that it was personal. I had twice been followed through the town.

And then there was that misleading message to my slave. The more I thought about that the more alarming it became. Someone in this town had sent it, in my name and quite deliberately. There was only one purpose served by doing so, as far I could see. It prevented the soldiers at the mansio from questioning my absence and sending out a search. That was sinister. It was clearly not intended that I should return. And, it occurred to me, the message had the additional effect of ensuring that my attendant was not outside the pastry shop when I went back for him, so I would be walking through the streets alone, deprived of the protection of a slave.

I wondered again where Promptillius was now. He had obeyed the 'message' on the writing tablet, presumably, supposing that it came from me, and had left the mansio with my clothes. The fact that my patron was being entertained at a feast was clearly common knowledge in the town – even Big-ears and his friends had known it – but how could anyone have guessed that I came from the military inn, and that Promptillius was attending me? By watching us, perhaps – that was distinctly possible, judging from my own experience.

I shifted on my pile of straw and groaned. I ached all over. As soon as I got out of here, I vowed, I'd send for Junio and some of Gwellia's balm. The comforts of my home seemed far away.

That brought me almost upright with a jerk. My home was far away. Who, in this town, could possibly have known my name to forge that note? Had I told anyone? I tried to think, but I was almost sure I hadn't. So who had sent the message? The red-headed expert with cup and ball who had delivered the message to my slave outside the pastry shop was Lyra's spy, Rufinus, I was sure of it. But how could she possibly have known my name, or that Promptillius was mine? I hadn't told her anything about myself, and besides, he was dressed in Marcus's household uniform.

So who had been behind all this? There was only one candidate that I could think of: Plautus. The man who was not dead. Who else could have associated me with Marcus and the military inn? Only Plautus, who knew from Glevum who my patron was. Most of Venta would know about the feast, and that Marcus had been present at the games – I had the evidence of the three young men for that – but no local resident could know my trade: yet the mansio guard had said that I was referred to as a 'pavement-maker' in the written note.

The written note. That was another thing. Whoever sent that message had access to wax tablets and a stylus, and sufficient education to produce written Latin good enough to look like Marcus's or mine. That didn't sound like Lyra or the butcher's boys. Plautus, on the other hand, had been a member of the Glevum ordo once, where reading and writing were necessary skills for any councillor.

Respectable, dull Plautus. It seemed incredible that he should want to kill me, but it was the only explanation I could see. I'd made it obvious that I recognised his face, and he did not wish it to be recognised. He had not wanted to waylay me and explain – he'd had the opportunity to do that, and had run away. So why would he follow me about, unless it was because I knew he was alive and he hoped to silence me? Boring old Plautus as would-be assassin? Was it possible?

I gulped. It would not have been very difficult, if that was his idea. An unprotected stranger on the streets at night, in a town where rival gangs are active – it would not be wholly surprising if I disappeared, or turned up in a gutter somewhere with my purse missing and my throat cut. If it had not been for the chance of that donkey blocking up the street, whoever had been on my heels would have caught up with me – it was possible that even my decision to accost Big-ears and his inebriated friends had helped to save my life.

Then another thought occurred to me: one which sent shivers down my already chilly spine. Was Lupus's murder

79

quite as unconnected with my presence as I thought? I had talked to Lupus, and a moment later – so his wife had said – someone had come out of the dark and slit his throat. Was that because I might have said too much to him? And was the follower also aiming to kill me?

I was still contemplating the full implications of this terrible idea when my thoughts were interrupted by the opening of the door. It was the warder who, true to his word, had brought a 'kind of blanket' – a length of coarse woollen cloth smelling overpoweringly of horse – and a hunk of bread. It was no more fresh than the blanket was, but I thanked the man sincerely and fell on my frugal feast.

He watched me for a moment. 'I'll get those oatcakes fetched in early,' he observed at last. 'I expect the prison governor will want to see you first thing. Now, if you've got any sense, you'll try to rest. I'll wake you at dawn.' So saying, he snuffed the taper, went out, and shut the door, leaving me in total darkness, except for the faint glow that filtered from the street.

I found that I was shaking with relief and weariness. There was nothing for it but to act on his advice. I took off my sodden clothes, wrapped myself in the makeshift covering, lay down on the straw-pile and – in spite of the terrors of the day and my attempts to think things through again – fell almost instantly into a fitful sleep.

Chapter Nine

The warder woke me shortly before dawn, but I was not conducted before the prison governor, as he had suggested I might be. 'That travelling magistrate has agreed to hear the case. You know, the one who's visiting the town. I hope you've got proper proof of what you say. He's a hard man, I hear, and he'll brook no nonsense if it's all a lie. Still, it's meant that our governor can wash his hands of you. He isn't even going to have you scourged – leave you to more senior men, he said. Doesn't want any trouble, if you ask me. Now, here's your oatcake. They'll be coming for you soon. Anything else you want to buy before you go?'

I looked up from my meagre breakfast – certainly the most expensive oatcake I have ever eaten in my life, and not entirely fresh. 'A bowl of water and a drying cloth.'

He looked astonished. 'Whatever for? Not thinking of trying to drown yourself, are you?'

'To clean myself a little. I don't want to look too much of a disgrace.'

He seemed unable to believe his ears. 'Where did you say you come from, citizen? They must do things very differently round there. Most prisoners here want just the opposite – beg me to send out for rags for them to wear, and dust and ashes to rub on their hair and face, so they can look properly penitent in court.'

I nodded. 'It's the same in Glevum too. Prisoners try to arrive before the judge looking as dishevelled and pathetic as possible. I know the idea is to whip up pity from the crowd.' When the accused man looks properly pitiful and contrite, if the verdict goes against him there is often an outcry from the onlookers and even nowadays that can be enough to affect the sentencing – although the kind of trial where the presiding magistrate refers the verdict directly to the mob is getting very rare, except in cases where public sympathy runs deep and it might avoid a riot. 'But it won't work for me.'

That was the understatement of the Empire. I knew Marcus. I was a member of his official party and the more disreputable I looked, the more discredit I brought on him, and the more displeased he would inevitably be. My appearance was profoundly disrespectful as it was. Bad enough that I was only in a tunic, but my brief sojourn in the lower-dungeon mud had not improved that humble garment, despite my attempts to sponge off the worst of it. In addition, I was rain-soaked and travel-stained and I could feel a big bruise swelling up above one eye.

The warder nodded, rather doubtfully. 'Don't suppose there's much point your appealing to the populace today. You won't have many supporters here, I suppose.'

That was another understatement. Nobody in Venta cared a fig for me – quite the opposite, it seemed – and anyway Marcus would be presiding as *iudicius*, directly on the departed governor's behalf. That meant that even the permanent jury had no say in anything – verdict and punishment alike were at his absolute, personal discretion. I did not want him too displeased with me.

After a little more discussion and a hefty bribe, I got my bowl of water and a drying cloth of sorts and dabbed at my face and ruined tunic where I could. Then, shortly after dawn, I was led out and taken to the forum under guard.

I was more than a little apprehensive, though. Judging by the cheering crowds along the way, my patron and his entourage had just arrived at the basilica, among all the pomp and ceremony which he so enjoyed – trumpets, heralds and a retinue of uniformed soldiers at his side, while he waved graciously to passers-by, resplendent in his laurel wreath and purple stripes. It made my dismal appearance even more acute.

I knew I was hardly looking spruce as I was brought in between two brawny-looking guards, but even so my lack of public penitential show was enough to draw hisses from the gallery, where a gaggle of young women had come to see the fun, though they hid their faces behind modest veils. That was a little bit unusual, I thought. Most of the spectators at such affairs are men.

The courtroom was bursting with other people, too. The public procession and the trumpet calls had naturally caused quite a stir in the town, and news of the trial must have travelled fast. Every inch of standing space was packed, and the adjoining area, which could be partitioned off to form another courtroom, had been left open to accommodate the crowd.

I was led – not chained, but still at sword-point – up the steps and down the courtroom to the dais. One of my guards was obliged to lead the way and force a path for us through the throng. I could hear the mocking and the whispering and I was jostled several times as I passed by. At least, I thought, because I had claimed to be a citizen, the trial was taking place indoors before a proper judge. Proceedings against non-citizens are still often conducted in the open air by lesser functionaries, to the hoots and jeers and heckling of the mob: it is a rough kind of justice and public humiliation is part of the ordeal.

There was nothing at all humble about this. I walked the whole length of the basilica. The building from outside might look relatively small, compared to the one in Glevum, but inside it was still an imposing edifice. The central nave was flanked by towering columns in the Corinthian style – doubly impressive in the narrowness of the space, which made them look much taller than they were – while the severely formal patterns on the plastered wall and the stark black and white tesselations of the floor added to the impression of humourless solemnity.

Marcus was already seated on the rostrum at the further end on a sort of judicial throne, flanked by two minor magistrates. I was brought to stand at the bottom of the steps, but for the moment he paid no attention to me at all. He was talking and laughing lightly, leaning back, as if he were enjoying the attention, as no doubt he was.

He was at his magisterial best, all purple stripes and laurel wreaths, with a heavy, jewelled torc of Celtic gold round his neck and his seal ring prominent upon his hand. I had never seen the torc before – it was not a thing he generally wore. I guessed it had been lent to him for the occasion – or given outright perhaps – by some local dignitary anxious to curry favour with His Excellence. Certainly my patron looked very well in it, and it gave him additional presence and authority.

Then a court official made a sign and Marcus clapped his hands. There was a little rustle through the crowd, and an expectant silence fell.

One of the court recorders stood up to read the charge. 'Excellence, in the name of the Most Imperial Commodus

Hercules Exsuperatorius, the Merciful, the Fortunate and the Dutiful, Emperor and God, I have the honour to inform you that the man before you stands—'

He got no further. Marcus had noticed who I was at last. He half rose from his seat and let out a startled roar. 'You? You ridiculous old fool. What by all the immortals have you been up to now?' His face was dangerously scarlet with anger and dismay at his own unstatesmanlike display. He sank back on his seat and turned towards the clerk. 'What is the meaning of this farce?'

A lean hungry-looking fellow at the bar stepped forward at these words. 'Excellence, this is no farce at all. An honest hot-soup seller was stabbed to death last night, and all his money taken. This man was on the premises, we have witnesses to that. And he was carrying a knife. The shop-keeper's wife accuses him and brings this case to your attention, Excellence. She seeks the right of *talio*, or compensation from the state at least.'

Marcus looked at me with obvious contempt. 'The keeper of a common hot-soup store, you say? Is this true, Libertus?'

If I could have dropped onto my knees and grovelled, I would have done, but I was still at sword-point and did not dare make an unexpected move. 'Your pardon, Excellence. I was in the shop, it's true, but I did not kill the man. He was alive when I last saw him, talking to his wife. As for the knife, it is not a weapon, it's a dining tool. A fine one, certainly, which my patron gave to me.' I essayed an apologetic smile.

He was not amused. 'Silence! Confine yourself to answering the questions which I ask. If I want your comments, I will ask for them. Your full name?' He sounded so unlike himself that I was seized with fear. I had taken for granted up till now that once before my patron I was safe, but it suddenly

85

occurred to me that this was by no means certain after all. Marcus prided himself on fairness and impartiality. It was not beyond the bounds of possibility that he would find against me, patron though he was. He had tried and executed friends before.

'Longinius Flavius Libertus, Roman citizen, from Glevum in the east.' I reeled off my Roman title with a tongue which almost refused to frame the words.

Marcus nodded briskly. 'Who brings the charges, here?'

The lean-faced man stepped up again. 'I do, Excellence. I am paid to advocate this woman's cause . . .' He indicated Lupus's wife, who I now saw was sitting close to him.

This was a surprise as well. Naturally, being female, and therefore a child in the eyes of the law, she could not bring the case herself, but advocates command substantial fees and I wondered how Lupus's wife had afforded the expense, especially after the cash chest had been stolen from the shop. Normally some male relative or guardian would plead on her behalf, but perhaps – since she was a newcomer to the town – she had no other family nearby. I wondered if there had been a contribution from the Venta Christians, though the sect is not a wealthy one: most of its adherents are among the poor or the slaves, more able to pray for things than pay for things, the saying went.

Wherever the money had come from, though, it had been well spent. Advocates know all the details of the law, and this advocate was an impressive one.

Marcus acknowledged him without a smile. 'Very well. What is he charged with and who are the witnesses?'

The lean-faced man set out the accusations one by one. He did it expertly. I had murdered Lupus and stolen the wooden cash box from the shop. Only I had any opportunity;

the woman herself had seen me there within a moment of his death, and – as the guards were prepared to testify – I had been carrying a knife, in contravention of civilian law. And later I had been seen escaping from the scene with haste and secrecy. A dozen witnesses could be brought in to confirm this evidence.

'Do you deny this?' Marcus said to me again.

'Only that I killed the man and took the chest. The rest of it is true.' I could scarcely deny my hurried departure from the scene, though I longed to ask who all these witnesses might be. The streets had been quite deserted as far as I could tell, apart from the footsteps which had followed me. However, I dared say nothing I was not asked to say.

The lean-faced man had rounded on me now. 'And look at his tunic. It has obviously been sponged. What was he cleaning off it? I say that it was blood. Blood from the wounds of the helpless victim he robbed.' He turned to Marcus. 'We want restitution, Excellence, and the full severity of the law.'

The mood of the spectators was getting ugly by this time, and there were cries of 'throw him to the beasts' – although I told myself that, since Lupus was not a citizen himself, this was not a likely punishment. More probably I would face a life exile on some barren island where I would gently starve to death, and – after a swingeing compensation paid to Lupus's wife – my possessions would be forfeit to the state. That was the good news. The charge of carrying a knife might carry a death sentence of itself, but Marcus was fair, however furious he was, and I was confident he would not find me guilty of possessing arms on the basis of a dining knife he'd given me himself.

The advocate was quite an orator and he knew how to play on the emotions of the crowd. He made a long, impassioned speech about how, if honest tradesmen could be robbed and cruelly killed . . . 'butchered, with fountains and rivulets of blood' . . . the whole authority of law was undermined. The crowd was listening to his every word. He finished by calling on Marcus to make an example of me, for the sake of Rome, and sat down to tumultuous applause.

Marcus nodded slowly. My heart sank to the pavement. He looked at me sternly. 'Have you anything to say in your defence?'

I had, of course, though I had decided that it was not a good idea to voice my suspicions about Plautus in the open court, nor to mention how the town appeared to be parcelled up between the rival gangs. Better to sound like an ignorant stranger, if I could. That way there was at least a chance that my unseen enemies would be lulled into security, supposing that I was frightened into silence by events and would just hold my tongue and go away. Otherwise, I had very little doubt, my life would be in danger if I was released.

My only hope was to convince the court that I was *alibi* – elsewhere. It would not be an easy plea to prove, since there is no way of telling time in most establishments, no water clocks or anything, and – since it had already been dark – there was not even a public sundial I could appeal to. But I did have one idea.

I kept my account as simple as I could. I had come out of the thermopolium when Lupus was alive, at the moment when his wife had entered carrying a new taper to be lit. She would attest to that?

A hurried consultation with the advocate. She would.

'When I went out into the street I thought that somebody was on my track – a thief with designs upon my purse, perhaps. I did not think of taking out my knife at first, but simply ran away and tried to hide. There are three young men in the town who could attest to this.'

'Their names?' Marcus was still curt and businesslike.

I gave their nicknames, which was all I knew, and an usher was sent out to summon them, while I continued with my narrative: how I had gone back to the mansio but the guard on duty would not let me in, and so I had returned to the thermopolium to seek a room. I didn't say anything about Promptillius or the note, or about my plans to find a brothel for the night.

At this point there was an unexpected interruption, as spotty Laxus was brought into the dock. I was astounded that he had been found so quickly, but the reason was soon pretty evident. He had been crowding round the doorway of the court and boasting of having spoken to me the night before. Now I was glad of the carelessness that had evidently earned Laxus his nickname. When I mentioned him by name and called on him to testify for me he took fright and tried to make off into the town, but the bystanders had laid hands on him and handed him over to the guard.

He confessed all this in sullen tones. He was looking frightened, too, and far more anxious to justify himself than be of any assistance to my cause. I had been skulking in a doorway, claiming to be a Roman citizen, and it was not his fault if I'd accosted them. He had no part in any homicide. He and his two friends had been at the public games all night, like model citizens, and in the tavern afterwards in full sight of everyone, where they'd had a skin or two of wine. They'd simply shown me to the mansio, as I had asked them to.

They had drunk a good deal more than a skin or two, I guessed, but I did not question it. His evidence supported me, if anything. It was easy to get him to agree that I had met them not long after the ending of the games.

'You see,' I said, to Marcus and the court, 'here is a witness who will swear that I was near the wine shop shortly after dark, and walked down to the mansio afterwards – there will be a guard there who can testify to that, as well. Now – follow this carefully – a home-made candle burns down in an hour or two at most. Agreed?'

There was a general murmur of assent.

'Yet, when I got back to the thermopolium, that new taper in the shop was not even half consumed. Ask the town guardsmen who arrested me. I noticed one of them had picked it up to view the corpse. You see what that suggests? Far from having time to kill the hot-soup seller and dispose of all his gold, I must have hurried directly through the streets to meet these people when and where I did. There was no gold in my purse when they arrested me – a small sum of silver only – as this young man can also testify. He saw me take it out to pay for some honey cakes from the pastry-cook. So what became of Lupus's treasure chest? I am a stranger to the town. Where could I hide a great big wooden box?'

The advocate was on his feet again. 'The fact that he hasn't got the money now is no proof that he didn't have it then. There is no doubt that it was taken, Excellence. I say he stole it, and he stabbed the shopkeeper.'

'That is another thing,' I said, turning to Laxus and looking him firmly in the eye. 'About the charge of carrying a knife.' The youth turned pale. He was guilty of that crime himself, and he was clearly terrified that I was going to accuse him of it now. 'Did you see me with a knife at any time?' I went on.

I saw him visibly relax. 'I didn't, citizen. I didn't know you had one. If I had—' He stopped, and was very anxious to be helpful, suddenly. 'Though it would hardly be surprising if you did – there are a lot of thieves and rogues about. People have been set on in the outskirts of the town a dozen times this year. Especially travellers or anyone with Roman ties. My own uncle disappeared a moon or two ago—'

'May it please Your Excellence,' I interrupted him. I did not want him to raise the matter of the rival gangs and perhaps divide opinion in the court. 'I am a stranger here, and did not know about all these unfortunate events. However, one possibility does occur to me. Perhaps the unhappy victim in this case was robbed and killed by the same band of criminals that did these other things. I thought I heard footsteps pursuing me, as I have explained. It all suggests there might have been a murderous thief about.'

There was uneasy muttering among the audience at this. One or two people began to look unsure – including one of the magistrates, I noticed.

The advocate for Lupus's wife was on his feet again. 'Then why has the wretch sponged his tunic, as he evidently has? Look at the dark stains and marks on it.'

The unexpected sally brought another hiss of discontent from some parts of the gallery. I thought of calling in the warder to speak in my defence – but Laxus was now firmly on my side. Before I had time to say another word, he volunteered, 'There was no blood on his tunic when he spoke to us. I can swear to that.'

'So, Excellence,' I said, seeing a chance and seizing it at once, 'if the killer was drenched with Lupus's blood, as by the advocate's account he must have been, then I am clearly innocent.'

There were louder rumbles now. The mood was beginning

to swing in my favour, and, seeing this, the advocate began another tack. 'There is still the question of the knife.' He produced it with a flourish. 'Here it is. The town guards took it from him at the scene. Carrying a weapon is a capital offence, and so is his claim to be a Roman citizen, if that is proved untrue. As I understand the matter, that is in dispute. He has brought no proof of it, of any kind.'

There was only one possible response to that. 'As to those charges,' I replied, 'I call upon my patron – His Excellence himself.'

I could not have caused more of a sensation if I had conjured up Jupiter in person. All eyes turned to Marcus, and even the soldier who had been guarding me allowed his sword to drop and swivelled round to stare.

Marcus cleared his throat and raised a hand. His face was mottled scarlet and I knew that he was raging inwardly, but he simply rose to his feet and said with dignity, 'What the man says on both these points is true. He is a citizen, and one of my clients. He is accompanying me to Isca, where – despite his present woeful lack of *gravitas* – he is to be an honoured guest. It is also true that I presented him with that dining knife in appreciation for a service he once rendered me.'

The advocate was obviously nonplussed by this, but he did not give up. 'Then what was he doing at that shop last night? Not once, but twice. He does not deny that he was there. And at the crucial time. He also had a knife, whether it is a legal one or not, and it is proved that he came back to the scene.'

Marcus ran a ringed hand through his tousled curls. 'There is no blood on that knife that I can see,' he said. 'You prove he had the opportunity—'

'And the means and motive – he took the treasure chest,' the man insisted.

He had interrupted Marcus, and that was a mistake. Marcus looked at him coldly. 'Do not attempt to give me lessons in the law. Mere opportunity is not sufficient proof – and the man has witnesses to say he had no blood or money on him afterwards. So, I will ask the question for the third and final time – Libertus, did you kill this man and steal his goods?'

The third time of asking was required in law, and I replied as firmly as I could, 'I did not, Excellence.'

'Then by the power invested in me by this court, I give my verdict. He appears not to have done it.' That was the official formula, and I found myself grinning helplessly, even before he uttered the final words. 'I've half a mind to fine him for improper dress – he has failed to wear his toga in a public place, which is an affront to his status and the name of Rome – but otherwise I find no fault in him. Let the prisoner go.'

There was a little stir which the herald quelled by shouting, in a high-pitched monotone, 'And that concludes the business of this court.'

Marcus turned and led the way majestically through the basilica, down the steps and into the official litter awaiting him outside. The other magistrates and officials trailed out after him.

I took a deep breath. I was free to go.

Chapter Ten

The soldier who had been guarding me throughout all this now put his sword away. 'Seems you are a lucky man,' he said. 'Now, do you want me to escort you out of here? Always a crush when someone's been released.' Without waiting for an answer he began to force a way back through the throng. 'Stand aside, there. Let us through.' The spectators reluctantly complied.

He was right about the crush. Now that the official party had departed and the spectacle was over, most people had lost all interest in the court and were simply anxious to get out themselves. There were a few people jostling at the door, to greet me as I passed with cheers or cries of 'Shame', but most did not give me a second glance. If anything, their attention had now turned to the gallery instead, where there was clearly some sort of altercation taking place. I was being borne along by the movement of the crowd and it was hard to see, but I managed to move sideways from the crush and get my back against a pillar for a moment so I could look up and glimpse what was happening overhead.

The disturbance seemed to be an argument between one of the young veiled women that I'd noticed earlier, and a skinny slave with acne who was waving a purse of coins in her face. He was shouting so loudly that I could hear his words, and so could all the others in the court.

'You tell your mistress that she is a cheat. You can't pay less because we lost the case. I don't care what you think we agreed. Just wait until the next time you come to court. You'll be sorry that you tried to cheat us then.'

I was wondering what all this was about when to my surprise the slave turned on his heel and bounded down the steps. He didn't join the departing multitudes but walked the other way, to join the advocate and Lupus's wife, who were still loitering beside the rostrum steps. When he reached the lean-faced man he bowed, handed him the purse and gestured fiercely to the women up above. I couldn't hear now what was being said, but Lupus's widow glanced at the gallery and I saw a look of fury cross her face. When I followed the direction of her gaze I got a shock myself.

The girl who had led the argument had now thrown back her veil and I realised that the group were not the modest maidens I'd imagined them to be. Nor were they a bunch of Christian matrons, come here to support Lupus's wife because she was a member of their sect, which had been my other guess.

On the contrary. The removal of the veil revealed a painted face: not merely showing a touch of chalk and white lead applied to face and neck, as women sometimes do for vanity, but flaunting a whole host of artificial tints. Even at this distance I could see bold smears of ochre on the cheeks, lines of sultry lamp-black round the eyes and lips dyed scarlet with the lees of wine. Given that her hair was also dyed an artificial blond and pinned up with jewelled trinkets in the curls, the lady's profession was not hard to guess. Why would such a woman pay an advocate? It seemed more likely that he'd be paying her.

I was still gazing upwards, wondering about this, when I

felt a sharp tug at my arm. My former guard was back. He followed the direction of my look and gave a mirthless laugh. 'You've spotted one of Lyra's girls, I see. No time for dreaming about that, my friend. I am to take you out of here as fast as possible. Your patron is awaiting you outside.'

I gave up on the little mystery and followed him at once. It is never wise to make my patron wait.

Marcus was indeed expecting me. He had given instructions for the official litter to delay, and another carrying chair to be fetched for me. However, he addressed no word to me, simply mounted his conveyance and left me to do the same. I returned to the mansio in solitary state, swaying in a hired litter borne by sweating slaves.

No question this time of a challenge at the gate; the sentry stood aside sharply to allow us in. Marcus had already dismounted and disappeared inside but, as soon as I had paid the litter-hire, a soldier came out to summon me.

I followed him, a little nervously, and found myself in the commandant's offices, standing before a table at which my patron was already seated on a sort of folding stool, with the optio beside him, looking flushed and grim. It was like appearing in the court again, except that I could tell from Marcus's face that this time I would not get off so easily.

'Well?' he said, tapping his baton impatiently against his palm – a sign that he was seriously annoyed. 'I'm waiting. I presume you have some explanation for all this? And what have you done with that young slave I lent to you?'

'I left him in the market, Excellence. And then I saw someone from Glevum that I thought was dead . . .' And I told him the full story, starting with following Plautus in the street and ending with the wax-tablet message which had reached Promptillius at the pastry shop and sent him hustling into Venta with my clothes. 'Meanwhile I went back to the hot-soup shop and got arrested, and they took me to the jail.'

Marcus waved the rest of my narrative aside. He was more interested in his valuable slave than in my recent plight, and obviously the name of Plautus hadn't registered. There are a good many people with that name. I tried to draw his attention to the point. 'Gaius—'

Marcus interrupted. 'Well, never mind all that. Where do you think Promptillius is now? He left here on your instructions, so he told the guard, but he did not come to the house where I was feasting yesterday.'

I nodded. 'I didn't think he would have, Excellence. And remember, those instructions didn't come from me – although presumably he thought they had. I imagine he obeyed them, whatever they might have been, and took my toga to some false address. No doubt the boy who brought the wax tablet told him where to go. The directions obviously weren't written down – that would have created suspicion from the guard on duty here. The mansio knew where you really were, and someone would have spotted that inconsistency at once.'

Marcus furrowed his brow in a frown. He was still wearing his magisterial wreath, and the combination made him look immensely stern. 'So where do you think they sent him?'

I could only shrug. 'That is the problem, Excellence. I've no idea. I left him waiting for me at a pasty-cook's close to the forum while I went to buy the clasp, but when I came back he simply wasn't there. He didn't even know that I'd set off in pursuit of anyone in the street. We'd already parted company by then.'

Marcus's scowl deepened. 'So you deliberately set off into the marketplace without a slave? Here, where you had been warned that there was discontent with Rome, and a degree of trouble in the streets? Don't protest – the optio assures me that he'd warned you about that. And after I had left you an attendant of my own! You seem to have been inviting problems, that's all I can say. I'm surprised the authorities permitted you to go.' He looked severely at the optio as he spoke, making it clear that his displeasure embraced both of us. 'Well, you have delayed us by a whole day as it is. We shall have to leave without Promptillius tomorrow, that is all, and have him sent after us when he is found. This is all extremely inconvenient.'

It was dangerous, but I knew it must be said. 'Supposing that he *is* found, Excellence.'

Marcus stared at me. 'What do you mean?'

'I think it is possible that someone wanted to kill me yesterday – and if there was an attempt on me, a citizen, then the murder of a slave would hardly bother them.'

He gaped. There is no other word for it. 'To kill *you*? I thought it was merely some shopkeeper who died.'

I spelt it out to him. 'Think about the sequence, Excellence. I see Plautus. He runs away from me. After that I'm followed through the town – first by Paulinus, then by someone else – and I only get away by accident. Then I find that my slave has been sent off on a false errand, so I won't be missed, and a man I simply talked to is slashed gruesomely to death – presumably in case I'd said too much to him. What does that suggest to you?'

He nodded. 'This Plautus fellow?'

'It rather looks like it. I know it is difficult to believe, but it is the only explanation I can think of which accords with all the facts. And what is he doing here in any case? You and I helped bury him not very long ago.'

This time it registered. '*That* Plautus?' He gaped. 'It can't have been.' He stared at me. 'You're sure that it was him? He might have had a twin.'

'With an identical scar across his face?' I shook my head. 'Anyway, he knew me. That was obvious. Why else would he run away like that? And who was it that we cremated in his place?'

Marcus looked horrified at this, as if that implication had just occurred to him. 'I can see your point. You think Plautus may have killed someone in Glevum and disposed of the body on the funeral pyre? I suppose it's possible. The face was covered for the ritual – horribly crushed under the falling masonry, they said. So it's quite possible it wasn't Plautus after all, although we all assumed it was. Dear Jupiter! What an amazing thought! Ah – dates!'

A military orderly had come bustling in, all importance, with a small bowl of these honeyed dainties which he offered to my patron first, as the senior person present. Marcus took the whole dish from him, selected the biggest fruit and ate it absently without relinquishing the bowl. The orderly looked bewildered and chagrined and – finding himself superfluous – backed out again.

Marcus picked out another juicy date. As I had eaten nothing but one measly oatcake since my stale bread of the night before, I watched him with envious interest. 'But why should Plautus come here in any case?' he said, taking another thoughtful bite. 'Venta is hardly the safest destination one would think of for a Roman citizen, especially one outside the protection of the law.' He laughed grimly. 'And since he is officially dead, I suppose, he is outside the law's protection, whether he killed anyone or not.'

'Perhaps that was the attraction, Excellence. It is the last place anyone would look,' I said. 'But there is one possible reason why he chose the place. Plautus only gained his citizenship late in life, by wealth and effort. He was not born to it. He has the red hair of a Silurian. Perhaps he comes from somewhere in this area and has family here. If so, what could be more natural than that, if he was responsible for someone's death – even if it was an accident – he should come home to hide until the threat was past?'

'If I may dare make a suggestion here, your mightiness,' the optio put in, with careful deference, 'it might be possible to search the tax records. You say this citizen is wealthy, so no doubt his relatives are too. If he or his family have property hereabouts, it must be liable for tax.'

Marcus rewarded him, not only with a smile, but by offering him the platter of dates. 'An excellent suggestion. I wonder I did not think of it myself. His full name is Gaius Flaminius Plautus. That should not be too difficult to find. Send for the keeper of the scrolls at once.'

'Excellence, with all respect . . .' I began. Why does it always fall to me to point out the obvious? Marcus was starting to look grim again. 'If Plautus holds property himself, there is no difficulty at all. It will be registered in his Latin name. But although he has a Roman name himself, his family may not be Flaminians, unless they are all citizens themselves. The name would have been bestowed upon him with his rank.'

Marcus was looking unimpressed by this. 'So what name do you think we should be looking for?'

'That is another problem, Excellence. It is impossible to

101

guess. It is possible he holds land here in his own name, of course. But his fortune was in Glevum, according to his will. And I'm only guessing that he has family hereabouts. But it is a smallish town. You could ask the tax collector if he has any recollection of dealing with a man who has a livid scar across his face – or if he knows a family which has such a son.'

Marcus snorted, but the optio signalled to a man beside the door, and a messenger was soon dispatched to find the keeper of rolls. 'In fact, if I might suggest it, Excellence,' the optio was still intent on demonstrating how helpful he could be, 'it is possible that one of my men would have some recollection of the man you seek. Or a member of the town watch, possibly. We know that he was in Venta yesterday – someone must have seen him pass the gates. Would you care to have me make enquiries?'

Marcus shrugged. 'It can't do any harm. Though – when I consider what Libertus says he saw – I'm not entirely convinced that it was not a sign or omen of some kind, rather than an actual living man. We should consult the augurers perhaps. I presume they will still be in session with the court?'

I looked at my patron with surprise. He is not usually a believer in such things. Of course, he is sometimes obliged to call the augurers – they are regularly consulted by senior magistrates when there is any dispute over the outcome of a trial and no decisive evidence can be brought on either side. But he is not usually much in awe of the result. Last time we spoke of it, he agreed with me that although the method is sometimes surprisingly efficient, this is usually because the guilty man, half crazed with fearing what the torturers will do, begins to believe in earnest that the gods will speak and hence confesses of his own accord, rather than as a result of anything the augurer actually concludes from inspecting entrails or the shape of clouds.

This time, however, he seemed in earnest. Even the optio seemed a bit surprised. 'I believe they are in session, Excellence. I will have them called.'

I risked a little joke. 'Perhaps the augurers can also tell you, Excellence, which spirit wrote that note? And what has happened to Promptillius and the treasure chest? Or would you prefer to make some enquiries yourself, and talk to that woman from the brothel, and the butcher's boys?' Although Marcus observes the public sacrifices to the Emperor, of course, and would not dream of dining without proper libations to the gods, he is usually fairly sceptical where the omen-readers are concerned.

This time, however, he was not amused. 'This is not a moment for your levity, Libertus. If it were not for you, we should not be in this dilemma now and I should not have lost a valuable slave. However, I suppose you're right. It would be sensible to talk to them. And since both the butcher and the brothel-keeper have premises in town, it's possible the drains-and-water tax might throw some light on them. Officer, can you see to that, as well?'

'At once, Excellence,' the optio said, getting obediently to his feet, though he looked less than delighted with his task. 'I'll deal with it myself. In the meantime would you care to have the mansio kitchen send in a little food? It is well past noon.'

Marcus looked thoughtfully at the dish of dates, and I thought for one awful moment that he would refuse, but after a moment he inclined his head. 'Since, thanks to Libertus, we have had to change our plans, I suppose it would be wise. And since we will not be in Isca till tomorrow night, I should also send a messenger to the commander there – and one to my home in Glevum too – to tell them of the alteration to our timetable.'

The optio was walking backwards, bobbing all the time, such was his desire to look industrious. I guessed that Marcus had made his feelings very plain about the wisdom of conniving at my market-trip, and the poor man was clearly desperate to atone. He ran an anxious tongue round his lips. 'I'll see that it's arranged at once. Leave everything to me.'

And, still bobbing, he backed out of the room. My patron looked at me, and for the first time since yesterday he relaxed his frown – although one could not pretend he actually smiled.

'Well, Libertus, I must say I'm relieved not to have been forced to find against you in the court. If I'd been obliged to have you exiled – or worse – I should have missed your company very much. Though I must say that I expected better of you than to go out, dressed like that, when you are part of my official retinue. How do you think these things reflect on me? That tunic is an absolute disgrace. I understand this mansio has a bath-suite of a kind – a cold plunge, anyway, for passing soldiery. Go and make use of it and find yourself something more respectable to wear.'

The rebuke was far less harsh than I had feared. I nodded. 'Excellence!' I was in the act of following the optio's example, and bowing myself, when another sobering thought occurred to me. I was obliged to stop and stutter out the words, 'Excellence, I'm very much afraid I don't have a toga to change into any more. From what I understand, Promptillius took my possessions with him when he went. Is there a member of our retinue, a slave perhaps, who might have a spare clean tunic I could use meanwhile? And do I have your permission to send a note back to my household, when you send your messenger? I have another tunic back at home, and an ancient toga too, of sorts. I can arrange to have it sent out after me.'

Marcus was looking furious again at my unseemly lack of suitable attire, but clearly there was no alternative. He gave a brusque, dismissive nod. 'Very well,' he muttered tersely, and applied himself to nibbling dates again. By the time I came back – glowing from the cold plunge, and wrapped in an old tunic of the optio's which was far too wide for me, and didn't reach my knees – he'd eaten every one of them.

He had, however, managed to obtain a battered writing tablet and a stylus for my use, so after a stout midday meal of army broth and bread, I sat down and drafted a letter to my wife and included some instructions for Junio, my slave. Since he was making samples of possible designs for the pavement of Plautus's memorial it occurred to me that, by calling to show them at the house, he would be well placed to make a few discreet enquiries. However, I knew that Marcus would not approve of that – it has never been his nature to stir up hornets' nests. So, after a little thought, I closed up the tablet at the hinge and, having tied it carefully, sealed the tapes with melted tallow-wax. It looked like the sort of makeshift fastening that anyone might use when sending a letter between distant towns: not a proper ring-seal, suggesting secrecy, but probably enough to stop Marcus from casually reading it before he passed it on. I reasoned that he could not overrule my instructions to my slave if he did not know that I was making them.

I need not have worried. Marcus handed my letter over to the messenger without a second glance, along with several missives of his own, and they were on their way to Glevum shortly afterwards. My patron was much more concerned with the information, brought by the optio, that neither the butcher nor his boys could be found. However, his men had rounded up the butcher's brother, who had been left to mind the shop, and he was waiting in a back room of the mansio. Would Marcus care to come and question him?

Marcus would. He made a point of not inviting me – evidently I was still in disgrace. However, the man must have said something to the soldiers who had brought him in. I waited for the optio to come back through the court and intercepted him, bustling and busy though he obviously was.

The optio looked dismayed at seeing me. 'Now what do you want?' he said ungraciously. 'I can't stop to talk. His Excellence is furious with me as it is – he seems to blame me for the whole event. Just when I was hoping to make a good impression on a man of influence, and perhaps be made up to centurion by and by.'

'This is as much in your interest as mine,' I said. I outlined what I wanted.

He shrugged. 'There isn't any mystery at all. The butcher, it seems, summoned both his sons last night and went out with his donkey cart at dusk. Took some skins out to a tannery a few miles down the road, and from there he was going on to visit a few of the larger stockholders nearby, to haggle for extra animals. There are some public feast-days coming up.'

'And that's not unusual?'

'Apparently he does the same thing every day or two. He keeps a large cart in a private stable not far from the gate, expressly for expeditions like this. It's a useful thing all round. It disposes of the waste materials from the stall and makes him a little extra on the side. He takes out the bones and 'block-bits' too, his brother says, all the ends and trimmings that he can't get rid of here.'

'Surely he could find somebody to buy the odds and ends?' I said, remembering Lupus and his thermopolium.

He laughed. 'He does. He sells them to forest-borderers, it seems, though he will hardly make his fortune doing that. Those people have no land: they scrape a living out of selling wood and bits of anything that they can scavenge by the road. They'll take anything he has: little scraps of flyblown meat – they boil that up for soup – or even bits of bone and teeth. The womenfolk carve ornaments from them and sell them to people passing by – I've seen them hawking the wretched things myself. Apparently they have a barter system with the butcher – he gets things like firewood in exchange.'

'So he went out there at dusk?' I said, and realised what a daft remark that was. Of course he went at dusk – wheeled transport could not operate by day. 'Is he not afraid of brigands, in the dark?'

'I suppose he's used to it. He and the boys sometimes stay overnight with relatives who have some land out there. They'll be home again tonight – or tomorrow at the latest – and then we can bring them in and question them. Till then, that's all the information that we're going to get. His Excellence is going all through it with the man again, but I really don't think he's got anything to add. He wasn't even at the butcher's yesterday: he's got his own stall selling something else – and, in case you were going to ask, his wife looks after that when he takes his brother's place. All quite a family affair – like everything round here. Look, there he is. I see they've let him go. He'll be pleased at that. We dragged him from the market as he was – bloodied arms and all – and he is obviously anxious to get back to the shop.' He made an exasperated face. 'And I must go as well. I am expecting a messenger to come from Lyra's house. I've been in enough trouble over you!'

He hurried off. I looked where he had pointed, and sure enough, there was the man in question scurrying away. He was a hunched and furtive-looking little man and had clearly been brought in straight from the market-stall: he was wrapped in the bloodied leather apron that all butchers wear and he still bore streaks of spattered flesh and fur. I grinned. Marcus would not have enjoyed his interview with that!

The fellow saw me looking and glowered fiercely back. I had a strong impression that I'd seen him somewhere before, though after all the anxieties of the last few days I couldn't for the moment work out where. I was still standing, staring after him, when the optio's other messenger arrived, saying that Lyra was nowhere to be found. She had been in her rooms this morning, it appeared, but now she had gone out and none of her girls knew where she was.

'Touting for business, probably, or visiting some special customer,' the rider said to me, with a suggestive leer. He swung down from his horse, and gave it to a mansio-slave who took it round the back to stable it again. 'I've left orders for her to report here as soon as she returns. That seems to be the best that I can do. Are you going to tell His Excellence the news, or do you want me to?'

'You tell him,' I said quickly, though I felt a little qualm as I watched him swagger off towards my patron's room with innocently cheerful confidence. I knew what Marcus's mood was apt to be when his plans were frustrated in this way. I made myself as scarce as possible, but even from the stables I could hear the bellowing.

Chapter Eleven

I did not see my patron again all afternoon: he had himself carried off in a private litter to the public baths where he was no doubt soothed and entertained by meeting the wealthy officials of the town, and the delights of hot plunge pools and steam. I had already had my chilly dip in the mansio bath-house and – ridiculous in my ill-fitting borrowed garb – could not go anywhere, not even to the market for that clasp. My tunic had been taken to the fuller's to be cleaned, but I knew that it would be at least another day before I could expect it to be returned to me.

There was nothing for it but to hang around the inn, and a very boring afternoon it was. Even the optio had no time to chat. I guessed that Marcus had been short with him. He had lost his air of polished eagerness, and hurried distractedly about, bellowing orders and ignoring me. A series of officials bustled in and out for hasty conferences in his private room and I guessed that this was part of an attempt to make the enquiries which Marcus had required. I would have loved to ask a question or two of these men myself, but the optio was quite abrupt when I suggested it, and without my patron to intercede for me there was nothing I could do.

In the end I went back to my room and went to sleep – a rare enough pleasure in the afternoon, but a welcome one, after the discomforts of the night before.

We dined in the optio's private quarters later on, at his request. He was clearly very proud of his domain, and if he had offended Marcus, this evening was intended to atone.

There was a proper dining couch – though only one instead of the more usual three, because his private dining room was small. Still, there were slaves to serve us with the meal, and the young officer fussed about to arrange us suitably on his solitary couch, as if he were presiding at a major feast.

'Your Excellence, if you would take the guest of honour's seat, there on my right hand, I, as host, shall have the central one, and I have also invited a town official whom I was sure you would be interested to meet. He will be sitting on my other side.'

He gestured to the individual in question, a stout, self-important man with gigantic sandy eyebrows as big as tufts of reeds – the sure sign of a provincial. I saw Marcus flinch. Like any pure-blooded Roman my patron would endure hours of discomfort at his barber's hands – tweezers, bat's blood depilatories, anything – rather than appear in a public place looking like that.

This apparition was the local censor, it appeared, the town senator responsible for keeping the taxation records for the civitas and the surrounding area, and he was blithely unaware of his offence. On the contrary, he was inflated, like a bullfrog, with his own self-importance and portentousness. Marcus rarely dined with town officials of such lowly rank, but the man was clearly oblivious of that: in Venta he was an important personage, and he condescended to us wonderfully.

Since all three places on the dining couch were thus accounted for, I was placed at one end of the table on an uncomfortable stool. I had swapped my borrowed tunic for a borrowed *synthesis* – the sort of combination robe and toga generally reserved for special feasts – in which I looked, if possible, even more absurd. In this setting it was wholly out of place. Even the optio wore informal dress. He was reclining in a simple yellow robe – and looking entirely at home.

The mansio kitchen had excelled itself. The food was pleasant and the servings liberal (though I noticed that pork and fennel was among the offerings again). By the time the optio's slave came round with watered wine even Marcus had shrugged off something of his bad mood. I almost wondered if our host would produce a lute-player or some other after-dinner entertainment, as there might have been at a civilian feast, but of course he did nothing of the kind. Instead, as soon as the final dishes were removed, he turned the conversation to the day's enquiries, and it became clear why the censor had been invited.

The optio cleared his throat. 'I have carried out your instructions, Excellence, and now I have the honour to report. I had the whole town searched this afternoon, especially the so-called Roman quarter of the town. I have also interviewed all members of the watch, but I fear there has been no news of the man with the scarred face whom you're looking for.' To my surprise he seemed secretly pleased, if anything – though since he had nothing positive to report, it was a little difficult to work out why. If I wanted to be promoted to centurion, I would not have smiled.

Marcus took another sip of wine and frowned. 'I trust your friend the censor has had more success? I presume you have made an examination of the tax records?'

The tax official inclined his head. 'I have. As you are well aware, Excellence, all private landed property is subject to a tax. It causes some ill-feeling locally, I'm afraid, but as I always explain, since all the land in the province is ultimately the property of the Emperor, the 'charge is effectively a rent.'

Marcus was nodding impatiently at this – he needed no instruction in the nature of the law. 'Of course. And all full citizens residing in the civitas are required to pay a contribution to the upkeep of the town. That is the object of the census officer.'

His irritation was quite plain to me, but the censor was imperturbable. 'Exactly so. As a result all local landowners and citizens should be registered. However, there is no mention of a Gaius Flaminius Plautus anywhere.' He delivered this information in a measured monotone, raising his enormous eyebrows skywards as he spoke. 'Nor is there any record of a Lyra in my scrolls.'

Marcus looked thunderous at this, but the optio seemed pleased, if anything. Indeed he flashed me a triumphant look. I wondered if there was more information still to come.

Sure enough, the optio turned to me. 'You talked about the street of the oil-lamp sellers, citizen. We have made enquiries. Most of the property in the area is owned by one individual, it seems. Censor, you have the information, I believe?'

The official produced a document from the folds of a pocket underneath his belt, with the air of a magician conjuring a snake. 'I've had my record-keeper make a copy for you.' He handed Marcus the scrap of parchment-bark on which the details had been scrawled in watery squid-and-lamp-black ink. 'The owner is a certain Nyros, the current head of one of the old Silurian tribes. Unlike most of the families that did not welcome Rome, his clan seems to have successfully maintained its wealth – judging by the tax on his estate. Not only does he have a farm some distance from the town, but he owns several buildings in the civitas. He has recently financed several public works, so he may consider seeking office soon, though there is no record of his ever doing so before.'

I squinted at the document as I best I could. It was not easy from where I sat, but if I craned my neck a bit I could make out the writing, more or less. Marcus saw what I was doing, and, aware of his own dignity, snatched the sheet away. 'I suppose he rents the building to this Lyra person, and takes a portion of the profits from the house. That's not unusual.'

The censor nodded. 'I agree. That is almost certainly the arrangement, although according to the record the rent is very small, no doubt in consideration of certain . . . hmmm . . . privileges with the wares.'

The optio looked horrified, but Marcus actually laughed. Before his marriage he had enjoyed a certain reputation of his own – though, given the rumours of his imperial lineage, it is doubtful he ever had to pay for services. 'He prefers the proprietor herself, perhaps?'

The censor looked comically shocked. 'Indeed not, Excellence. The keeper of the lupinarium is not . . . hmmm . . . a practitioner herself – at least not to the general populace. It is rumoured that she does have one wealthy customer – most wolf-house madams do – who keeps her for his own exclusive use.'

'Do we know who he is and where he lives?'

He shook his head. 'The girls refer to him as Optimus, but that is most likely a name he gave himself to cover up his true identity. These men insist on anonymity – it keeps their dalliances from their wives. According to my understanding, anyway.'

Marcus said, 'How do you know all this?' and the censor had the grace to look abashed.

He coughed. 'Oh, it is general gossip in the town. And she goes to him, he doesn't come to her, which keeps it all discreet. He must be someone rich and powerful to afford that sort of service. It's what every customer would like – someone experienced but not diseased. Not that I have any familiarity with that sort of thing, of course.'

The optio said, 'Really?' in a chilly tone.

The censor seemed to realise that he'd said too much. His bullfrog cheeks turned dully red and he added hastily, 'However, as I say, Lyra is not mentioned anywhere in the records. The building is officially rented to a Tholiramanda, or something of the sort.' The eyebrows indicated his disdain. 'You will see it on the copy I have given you.'

Marcus glanced briefly at the document and handed it to me. 'And what do you think is the significance of that?'

I saw the obvious immediately. 'It's the same woman. Tholira-manda – Lyra for short – it trips more easily off the Latin tongue. I'm sure that is the answer, Excellence!' I exclaimed. 'That's simply the Latin of her full Celtic name. She rents the house and runs it for her patron.'

I was pleased with my deduction, but Marcus seemed unmoved. 'I suppose she does. Most brothel-keepers do. There's nothing to prevent that, under law. He might even be this Optimus.'

The censor shook his head. 'Nyros lives out of town. She goes to see her client overnight, sometimes, so he must live in Venta. Or that's what I've been told!' He saw that he'd betrayed himself again, and hid his discomfiture in another drink.

'We'll find out soon enough when she arrives,' my patron said. 'Has she been found yet, optio?'

The optio was agitated now. 'Not as yet, Excellence. I sent a guard to the wolf-house, but she had not yet returned. But never fear. She will not escape us very long.'

Marcus hummphed. 'She seems to be elusive, suddenly. I wonder why? The brothel itself is legal, I presume?'

The tax-recorder was still scarlet-faced. 'Your Excellence is quite correct. It is all entirely within the law. I've looked into it before. Her girls have all got proper licences. She does not receive general customers herself, but even if she did she is not a married woman or a citizen so there would be no case for impropriety. And it's all quite clean and organised – or so I hear, though naturally I've never patronised the place.'

That wasn't how Lupus had described the place to me. I saw what he meant about Lyra's having influence with the authorities. I glanced towards the optio, but he was at pains to make it clear that he was not interested in the censor's private vice. He signalled to the slave to bring another jug of wine, saying at the same time, with a puzzled frown. 'But it is odd. If the citizen Libertus is right about the name – and of course that remains to be investigated – one would expect this Nyros to be her guardian in matters of the law too. But that is not the case. There is a butcher, from the bath-house end of town, who claims to be a sort of relative and acts as her representative in court.'

'Court?' Marcus demanded sharply.

I had an answer to that one myself. 'I've heard that she's been summoned to the law-courts once or twice, when customers have complained of being robbed while on her premises.'

'So she has family?' Marcus swallowed almost all his wine, clearly startled by the picture this had conjured up – the kinswoman of a respectable tradesman running a wolf-house on the side. 'Doesn't this fellow put a rein on her?'

'Not that I'm aware,' the optio answered. 'On two occasions he appeared in court on her behalf, and both of the complainants dropped the charge.'

'So his connection with Lyra is well known in the town?'

The optio inclined his head. 'Indeed, but it is obvious that he tolerates her trade. More than that, he positively helps. He's a big man, and she calls on his physical protection too from time to time – no drunken client of her establishment would ever argue with him more than once.'

Another possible candidate for Optimus, I thought – but again the details didn't seem to fit. A butcher was not a wealthy citizen, and a relative would hardly be a client. It did occur to me to wonder fleetingly if Plautus might be the man, but I dismissed the thought. Until his theatrically staged demise, Plautus had lived in Glevum, more than a day's journey to the east. Lyra could scarcely have visited him 'overnight'.

The censor gave a pompous cough and cut across my thoughts, trying to overcome embarrassment by showing how efficient he could be. 'However, there's something else which might be relevant. I traced this Tholiramanda through the tax records and found her mentioned elsewhere – as a landowner. It appears that she is the legal holder of a whole block of property down in the bath-house end of town. She inherited it when her husband died: a licensed fuller's shop and several stalls – including a butcher's shop, as I recall. If this is the same butcher, then she would own his shop – that might explain his acquiescence in her activities.' He was preening now.

The optio was looking horrified at this. It is one thing for a woman to run a brothel from necessity, quite another for an otherwise respectable widow, well provided for by her husband's will, to do so out of choice. 'Great Mercury! Why did you not mention this before?'

Marcus, too, was trying to cover his shocked astonishment by gesturing to the wine-slave to refill his cup. 'Surely it's unusual, to say the least, that a woman of that kind – a widow with property of her own – should rent a building in another part of town and use it for such . . .' he hesitated before he found the word, '. . . commercial purposes?'

The censor said stiffly, 'We never had occasion to connect the two before: there has never been any difficulty in collecting tax, so there was no need to question who the tenants were. They're only townspeople. It's not as though they were Roman citizens.' He clearly felt that he'd absolved himself and he consoled his wounded dignity with another sip of wine.

'But why should a woman with income of her own be running a lupinarium at all?' Marcus drained his goblet and looked expectantly at me. 'Well, Libertus? What do you make of it? You look as if something has occurred to you.'

In fact, I was remembering what the now dead keeper of the thermopolium had said – that rival families, both pro- and anti-Roman, owned large portions of the civitas, and secretly controlled the businesses within their area. Presumably Lyra enjoyed 'protection' from one faction, then. But if so, which?

According to Lupus she had good relations with the town authorities. That made a kind of sense because the wolf-house was in the pro-Roman area of town: her landlord, Nyros, funded civic works and seemed to be hoping for a council post, and her special client was a man of influence.

Besides, I was convinced that she had some connection with my mysteriously resurrected friend – that most Roman of Roman citizens. It was obvious that she had pro-Roman links.

Yet, according to what we had learned tonight, she also had connections with the 'bath-side' faction, which – according to Big-ears and his friends – was the unofficial territory of the opposing side. That was where I'd met her first, it was the home of her kinsman and his two red-headed spies, and it now seemed that she even had property in that area herself.

I was still running these ideas around my head and trying to make sense of them when the meal was abruptly interrupted by a loud disturbance just outside the door. There was the sound of furious, muffled argument, and then a flushed and flustered menial appeared. 'There is a messenger to see you, optio.'

He had hardly managed to blurt out the words before the messenger appeared behind him at the door – a cavalry officer by his armour and his cloak, though he was dusty and dishevelled and limping on one foot as though it pained him.

The optio was already struggling to his feet. As commander of a military inn – especially in a border area like this – imperial duty obliged him to attend at once to any messenger, but he seemed almost relieved at the excuse. 'My apologies, citizens,' he murmured. 'I shall not be long.'

But the horseman had by now advanced into the room. He ignored the optio and flung himself abjectly in front of Marcus. 'Your indulgence, Excellence. I regret this interruption to your meal, but this is too serious to wait. I bring distressing news.'

Marcus looked startled, but he stretched out his hand and

signalled to the messenger to rise. 'Who are you and what is your business here? I hope it is as urgent as you say, to merit this intrusion.' If not, you can expect the consequences – he did not speak the words but they were understood.

The soldier nodded. 'My name is Regulus, Excellence. I am a member of the Isca garrison – an auxiliary spearman with the cavalry. There were four of us. We were detailed to come and find you here and accompany you, as outriders, to the garrison. There have been renewed attacks on army patrols and personnel of late, and the roads between here and the border are not wholly safe.'

'You are very late about it,' Marcus snapped. 'If it were not for an unhappy incident which delayed us here, we should already have been in Isca by this time. In view of all the troubles I've been hearing of, I was proposing to organise an additional armed escort from this end. Though I must confess I had expected that your commander would have provided one – I've just sent a message to him, saying so.'

The soldier's face turned scarlet at the implied rebuke, but his discipline did not fail. 'We should have been with you by noon, Excellence, but I regret to tell you that we were delayed – set upon by a marauding band. It was a lightning ambush and we were unprepared. We suffered only lightly – a few cuts and bruises, none of us seriously hurt – but our horses were captured and our equipment seized and we have been obliged to walk. I regret if you have suffered inconvenience. A messenger was sent here to the mansio ahead of us, to advise you that an escort was prepared—'

The optio interrupted him. 'We've received no messenger.'

'Indeed, sir. I am now aware of that. It appears that the man concerned was ambushed too. I fear he was killed. Only

119

of course there was only one of him, while there were four of us – and even we had difficulty fighting ourselves free.'

Marcus frowned. 'And you lost your army mounts, you say? How did a detachment of the Roman cavalry come to be so easily overwhelmed?'

The soldier's colour mounted and he kept his eyes fixed resolutely on the wall. 'I crave your indulgence, Excellence. We walked into a trap. There is one portion of the road which is extremely steep and wooded. We were riding through it this morning, single file, when one of our number spotted something hanging from a tree a little way down a forest path. It appeared to be a naked human form, but there was a Roman cloak and helmet dangling nearby. Naturally we dismounted and went to look at it . . .' He tailed off in dismay.

'And that was when a group of armed assailants jumped out of the trees at you?' I finished for him.

He nodded gratefully. It was a guess on my part, but a likely one. If I had been a rebel, I would have set up exactly such a scheme.

'There must have been half a dozen men in all,' the soldier said, returning to his tale. 'Two of them seized the horses and made off with them, but one of our men spotted what they were up to and called on them to halt. They ignored us, naturally, just went on leading them away. We drew our swords and started to pursue them down the path, but all at once another, bigger group leapt out on us and attacked us from behind. We formed a square and managed to protect ourselves – held our ground and even succeeded in wounding one of them. Then, when their companions had made good their escape, our assailants simply turned and faded off in all directions through the undergrowth. We tried to crash through after them, but we were wearing armour and they were lightly dressed. They were too quick for us.'

'Meanwhile, you'd left your equipment with the horses, I presume?' The optio sounded scornful. 'You left them standing there without a guard? If so, I shall report it to your commandant. That amounts to simple negligence. You will be put on punishment fatigues and the cost will be deducted from your pay. You understand?' There is always a rivalry between legionary officers like the optio, who are citizens by birth, and auxiliaries like Regulus who only earn the status after forty years of service, usually on a fraction of the pay.

'Understood, sir.' The soldier was getting more crimson by the minute. 'But, if I may make so bold, we felt it was our duty to investigate. The cloak and helmet looked like Roman ones, and there was a lot of blood spilt on the ground.'

'Never leave horses and equipment unattended, even on the edges of a battlefield, without one of your number standing guard,' the optio said. 'What kind of training do they give you lads nowadays?' He sniffed. 'Well, it's too late now. Your steeds have fallen into rebel hands, and they'll no doubt be used to harass Roman soldiers later on. You can think of that when you are cleaning out latrines. So, what did you do with the body of the messenger? Did you cut it down and bury it?'

This time the soldier did meet the optio's eyes. 'That is the extraordinary thing,' he said. 'The cloak and helmet were the messenger's, I don't think there is any doubt of that. But the body wasn't his. This was no soldier. A pasty sort of fellow, when he lived, with soft hands and flaccid muscles and a slave-brand on his back. He seemed to be some kind of personal serving-boy.'

Chapter Twelve

A rustle ran around the table at these words, and Marcus half rose to his feet. 'A slave-brand, did you say? What kind of brand? And what have you done with him?' He seemed to recollect himself and added with a smile, 'I ask, because it is just possible that he might be mine. Thanks to a' – he flung me a reproachful look – 'local, regrettable event, I seem to have lost a valuable slave.'

The soldier looked alarmed. 'Your pardon, Excellence. We haven't done anything particular with him – just cut him down, wrapped him up and buried him under some soft leaves in a ditch. Forgive us if we have given you offence.'

Marcus was looking really furious at this. I knew that he was unlikely to grieve very long over the possible loss of a single slave, especially one like poor Promptillius, whom he clearly did not value very much – after all, he'd lent the boy to me. However, he was not a heartless man and, besides, he was irritated as anyone might be at the unnecessary loss of something that was his.

It was if anything a deeper blow to me: not only was I appalled at what seemed to have happened to the lad, but technically, since he was loaned to me, I was responsible for replacing him, as I would be for any chattel I had borrowed and was not able to return in working order.

Regulus saw our faces and was apologetic now. 'Forgive

ROSEMARY ROWE

me, Excellence. We had no notion who his owner was –
certainly we never dreamed it might be someone of distinction, like yourself. In fact, we concluded that he was merely
the attendant of some hapless citizen who had been travelling
through the woods – perhaps on some trading venture, since
he clearly wasn't rich – and been set upon by these vagabonds
and robbed. We found a package of used clothes nearby
which seemed to suggest something of the kind.'

It was my turn to sit up sharply. 'A toga and a green linen
tunic with a woven band, by any chance?' I asked.

The soldier stared at me. 'How did you know that?'

'Because I rather think that they're mine,' I said. 'As you
can see, I'm wearing borrowed clothes. The slave that His
Excellence lost had taken my spare clothes . . . don't ask for
explanations. It's a complex tale.' I sighed. 'So it was
Promptillius, it seems. Poor fellow – he went out to his death,
supposing that I'd summoned him. I hope his end was quick.'
I felt very guilty about this, in fact. If I had not left him in the
marketplace it seemed quite likely that he would be with us
now.

The soldier nodded. 'I think I can assure you that it would
have been. He clearly died without a struggle, citizen.
Someone slipped a thin cord round his neck from behind
and pulled it tight – the marks were clearly visible. He would
scarcely have had time to know that it was happening.'

Marcus frowned. 'Strangled? I thought that he was hanged?'

'Killed first and strung up afterwards, I am fairly sure. We
discussed it at the time. The rope was in the wrong place and
the wrong size for the mark – there was no attempt to hide
the fact and make the two things match. It all seemed very
odd. He may have been put there in a hurry – it looked as
though he had – and he may not have been dead for very

124

long. We decided that he was most likely killed elsewhere and simply slung up to dangle where he was – together with the helmet and the cloak – just to get our attention and entice us from the path.'

I glanced at Marcus, who was scowling doubtfully. I had already offended proper protocol by interrupting twice without being invited to speak, and I had no wish to increase his irritation by doing so again. However, I was impressed by this soldier's clarity of mind. He was clearly capable of cogent reasoning. 'If I may ask something further, Excellence?' I ventured. Mercifully, Marcus gave me permission with a nod, and I turned to the soldier. 'I thought you said there was a pool of blood?'

'There was. It wasn't his. There was no wound on him. That is what made us suppose that he had a master with him, who was stabbed and dragged away – just as, I suppose, the messenger had been. We found the marks of heel-tracks in the mud as if a body had been dragged that way, but we couldn't trace them very far before they disappeared in puddles and leaves. We even left a man on guard and searched the area, but we found no sign of any other corpse.'

'Nor of the slave-boy's tunic?'

He looked perplexed. 'I hadn't thought of that. I wonder why the raiders stripped him naked and took his things away, then left the other garments lying there? They were loosely tied up with a strip of cloth. It was quite evident that they were clothes – though they were of no great value, I suppose.'

Marcus, with faint signs of impatience, cleared his throat. 'Is all this significant?'

'It is significant to me,' I said humbly. 'And possibly to all of us, in fact. If I might make a suggestion, Excellence, do you not think it would be wise to make a foray out that way tomorrow, perhaps with a detachment from the garrison as guard, and make an examination of the spot?'

Marcus looked extremely sceptical at this. 'And delay ourselves still further? For the sake of some old clothes?'

'For the sake of the administration, Excellence. It seems that an official messenger has been killed, carrying a letter for you from the Isca garrison – which was no doubt sealed?' I looked towards the soldier, who confirmed this with a nod. 'Then surely we are dealing with a serious matter here – interfering with the imperial post. Isn't that a capital offence? I'm sure the Emperor would not be pleased, and would expect you to investigate.'

Marcus nodded wearily. 'I suppose you're right.' He brightened. 'Though there's no proof the messenger was killed.'

'Only the bits of uniform,' I said. 'And don't forget the heel-marks and the blood. Who else did they belong to? Not to the owner of the slave, as the soldiers quite reasonably thought, because you are his owner and he'd been serving me, and clearly it wasn't one of us.' I shook my head. 'I suspect it was our poor messenger all right.'

'Oh,' Marcus said gloomily. He was obviously disinclined to bother with all this, but – as I had judged – his sense of duty compelled him to do something now.

The optio, who had been listening to all this, sprang suddenly to life, anxious to show that he could think as clearly as any mere auxiliary. 'Dear Jupiter, you see the implications of all this? Supposing that the letter had not merely concerned arrangements for your escort to the fort, but private information about the movements of the troops? All that would be in rebel hands by now.'

I nodded. 'Precisely. And he had a horse and uniform.

Anyone could use those to impersonate an imperial messenger. We would not expect to recognise the face. And he had a letter with an official seal – probably on a simple ribbon-tie, which could have been prised off and used again, with care.'

The optio was looking horrified. 'To send a different message here, if they chose?'

'Or to any other border garrison,' I replied. 'I doubt that, in the circumstances, anyone would examine the seal too carefully. And now they have Promptillius's household uniform as well, which anyone who knows my patron well will recognise at once, and take to be proof that the wearer is His Excellence's slave – another way of carrying false messages. You see why I think it worth our while trying to find out what happened in the forest last night?'

Marcus was looking suddenly alert. 'Of course, from the administration's point of view, there's also the question of the thefts involved. At least five army horses, as I understand it, and some equipment too. The incoming governor will no doubt be extremely pleased if we can discover who perpetrated this and bring the men to justice.' He made a thoughtful face. 'It occurs to me that we should be travelling past the spot where all this happened on our way to Isca in the morning. You, optio, could ride out with us, perhaps – your men can provide us with a proper escort too. I understand there is a marching-camp nearby that you can call on for some extra men?'

The optio nodded. 'There has been one stationed here ever since the raids on Roman travellers began again – a show of force to keep the dissidents at bay, though they're not a lot of use against these ambushes because we don't know where these rebel groups are based. I'm sure the commander will be pleased to help – it will give them something positive to do, apart from route-marches and stabbing at practice posts with wooden swords. I will send to the centurion in charge at once – if you will honour me by sending the request under your seal, Excellence. He is superior to me, of course.'

My patron looked flattered. 'Certainly I will. We'll make a thorough examination of the murder site and see if there is anything to learn.'

He spoke as if the whole idea had just occurred to him. I smiled, but knew better than to say anything except, 'A splendid notion, Excellence. I'm sure the new governor when he arrives will be appropriately grateful for your help.'

Marcus preened. He nodded to the auxiliary cavalryman, who was still standing stiffly at attention near the door. 'Very well, soldier, that will do for now. You may dismiss. Get some food and find yourselves a bed. We shall expect you to accompany us at dawn. I think you said that there were four of you?'

The soldier nodded. 'Myself and three other unhorsed spearmen, Excellence. Though two of us no longer have our spears.'

'Then I imagine that replacements can be found for you. But you will have to march. I don't expect the mansio to have four horses free – at least not four that could easily be spared.' He said this quickly, before the optio could intervene and offer to find animals from the marching-camp. They would almost certainly have spare mounts there, but it was clear that my patron preferred to have the Isca men travel ignominiously on foot, to remind them not to lose their horses again so carelessly.

The cavalryman looked properly dismayed at this, but he

said humbly, 'As you command, Excellence.' And he withdrew.

Marcus was in high good humour now. He called for another jug of wine and turned to us. 'These moments of transition are always dangerous. When there is no appointed governor in place, the rebels take the opportunity to strike. The same thing once occurred in Gaul, I understand . . .' and he treated us to a rambling lecture on the recent uprisings.

I have no head for Roman wine and even less for foreign politics, so I was glad when the evening came to a close at last, and I could stretch out on my comfortable palliasse again. As I drifted into sleep it occurred to me that, after all, I had not been reunited with my clothes. Perhaps the soldiers had them. Well, it was too late now. I would have to wait till morning to make enquiries.

I must have slept extremely well, because it was broad daylight when I woke and there was already the sound of movement in the court outside. With no Junio to wake me I was almost late – and (having already lost Promptillius) I had not been offered another of Marcus's slaves. I splashed my face quickly in a little of the cold water from the jug on the stone bench in my room, bolted down the apple and the crust of bread provided as breakfast dainties by the mansio, and drained the welcome liquid in the jug. Then I straightened my borrowed tunic, put on my shoes and cloak and hurried out into the morning light.

Marcus was already in the court, looking as elegant as he always did. I hurried to his side, and dropped uncomfortably to one knee on the cobbled yard – Marcus expects the proper obeisances, even in circumstances like these.

'Ah, there you are,' he said, extending a ringed hand for

me to kiss and waiting impatiently for me to rise. 'I was about to send a guard for you. We are almost ready to depart.' He gazed at me. 'What's happened to your toga? I thought that it was found?'

'I thought so too, Excellence,' I said. 'I presume the soldiers brought it when they came, but it hasn't been returned to me as yet. However, here's the leader now. Perhaps he can tell us what they've done with it.'

The cavalryman, looking a little more refreshed, came over at my patron's signal and bowed in brisk salute. 'Spearman Regulus at your service, Excellence.'

'We were wondering,' Marcus said, with that little smile which made the seemingly polite enquiry something far more dangerous. 'The parcel of clothes that you found. They belonged to my friend the citizen here, as I believe you know. Where are they? He would be glad to change into them to travel on.'

The soldier had that hunted look again. 'I fear I don't have them, Excellence.' He looked desperately around, as if his companions might be summoned to share the blame with him. 'You see, we used the toga to wrap the body in. It didn't seem proper to leave it as it was, and we didn't expect the parcel to be claimed. And as for the tunic – I'm sorry, citizen – we gave that away.'

'Gave it away? Who to?' I was too upset to be grammatical.

He was deploying that military trick again, of standing stiff and staring past you as he spoke, while his face got steadily more scarlet with embarrassment. 'I'm afraid we gave it to a peasant, sir. A fellow with a herd of pigs, who helped us in our search. He'd got a little hut place in the clearing there, where he kept his herd, and he'd obviously been camped there overnight. He was very helpful – gave us water and bound up my foot, and even came out to search with us when we were trying to discover where those heel-tracks went. He had a grudge against the raiders, too: said they'd broken into his enclosure overnight, stolen one of his pigs and let the others out. He was rounding them up when we discovered him.'

'You gave it to a swineherd?' I exclaimed. 'That was my second best tunic!'

Regulus looked properly abashed. 'Well, he was extremely helpful, citizen. We offered him the tunic as reward. He was the one who located it, in fact – the parcel had been hidden underneath some leaves, and though he did not exactly ask for it outright, it was obvious from his manner that he wanted it. It was easy to see why. His own garment was a pathetic mess – a dreadful greenish tunic, torn and stained and, frankly, unpleasant to be near. I suppose it comes of dealing with the pigs.'

Marcus nodded judiciously. 'No doubt it seemed a better bargain at the time. A tunic which nobody seemed to want, instead of offering him your hard-earned cash?'

'Exactly, Excellence,' the man said eagerly. 'It would have fetched a few *quadrantes* in the marketplace, at best.' He realised that this was an unfortunate remark and went on hastily, 'We could go and demand to have it back – explain that the owner had been found and wanted it. Not force him to give it up, exactly – we have enough enemies around here as it is – but we could offer him a few denarii instead.' He had cheered up and was quite animated by his own suggestion now. 'It would be an easy matter to locate the man. We know where his portable enclosure was last night, and even if he has moved on by now, he should not be difficult to find. He's got a great big jagged scar across his face.'

131

There was a silence. Plautus! Could it be? I looked at Marcus and he looked at me: obviously the same thought had occurred to him. He raised an enquiring eyebrow but I tried to signal caution with a quick shake of my head. The fewer people who knew of our suspicions, the better.

Marcus gave me a swift, comprehending nod and raised his hand, preventing the optio from saying anything. 'Enough of this discussion. We are wasting time. Let's get moving as soon as possible.' He turned to Regulus. 'You march in the front. We'd better find this pig-keeper of yours. I rather think Libertus wants to talk to him.'

Chapter Thirteen

It is an eerie feeling travelling through empty countryside, escorted by half a century of soldiers on the march – eight rows of five abreast. (There are eighty soldiers in a century, of course, despite the name!) There were a dozen mounted outriders as well, hastily co-opted from the nearest marching-camp in case we encountered trouble on the way. The optio, still anxious to give a good impression, took care with posting them: six of them well out in front as scouts, and the other six just as far behind to guard the rear. The cavalrymen from Isca might have helped with the task but following what Marcus had ordained they were simply re-equipped with spears and thus obliged to march.

It was a military operation and an air of businesslike precision reigned. Marcus's private mounted bodyguard, which had accompanied us all the way from Glevum, was not now deemed sufficient to protect us, so instead of cantering up and down alongside our carriage they were obliged to fall in behind the two domestic carts which carried all Marcus's serving retinue and other equipment for the trip. There was none of the cheerful jingle of their harness and shouted banter now, and the whole atmosphere was much more tense.

There was only the measured ring of hobnailed sandals on the road, the creak of armour and the groan of carts and an occasional snort from one of the horses. The lack of any human voice was almost sinister: the rhythmic pounding of the feet so perfectly in time that it seemed that the whole column was a single animal. And quite a swiftly moving animal. If you have ever seen a phalanx of advancing Roman troops, you will know that they can move with startling speed. It is said that a legionary can march twenty miles a day fully armed, and with his entire equipment on his back. Our escort were not carrying their packs today, only their fighting weapons and their shields, and although obviously our progress was not as quick as it had been when we were unaccompanied by men on foot, we were still jolting through the countryside at surprising speed.

We passed through the cultivated area which surrounds the town, where a few Roman-style villas could be seen, each with its contributory farm and all much like similar home-steads I was used to further east – except that here the houses were built, not in sheltered places, but on the tops of hills where they were exposed to wind and weather but had commanding views of the countryside about. They were surrounded by high protective walls, and there were similar defensive enclosures round many of the fields. We even saw a small party of slaves, armed with pointed staves and clubs, patrolling the borders of one villa-farm.

As we moved further from the town the substantial dwellings gave way to humbler ones: first Silurian round-houses in cosy villages and then – as we travelled increasingly through woods – more isolated huts. In one dank clearing by the road we saw a wretched cluster of miserable shacks, where scrawny chickens mixed with scraggy goats and naked children ran about unchecked, while skinny women with suspicious eyes stopped their work and put down their querns and hoes to watch us pass. I thought about the butcher peddling bones and scraps of fly-blown meat – these people were among his customers, no doubt.

The road got hillier and more wooded as we went along, until we reached the outskirts of unbroken forest, stretching in all directions as far as we could see. There we found a wretched hovel, masquerading as a civilian inn. It was little more than a filthy staging-post, where a few flea-bitten horses could be had for hire, but at the sight of Marcus's insignia on the coach the landlord came bustling out with gifts of cheese and some of the foulest wine I had ever tasted. Nothing would have persuaded me to go inside, but we did consent to water our own animals at his trough and listen to his whining voice complain of how even his mangy steeds had been attacked, and how he kept a dagger ready, just in case.

The forest looked forbidding but the front outriders had scouted on ahead and, having found nothing untoward, had galloped back and were waiting for us at the inn. The optio came back to tell us that – to all appearances at least – the way was clear, and asked for permission to proceed. Marcus gave it with a silent nod and our procession jolted off again, with the riders now formed up close in front of us to afford us extra protection from surprise attack.

Then we were in the forest. It was far more disturbing than the open road. Here the feeble sunshine could not penetrate the trees, and after the heavy rainfall of a day or two before even the military road was dank and treacherous with mud and fallen leaves. We jolted forward into shadowed gloom where grey light filtered only patchily through the tangle of naked branches overhead, and then through a dense, forbidding stand of evergreen, which created a dim green half-light that was even worse. The clanking of our marching passage stilled the winter birds, but there was a wind and the woods were full of rustling movement. It was easy to imagine that each falling leaf or stirring branch was set in motion, not by a freak of breeze, but by some hiding enemy. And there were always wolves and bears to think about.

I was glad of our elaborate escort now. The thought of travelling through these threatening woods without our armed protection was an alarming one. As it was my heart was thumping uncomfortably in my chest, and beside me Marcus began to fidget too, though he did not say anything to me. The purposeful silence of the marching men outside had somehow communicated itself to him, and he had not addressed a word to me for miles.

Of course I could not start to talk to him, unasked, so I turned my attention to the last few days – anything to take my mind off bears and bandits. In any case, something was obscurely troubling me.

I had not killed Lupus, but somebody had done. Up until this morning I had more or less concluded that it was Plautus, however unlikely that appeared. Paulinus, whom I had taken for his spy, had followed me almost to the door, and it had seemed logical that – since I'd clearly recognised his face – Plautus might have wanted to silence me, and anyone I might have spoken to. But now I was wondering if I was right.

If the swineherd with the scarred face was really Plautus in disguise, as seemed highly probable, then – according to what Regulus had said – he had been in this forest all night with his pigs. In that case he could hardly have killed Lupus after dark, much less followed me around the town. The civitas was simply much too far away. Nor could he have done it and walked here overnight. Apart from all the normal dangers of night-time travel, the town gates were always closed at dusk and anyone going through them after that would be noted by the guard, yet we knew that no one of Plautus's description had been seen to leave – the optio had made particular enquiries on the point.

But if Plautus had not killed Lupus, who could it have been? Not Paulinus – the child would have been far too terrified to be entrusted with such a task – and not his brother either, since he was intercepting Promptillius at the time. Was there some other explanation, unconnected with my visit to the thermopolium? Had Lupus simply failed to pay the protection fee, or in some other way aggrieved the rival gangs? I shook my head. It was too much of a coincidence. Unless . . . I sat up with a sudden start. Was I looking at all this back to front?

Plautus was after all a Roman citizen. What was he doing in the bath-house part of town? What was he doing in the civitas at all? Obviously he was somehow on the run, but I had just assumed that he was fleeing me. Suppose that by calling out his name, far from his being any threat to me, I was in danger of betraying *him*? That might explain why he had hurried so furtively away, and perhaps also why Lyra and her boys had shown such interest in me when I followed him. I had supposed that they were friends of his, but I had no proof of that. They didn't even seem to know his name.

I was just deciding that I ought to voice these thoughts to Marcus, and run the risk of a rebuke, when the whole marching column came briskly to a halt. Regulus, who had been marching in the van, came hurrying down between the ranks to speak to us. He was streaked with sweat and breathing heavily and limping very badly – the pace maintained by the trained infantry was clearly making great demands on him, though his pride had somehow forced him to keep up. The optio, who had accompanied him, looked as fresh and unconcerned as if he had merely been out for a stroll.

'In the name of His Most Imperial Divinity, Commodus Fortunatus Britannicus, the Earthly Manifestation of Great Hercules, Emperor of Rome and all the provinces . . .' the optio began, approaching our official carriage, and presenting his baton with a bow.

Marcus leaned forward and touched it graciously, thus cutting short the lengthy formula. 'You have my permission to report. I presume we are getting near the spot where the ambush happened yesterday?' He looked at Regulus.

'Just . . . bottom . . . of . . . the valley . . .' the cavalryman managed to pant out. He waved a hand in the direction he had mentioned. 'Very . . . steep.'

The optio took over. 'I have sent a pair of mounted soldiers on ahead, to check that it is safe for us to proceed. All the same, with your permission, Excellence, we will deploy your mounted bodyguard as extra scouts, and move up in close formation around the carriage as we go, to give you as much protection as we can. The rebels have struck in this valley several times so far. It's possible they have a base nearby. There's still a risk of ambush in the area.'

This was not a comfortable thought. Marcus nodded. 'Very well. As you suggest.' Another barked command and the convoy surged forward, though more slowly now.

The road seemed a good deal narrower here, hemmed in as it was by tall trees on either side, and the marching troops closed ranks and pressed in around us, so that we found ourselves the centre of a moving box. When I looked out through the leather curtains of the swaying vehicle, I could see that the men had drawn their swords and raised their shields and so were forming a sort of defensive outer wall. I craned out to see behind us, and realised that the last two rows had fallen back, and were marching in diamond formation, still perfectly in time, so as to protect us from the rear. Further behind them still, the mounted horsemen rode with daggers drawn.

It was an impressive display of discipline, and it occurred to me what an awesome sight the Roman army must present to any enemy confronting it. If I had been a Silurian rebel hiding in the trees, I would have been thoroughly intimidated by this time, especially when the men began a rhythmic beating of their swords against their shields. It was a tactic that I'd heard about, intended to strike terror into the enemy.

There was a definite feeling of expectancy and threat. I held my breath, half waiting for an ambush to leap out at any time, but we reached the bottom of the valley without incident. There, where a little path led off into a clearing on the right, we stopped a second time. This was our destination, it seemed. The optio appeared to help us from the carriage and we dismounted on the verge beside the road, to find ourselves ankle deep in fallen leaves, among a little stand of ancient oaks. The troops were drawn up silently on either side, so that we were still the centre of a protective square. There was no wind now, but there was a chill damp in the air, and despite myself I shivered.

The officer gave a stiff bow of salute. 'Permission to report? The lookouts have made an examination of the site and found no intruders in the area, though there is lots of evidence of recent tracks. We therefore await your orders, Excellence.'

There was a pause, then Marcus turned to me. 'Well, Libertus? This trip was your suggestion, I believe? What do you propose we do now?' As he spoke he tapped his baton on his palm – a sure sign of stress and irritation, as I knew.

I was just as anxious. The forest was a menacing place, but I tried to sound as confident as I could. 'I think I should inspect the site with Regulus,' I said. And then, fearing that he might feel overlooked, I added, 'With you two gentlemen as well, of course, if you would condescend to help our humble search. Your intelligence and experience would be invaluable.'

I saw my patron preen at this, so I turned my attention to the optio. 'I'm sure you will agree that a small group searching the area on foot may find more than a larger number would.' I did not want forty men trampling on the evidence, I meant, but I did not have to say the words. The optio understood.

He sniffed. 'Well, perhaps you're right. But if His Excellence is to participate, I insist that he shall have a bodyguard. I am charged with his safety and, with due respect, cannot consent to let him wander around the forest without armed men at his side. Not after what happened yesterday. There have been too many other incidents on this road of late. It's almost as if the wretches know where we're going to be.'

I was afraid that Marcus was going to protest – he prides himself on Roman nonchalance in facing dangerous situations of this kind. But to my relief and amazement he was already saying, 'As you wish. But if we are to do anything at all, let us do it quickly. This forest is most unpleasantly cold and dark.'

It is not like Marcus to complain of physical discomfort in this way, so I knew that he too was feeling seriously alarmed. The presence of an extra pair of guards was just as likely to obliterate what I was looking for as any other set of marching legs, but I held my tongue and our little party soon set off –

myself, my patron and the optio, together with Regulus and two mounted guards and a couple of extra foot soldiers to guard our rear.

I thought our task was likely to be a fairly hopeless one – the scouts had already ridden up and down the military road, so there was no hope of following any tracks imprinted in the mud, and according to what Regulus had said himself, the rebels yesterday had disappeared in all directions through the undergrowth with the unhorsed cavalrymen plunging after them. There was little chance, at this distance, of learning anything. However, Regulus led us down the forest path, leaving the other men to search beside the military road.

'This is the branch where he was hanging,' Regulus said, pointing to a massive overhanging tree. 'And over there, look, in the ditch – under that pile of earth and leaves – that's where we buried him. It looks as if the grave has been disturbed.'

Marcus shot a look at me and nodded to one of the foot guards at the rear. The man stepped forward, gulped, and – using his dagger as a spade – began to move aside the loosened earth. There was something lying only an inch or two below the surface, and it was soon revealed: first, something that had once been my toga, and then, when that sorry wrapping was removed, something that used to be Promptillius. Enough of him remained for me to have no doubt of that, although something – rats or bears, perhaps – had already been gnawing at the bones.

The man who had been doing the digging-up looked pale. Death is a routine matter to a legionary, perhaps, but there is something particularly unpleasant about uncovering a corpse. Marcus nodded brusquely at him.

'Wrap that up and have it taken to the cart. I'll see that he has a proper burial later on. Nothing elaborate – he was just a slave – but he was a member of my household, after all.'

The man nodded, and bent to wrap the figure up again, using my ruined toga for the task. That would benefit from burial too, I thought – the rats, or whatever they were, had damaged it as well, and it was no longer fit for any other use. Secretly, I was rather glad; otherwise Marcus might have suggested that it be returned to me.

The optio briskly sent a rider back with orders to conscript four men to come and lift the corpse. He supervised them as they carried it across and laid it in the second cart, which held our belongings and two of Marcus's remaining slaves who were travelling as guards. I hoped they were not superstitious lads. They would have to share the cart with that grisly burden from now on, and it was already none too fresh. However, no one spared a second thought for them. Regulus was already striding on.

'That's where the helmet and the cloak were hanging,' he explained, pointing to the overhanging branch, 'and this is where we found the heel-tracks – see? You can just make out the marks, although of course they're fainter now. We followed them right over to that copse of elms, but then we lost them in the leaves and mud.'

'You'd better show us, now we're here,' Marcus said ungraciously, and Regulus led the way again.

'There you are, you see?' he said, stopping to indicate faint marks on the ground and a trail of broken branches through the undergrowth. He led us on, following the trail through fallen leaves and over jagged roots until we came to another faint pathway winding through the trees. 'This is where the heel-marks stopped. It may be that the rebels have some secret base nearby. They must have done something with the messenger's body when they dragged it off. They didn't come this way by accident. But after that the trail is too confused.'

Marcus was looking, frowning, at the ground. 'But there has been someone this way recently. There is the print of hobnails in the ground.'

Regulus went over to the spot. He seemed to brighten, but a moment later I saw him colour ruefully and shake his head. 'Those are my sandal-prints from yesterday, I fear. See where I've just trodden in the mud? The pattern of the studs is just the same – including the one missing on the edge.'

I peered down at the path. The man was right. 'But what are these other little tracks?' I gestured to dozens of faint pointed marks. 'They look like animals'.'

'The pigs, perhaps?' the cavalryman said. 'They might have come this way. They had escaped from their enclosure – just down in the valley over there – and were swarming everywhere.'

'Is this where you met the swineherd?' I enquired.

He shook his head. 'That was further on. We were searching up and down the path, in case there was any sign of anyone, but he was the only person we met. We questioned him for quite a time – and not too gently either, once or twice – but in the end we had to let him go. He was clearly sympathetic to our cause. After all, he was a victim of the rebels, too. He helped us search.'

Marcus said loftily, 'All the same, we want to interview the man again. Can you take us down to where this pig enclosure was?'

The optio looked concerned at this. 'But, Excellence, we are moving a long way from the troops . . .'

Marcus quelled him with a look. 'You heard my instructions, I believe.' He turned to Regulus. 'Lead on.'

The optio was right to be doubtful, I thought privately. The path was a narrow, winding one and the trees around us were extremely dense. Every step took us further from the safety of the legionary force, and although we had an escort with us, it was small. I began to wonder how effective it would be against a band of armed attackers. But one cannot argue with a man of Marcus's standing. As the governor's representative he outranked the optio, and we found ourselves moving down the little track, reluctant as a troop of conscript slaves going into battle for their overlord.

There was a lot of rustling in the undergrowth, and I held my breath. Nothing happened. That was almost worse.

It was almost an anticlimax when we reached the spot and found the small enclosure, constructed in the ancient Celtic way: a stout little fence of woven hazel wands supported by scores of pointed stakes, so that when the acorns in this part of the forest were all gone it could easily be dismantled and removed to somewhere else. There was a little makeshift shelter in the midst of it, and a wisp of smoke emerging from the hole in the centre of the roof suggested that the owner was at home.

The optio looked at Regulus and gave a nod. The cavalryman stepped forward and raised his voice. 'Pigman, come out here. In the name of the Emperor Commodus and the Empire, we wish to speak to you.'

There was a rustling in the area behind the hut, and a figure came towards us through the trees – a greying redhead, carrying a pail. A half-dozen largish pigs came snuffling after him, but I saw that they were each tethered by a hind leg to a tree, so that they could not escape again, though they were straining at their leashes and the ropes were long. The pigman paused and emptied water into a sort of makeshift trough formed by a fallen hollow tree and for the first time I got a proper look at him.

He was wearing my green tunic: I recognised its distinctive braided edge. I was startled to see it already sadly torn and grimed with mire, but the greatest shock was when I saw his face.

This wasn't Plautus. It was a man I had never seen before – slow, grimy, weather-beaten, and with a vacant expression on his eager countenance. He was a simpleton, by the look of it. Dirt streaked his cheeks and he wore a straggling beard, but it was still possible to see that there was not the slightest sign of any scar.

Chapter Fourteen

He grinned foolishly at us and spoke, in Latin of a kind –
though it was so slow and accented that it was quite difficult
to work out what he said. Roughly, though, the message was
quite clear. 'Hello, Romans. You've come back very soon. We
managed to find all my pigs again except for one. And thank
you for my tunic – it's a lovely fit.'

I glanced at Regulus, but he was looking just as startled as
the rest of us. 'This is not the man I saw before,' he said to
me. He turned to the pigman and said, very slowly and with
emphasis, 'Who are you? And where's the other man?'

The pigman gave another of his grins, flashing a surprising
display of sturdy teeth. 'My name is Subulcus,' he managed
in his tortured Latin, and thumped his chest with pride. 'I
am the keeper of the pigs.'

The name means 'swineherd' so this was not altogether a
surprise. Marcus gave a deep, exasperated sigh. 'Where is the
other pigman?'

Subulcus shook his head. 'I am the only Subulcus here.'
He grinned again. It was impossible to tell whether he was
referring to the name or to the job.

Marcus tried again. 'A man with a scar?'

Subulcus pushed back his sleeve to show his arm. There
was a long jagged mark along the length of it, as if someone
had slashed him with a sword. 'Scar,' he said, exhibiting it

with a smile. He tapped his neck and shoulder. 'Scar,' he said again.

Marcus turned to me. 'Try him in Celtic, my old friend. It's obvious his Latin isn't good.'

I nodded. The pigman's dialect would not be exactly like my own, but there was a fair chance I could make him understand. 'There was another man here, yesterday,' I said, enunciating each word carefully.

My Celtic did the trick. Subulcus flashed his teeth again, and launched into delighted speech. 'I know. They stole my pig. I had to run off after them. And there was the Roman man who left this tunic for a present. I like Romans now – that's why I'm not afraid to talk to you. He was kind. Not like the nasty ones my master talks about.'

I translated this. The optio turned to Marcus with a shrug. 'This is hopeless, and we're wasting time. Should we take him back and have him questioned properly by the torturers? I'm sure Libertus could translate for us.'

Marcus shot me an enquiring look. He knows my views on this. Handing a man over to the torturers may be useful in extorting information from his lips, but that is not necessarily the same as getting at the truth. After an hour or two of torment the victim will usually admit to anything at all, simply to make the anguish stop, even if he has to make up the facts they want to hear.

It is never a process which appeals to me, and I particularly loathed the idea of causing pain to a poor simpleton like this, who would hardly comprehend what was required. Better to try to gain his confidence. I shook my head. 'I think he's telling us the truth,' I said. 'He hasn't got the wits to tell a lie. You could torture him for hours, to no avail. I don't think he knows anything at all.'

My patron sighed. 'Very well, Libertus, question him and see what you can do.' His tone suggested that it was beneath his dignity to question swineherds in the woods. 'If you can make no progress, we'll try flogging him.' He had spoken in Latin, but the pigman got the drift. His face crumpled and he was near to tears. His filthy fingers were plucking at my sleeve.

'Don't let them hurt me,' he whimpered. 'I didn't mean to lose the pig. I wouldn't have left them for a minute – I don't usually – but my master sent for me to come up to the house. Then when I got there it was a mistake, and he didn't want me after all, so I hurried back. When I arrived, I saw some horsemen here. They had one of my pigs and they were driving all the others off into the woods. I ran off after them but they just laughed at me. And then young master came by, and he was cross with me because the pigs were loose. He told me to run up to the round-house right away and fetch the children to help to round them up.'

'And that is what you did?'

A vigorous nod. 'I have to do what he says now. My master tells me so. I have to do what all the family says, because my proper family aren't here.'

It made a kind of sense. Pigs have a special value in the Celtic world. Roast boar is the universal meat at feasts – together with goose and venison – and the animal is sacred to the gods. Those with simple, trusting minds like Subulcus are believed to have a special gift with animals and also to be favourites of the moon goddess, whose caresses have deprived them of their brains. So such a child, though rejected by his parents as a normal son, might well be 'adopted' by the tribe and housed and protected in return for tending to the pigs – though in truth, his condition was not much better than a slave's.

Subulcus was still finishing his tale. 'I found three of the children from the farm, and brought them back, but when we got here all the pigs were gathered up, and there was a tunic for me in the hut.' He looked down at my pathetic garment, mired with mud. 'Young master said it was a present from a Roman man. It's a nice one, isn't it? The best I ever had.'

'This young master – does he often give you gifts?' I said.

He dropped his eyes. 'I don't see him very much. He says I know nothing about anything. But it isn't true. I know about the pigs. My master says there's nobody who knows more about pigs than me.'

'I'm sure that's true,' I murmured soothingly. 'Tell me, who told you that your master wanted you? I suspect, you see, that you were sent away on purpose, so those bad men could get in and steal your pig.'

He thought about this gravely and then shook his head. 'It was a big man on a horse. The Roman man. But it can't have been a trick. He had a big ring with a seal – and a sort of uniform like that.' He gestured towards Regulus and screwed his grimy face into a frown. 'I thought that you were him again, at first, but I can see now that you're not.'

'It wasn't one of us,' I said gently. 'I don't think it really was a Roman man at all. I think he was just dressed up as if he was. But you thought he was a soldier, so you did what he said?'

He nodded. 'I have to do what soldiers tell me – there'll be trouble else. My master always tells me that. And I mustn't spit at them or call them names – even if they did come in and take our land away.'

It was as well that Marcus couldn't understand all this, I thought, or poor Subulcus might find himself enduring a flogging after all, for speaking out against the Empire. I said, 'Your master tells you that?'

More vigorous nodding. 'He's taught me that since I was very young, when he first took me in the family. He says I have a special right to know.' Subulcus held out his arm, and pointed to the scar. 'You see this mark? This is where someone hurt me when I was very small – for nothing. I wasn't fighting him. I was just a baby and was in the way. But that was a naughty Roman man – he killed my proper mother, and he hurt my uncle's son as well. He wasn't a kind Roman like the one yesterday. That one left me a new tunic.' He looked suspiciously at the optio and his men. 'Are these kind Romans too?'

I took a deep breath. 'Listen, Subulcus. The man who sent you to the farmstead yesterday was not a proper Roman, and he wasn't kind at all. I think he stole that horse and uniform and ring, and killed the man who owned them, and more than likely murdered my poor slave as well. This soldier found him hanging from a tree.'

Subulcus was struggling with this information. 'Then he was a bad Roman too? But he was kind to me.'

'I don't think he really was,' I said. I was beginning to despair of ever making the pigman understand. 'I think he told you to go up to the house, just so that the other men could come and steal your pig. I'd like to know about that tunic, though. I want to know how he got hold of it. It was mine. My attendant brought it to the woods and this soldier . . .' I indicated Regulus, 'was the kind one – he gave the tunic to a pig-minder who helped him in the woods. Not you. But that's the man we're looking for today.'

Subulcus shook his head. 'I'm the only Subulcus round here,' he repeated stubbornly. 'And you can't give the tunic to another man. It's mine. Young master told me so. It was waiting for me in my hut. He said the Roman man had left it, and it was for me.'

We were going round in circles. I glanced at Marcus, but of course he couldn't understand a word. He was chatting to the optio, looking bored and tapping his baton impatiently against his thigh. That was a danger sign. I turned to Subulcus. 'It's all right. You can keep the tunic – if you help us as the other pigman did. So tell me, where's young master now?'

'Down at the homestead,' he replied, as though I were the idiotic one.

I explained all this to Marcus, and was about to ask the pigman for directions to the place when we were interrupted by the sound of hooves. Our escort drew their swords at once and whirled round to form a square, ready to protect us if need be. Subulcus darted back towards his pigs. But the men who galloped up to us were not an ambush group, only the outriders from the marching-camp who had accompanied us on our journey here. The leader called out the password of the day, and our would-be defenders sheathed their blades and let them through.

The leading rider dropped from the saddle and presented himself before Marcus and the optio. 'Your pardon, sirs. We are relieved to find you safe. We were beginning to become alarmed. The sub-officer you left in charge ordered us to come and see what had occurred – we feared you had been ambushed and attacked. He's marching the rest of the men over here to offer you support – though it will take them a little longer to arrive.'

Marcus looked extremely vexed at this. 'And leave my carts and carriage to be a target on the road? You can report back that we are entirely safe and that we are going to the farmstead to interview the owner of these pigs. There must be a farm track somewhere. Two of you must go back and guard the vehicles while we complete our business.' He scowled. 'How did you find us, anyway?'

The horseman almost smiled. 'We tracked you through the trees. It wasn't difficult.' He saw the look on Marcus's face and added quickly, 'Where is this house, Excellence?'

Marcus looked at me. 'Libertus?'

But Subulcus had already understood. 'On the outskirts of the forest, down this track. You come to the main track, where the big oak is . . .' He gabbled directions in such garbled Celtic that I could hardly follow them.

I nodded. 'I think you should come with us, Subulcus, and show us where it is. We'll leave some soldiers here, to guard your pigs.'

Subulcus looked most disturbed at this. 'My master told me I must stay here all the time.'

'You left here yesterday,' I pointed out.

'But that was different. The soldier told me that my master wanted me. And even then look what happened when I left the pigs. But you have to do it, if a soldier says.'

I saw what was required. I turned to Regulus. 'Would you tell him, very slowly, that he has to come with us? He'll only do it if he's asked by someone with the right authority. I think your uniform might do the trick.'

Regulus looked doubtful, but he did as I asked and it worked exactly as I'd hoped. Subulcus reluctantly agreed to leave his precious charges in the care of the optio's men, although he was clearly very dubious about this. It was almost laughable. Instead of shambling Subulcus, there would be a party of professional soldiers guarding them with their daggers drawn. Rarely could a herd of pigs have enjoyed such good protection in the whole history of swine.

The crash of military sandals through the undergrowth alerted us to the arrival of the larger troop. Marcus was for dispatching them straight back to guard the carts, but the optio argued fiercely that half of the company should come with us, and the rest should be left behind to guard the carriages and the pigs. Before he could be briskly overruled, there was a rustle in the trees – which might have been an ambush, but was probably a bear – and Marcus abruptly changed his mind. Subulcus, the optio and I would lead the way, while he, his bodyguard and a score of the foot guard would follow on behind, along with the ten remaining outriders.

In this military formation we set off down the track. The appearance of so many Roman uniforms had reduced the poor swineherd to uneasy silence now, and despite my best attempts at questioning him about his master and the nature of the tribe, I couldn't get another sentence out of him until we reached the oak.

'There it is,' he said. 'Just as I told you.' He gestured to a massive tree, set back a little from the road. It was partly screened by lower bushes, but there was a clear space carefully maintained around the bole, and even from here I could see the sacred mistletoe in the upper fork and the strips of tell-tale rag tied and left hanging from the boughs.

I caught my breath. This was not a simple marker on the corner of a lane, as I had thoughtlessly expected, but a proper sacred oak – a Druid shrine. As we reached the entrance to what was effectively a grove, I could see that there were statues planted in the ground and that the great trunk was daubed with something red and darkening. I gulped. I had not seen a sacred tree like this for many years, but when I saw one last, the branches were adorned with severed human heads. The gruesome spectacle had haunted me for years – though of course my own ancestors would once have worshipped somewhere very similar, hung with the heads of their enemies.

Thankfully, there was nothing of the kind in evidence this time, at least from where we stood – although I did not care to wonder what the daubs might be. I knew already what the little statues were: symbolic faces made of rock or wood, some with cat-like ears and furrowed brows – a sort of substitute for proper heads. I debated for a moment what I should say and do. Druidism is forbidden under Rome on pain of death, and if Marcus realised what this tree signified he would set the soldiers on to it at once, to cut down the rags and hew the branches off, and order that the countryside be searched for devotees.

I glanced at Subulcus. It was obvious that he was one of them. He was edging past the grove with awe, and I knew that any desecration of the shrine would not only cost us any trust he might have had in us, but terrify him into speechlessness as well. He would not help us if we touched the tree.

I tried to strike a note of bored contempt. 'Some sort of local altar, Excellence. You know these people worship streams and trees.' I gestured down the track. 'I imagine the homestead is along this path.'

'Then lead us to it,' he said icily. He didn't glance again towards the oak.

It was a good deal easier marching on the lane, but it was still some time before we reached the limit of the trees and saw the farmstead nestling on the raised ground opposite: a small gathering of roundhouses, perhaps ten or twelve –

almost a tribal hamlet – built of stone and protected by a stout fence of triple stakes within a ditch, the smoke of wood fires rising through the thatch.

The place was almost fortified and had clearly been constructed for defence, but today there was no guard in evidence. A pair of tethered dogs set up a bark at our approach, and a tall thin woman in a shawl came out to gape suspiciously at us. Subulcus called something that I could not catch – it sounded like a password – and she scurried off, returning in a moment with one of the most striking men I've ever seen.

He was clearly a person of importance in his tribe. He was not tall – no taller than myself – and was no longer young, but he had enormous presence. He wore old-fashioned Celtic dress: plaid trousers, belted at the waist, and a jerkin of the same fine-woven coloured cloth, adorned by a single mighty silver brooch of intricate design. His hair, which had been shaved to halfway over his head, was long and flowing at the back, bleached fair with lime, and though he wore no beard the length of his moustache was wonderful.

He looked at the company outside his gate. 'I am Kiminiros, keeper of the fire and by the grace of the gods of tree and river elder of this tribe. What do you want with me?'

Chapter Fifteen

I glanced back at Marcus and the optio to see what their reaction was. To appear cowed or threatening would be a mistake. However, I need not have been concerned. Already my patron was striding forward through the ranks of guards and coming to address the Silurian elder face to face.

This meeting of two representatives of different ways of life was an imposing sight: Marcus magnificent in his spotless toga (the gods alone know how he managed to keep it so effortlessly white – mine would have been stained with grass and travel long ago), his rank emphasised by the width of purple stripe, and the bevy of armed men at his back; and the thin old man in his tribal plaid standing with a simple dignity quite alone on his side of the gate. Even the woman had slipped away and gone back to the dwelling huts by now.

I had been ready to translate for this minor chieftain, as I had done for Subulcus before, but when he spoke it was in faultless Latin – his deep voice as impressive as his appearance was.

'You come in peace, I trust? It is many, many harvests since my tribe fought with yours, and longer yet since there were swordsmen at my door.' We were a large group and our troops were armed, but he behaved for all the world as if he were favouring us by granting audience. He gestured towards

Subulcus. 'I see you have my swineherd with you. I hope he has not contrived to offend you in some way?'

It was an unspoken declaration that he was not afraid of us. Marcus met it squarely, throwing back his head and saying, in his most authoritative tone, 'We come here seeking information. My servant was murdered in the forest yesterday, several army horses have been stolen and an imperial messenger has disappeared. In the name of his most divine majesty, the Emperor of Rome and all the provinces, I require you to assist us if you can.'

The elder's expression did not change, but he inclined his head. 'Of course. I know my duty and will do it, as far as age and frailty permit. Although I doubt if I can help you very much. I am an old man, and these days I confine my attention to the farm – and certainly there's been no disturbance here.' He was still not bowing to our authority and I saw Marcus bridle, but suddenly the old man seemed to change his attitude. He gave a bitter smile. 'However, my nephew tells me that there were raiders in the forest yesterday. We ourselves have lost a pig, I hear – a boar that I was saving for a feast. We are poor farmers, Excellence, and I can ill afford the loss. I should be glad to help you if I could. Come, we will talk of this indoors.'

He clapped his hands and the woman reappeared at once. 'Tell them in the common house that we have Roman visitors. Have them prepare appropriate refreshments for our guests. And tell my nephew Thullero – he is with the horses in the farther field.'

She looked at us with eyes as big as water-bowls, but nodded obediently and hurried off. I looked at Kiminiros. He reminded me of elders in my own tribe long ago. I said deliberately, in my own tongue, 'Do not fear if some of your people don't speak Latin. I'll translate for you.'

He turned towards me then, and for the first time I looked into his eyes. They were disturbing: piercingly intelligent and blue, and regarding me with such overt suspicion and dislike that it made my blood run cold. 'Ah,' he said, after a little pause, 'a Celtic speaker. How very convenient.' Then there was that softening of his manner, as he added suddenly, 'But you are not from this area, I think? Not even a Dobunni, from the look of you.'

'Indeed,' I said. 'I live in Glevum now, but my home was in the far south of this province, many days from here. They call me Libertus. I am a Roman citizen and client of this exalted gentleman, but I was born a Celtic nobleman myself.'

He bowed. 'Then, if you will lay your weapon on the step, I am honoured to welcome you beneath my roof. There can be no quarrel between your tribe and mine. But these men who come to my household bearing arms – that is another thing.'

I took this as a kind of compliment. 'I do not carry weapons, and I have lost my dining knife,' I said, throwing back my borrowed cloak to show my empty belt. 'And this escort is for our protection, nothing else. We mean no threat to you. I am here entirely in the service of my patron, who – as you have heard – has lost a valued slave. The boy was found here in the forest hanging from a tree. Unfortunately he was on loan to me, so I have a double responsibility.'

The old man looked doubtfully at the serried troops, and all trace of a smile vanished from his eyes. 'In what way, exactly, do you think that we can help?' His voice was wary.

'That tunic which Subulcus is wearing used to be my own. The murdered slave had charge of it before he died. I'd like to discover how your pigman came by it.' I switched to

Latin this time, so that Marcus (who was fidgeting again) could follow what was said.

Kiminiros said in the same language, 'You think he stole it from your murdered slave? I doubt that, citizen. It is not in his nature to become a thief. And, as for killing anyone for such a trivial thing . . .'

I interrupted him. 'It was given as a gift – but not by me, and not to Subulcus. It was given to a different pigman yesterday. And that is another little mystery. That pigman has now completely disappeared.'

He looked incredulous. 'There is no swineherd here but Subulcus – though the land-slaves sometimes help him out.'

I nodded. That accorded with what I'd heard before. 'It seems that "young master" might be able to explain.'

'Then you must come and ask him for yourself. I have already sent him word that you are here,' the old man said, stepping forward to unlatch the gate. 'Please, citizen, bid your patron and the officer be welcome to my home. And you, yourself, of course.' He gestured towards the large roundhouse in the centre of the compound, where a group of women were now standing at the door. 'The other soldiers, I regret, must stay outdoors – there is not room in the roundhouse for so many men, but I will see that there is bread for all of them, and they may refresh themselves by drinking at the well. My swineherd will show them where it is.' He turned to Subulcus, who nodded eagerly to indicate he'd understood.

The optio gave his men the order to stand down, and the pigman led them confidently away to what was obviously a spring that served the farm. Marcus did not dismiss his private bodyguard, however, and when the old man at last unlatched the gate and we went through the triple palisade into the enclosure on the other side, they stayed to keep watch outside.

The women came forward to greet us now. They were formal, silent and unsmiling, and clearly either terrified or shy, but they gestured us to follow them and led us to the largest of the buildings on the site. It was a handsome roundhouse, with a low-lintelled door, so small that it was necessary to bend as one went in, but once we straightened up again and our eyes became accustomed to the gloom, we found ourselves inside a spacious room.

It was much larger than the roundhouses I am accustomed to, and clearly some kind of common meeting space. There was no sleeping area, but wooden benches draped with bearskins stood around the walls, which in turn were hung with furs and spears and woven cloths of elegant design. On a stone hearth in the centre was a glowing fire, with a large Roman-style pot of something savoury bubbling over it. From a clay oven broken open near the fire I caught the warm aroma of fresh oatcakes, too. If this tribe were 'poor farmers', they were successful ones, I thought.

I turned to Marcus with a smile, and saw to my dismay that his eyes were watering and he was choking in the swirling smoke. I am accustomed to central cooking-fires and to the fumes from sheep-fat tapers; he is not. I hurried to his side before he could say anything unfortunate – it is the worst kind of insult to a nobleman to criticise his house and so insult his hospitality.

'This is a fine room, Excellence,' I whispered. 'No doubt the best they have. And they have prepared refreshments for us, too.'

Marcus was still coughing but he understood. As Pertinax's representative he has often been obliged to handle ceremonial occasions with tact, and avoid offending tribal sensitivities. He nodded his assent with streaming eyes, and permitted himself to be seated on an embroidered stool which one of the women now produced for him, together with a fine-chased silver cup. Other females brought in lesser cups and stools for the optio and me. The chieftain was installed upon a wooden chair, with carving on the back, and given a splendid goblet which was obviously his own.

My patron looked rather dangerous at this. He was not used to taking second place. So when a girl came in with a jug of warm, spiced mead, and offered it to her master first, I felt it opportune to murmur an explanation into Marcus's ear.

'A courtesy to you, Excellence, and a gesture of good faith. To show there is no poison in the cup.'

'Of course,' he snapped at me impatiently. Like any wealthy Roman he kept a slave at home to serve as poison-taster every time he ate. I did not mention that he did not have one here, or tell him about the day, much famed in Celtic legend, when a chief had entertained an ancient enemy and, knowing there was hemlock in the jug, none the less drained his goblet first: quite prepared to die himself, provided that he killed his visitor as well. I watched the woman filling Marcus's cup and hoped there was no such heroic deviousness today.

Marcus nodded sagely at me, and took a tiny mouthful of the mead. I knew that the sweet honeyed wine would not be to his taste, but he sipped at it with an appearance of good grace, and at his bidding the optio did the same. I needed no encouragement myself. There was no chance of our passing into legend now, and it was delicious mead. A pity, really, to waste it on those who preferred the sourer taste of Roman vintages.

Kiminiros noted my approval with a smile. 'Now, you wish to speak to my nephew, I believe. I have sent to let him know, and no doubt he is already on his way. In the meantime, I have ordered these oatcakes to be brought for you, and there is stewed venison, if you would care for some.' He signalled to the girl, and she disappeared again to return a moment later with a ladle and a beaten metal plate.

I saw at once that this was a deliberate display of wealth and rank. These were no humble kitchen implements – they were impressive things. The spoon was Celtic, from the intricate designs upon the handle, but the platter was a solid Roman one, with hunting deities incised around the rim. The woman scooped out a ladleful of stew, and offered it to Marcus with a smile.

I sent up an inward prayer to whatever gods there were that Marcus might depart from his usual custom, and accept the food. Clearly I could not partake if he did not, and it looked and smelled extremely tempting after all the rigours of the day. However, he dismissed the offer with a smile.

There was a long, uncomfortable pause. I broke it by saying, 'That is a splendid copper dish you have. Your household has trade links with the Romans then, I see?'

The old man bestowed a searching look on me. 'Indeed, my friend – or citizen, I think you said you were. That is the only future for us. It is regrettable, perhaps, but Rome has wealth and power and if we wish to prosper, we must trade with her. And as you say, there are fine artefacts to be found. And lessons to be learned. We have set up a little aqueduct, for instance, on the Roman style to bring water from the spring up to the house. I have a brazier in my private roundhouse, too: and some of our young men wear tunics nowadays, and shave their faces like Roman emperors.'

'And you speak good Latin, I observe.'

He smiled to acknowledge the little compliment. 'Most of the members of the household do – though not usually at home. I saw that they were taught. We grow a little spelt and barley for the town, and Latin is a necessary language in the marketplace.'

Marcus was still struggling with his mead, and seeing that his concentration was elsewhere, I risked an observation. 'It is a pity that all Silurians do not think the same. There is still some opposition to the Empire here, I think?'

I saw that momentary stiffening again, before he turned towards me with a smile. 'Unlike some others in the area, my forefathers were treated with respect. True, they were enemies to Rome – heroic ones – but in the end they lost. They were captured, certainly, but they impressed their captors with their dignity. My own ancestor was said to be so noble in defeat that he was not sold into slavery, or killed for sport, and although the family were deprived of all their land we have been able to work hard and buy it back again – or some of it at least. And we have prospered since, as you can see today. Besides, all that was long ago. We must accept the fate the gods ordain for us.'

Marcus had put his cup aside and taken a sudden interest in all this. 'One of your forefathers was actually reprieved, although he actively resisted Rome? That is unusual.'

'Indeed. Others were much less fortunate. But our family has that to thank the Romans for – and we have not forgotten it, although it was over a century ago.'

'So you teach Subulcus that he must not spit and call the Romans names, but do what any soldier tells him to?' I said.

He nodded gravely. 'Precisely, citizen.'

'Even though the conquerors took your land away?' He

looked so affronted at my insistence on the point that I felt prompted to explain. 'I ask because your swineherd told us that "a naughty Roman man" had scarred his arm and neck, and killed his mother.'

Kiminiros looked first startled then amused. 'He told you that? Well, it is partly true. No doubt he told you what he took to be the facts – he does not always understand complexity. There was a raid here, many years ago. The raiders torched the houses, stole the cows, and raped and killed the womenfolk who didn't flee in time. They even slashed the children who were in the women's hut – left several of them dead and scarred the rest.' He was entirely unsmiling now: clearly this was a memory which still angered him.

He picked up an oatcake and crushed it in his fist, as if he could crush the perpetrators by the action too, then let the crumbs fall slowly in the fire. He watched them burn and turn to ash before he went on, in an even tone, 'The man who led the raiders was Silurian by birth – a member of another family which has a feud with ours. He was none the less a "Roman" man because – like you, Libertus pavement-maker – he was a Roman citizen. It is a distinction that my poor swineherd finds hard to understand.'

There was silence for a moment, and then the optio spoke. It was the first time that he had ventured a word, and he sounded grim. 'But if the fellow was a citizen, surely he should have been an ally of your tribe? You declare yourself, if not quite a friend to Rome, at least no enemy.'

The old man smiled. 'You are not a Silurian, my friend. Perhaps you do not understand these things. Not everyone had ancestors who were reprieved like mine – many house-holds saw their sons and fathers die. There were atrocities, I have to own the fact – the Romans did appalling things to other families, even to the womenfolk sometimes. We were the lucky ones – or it seemed so at the time. But of course there were accusations later on, of treachery and cowardice and perfidious support for the invading force, and some of the survivors vowed to wreak revenge.'

He had the Celtic gift of storytelling, making the narrative a sort of poem and declaiming it with feeling as he stared into the flames. The effect was extraordinarily powerful and none of us moved until he spoke again. Only the optio swallowed down his mead, as if he felt the need of sustenance.

'A wound for every wound, a life for every life. Kinsman against kinsman. Adult against child.' The old Silurian looked keenly at our faces one by one. 'These things leave lasting hatreds. There are still men who kiss their swords each day and swear the ancient oaths – not to rest until every tribal wrong has been avenged.' He paused, and went on in a different tone. 'Of course, that means that new wrongs are perpetrated all the time. There will be deaths for generations yet.'

There was another awkward moment. The old man had spoken with such force and feeling that I think we all felt a little disconcerted.

Then Marcus cleared his throat. 'I see. All most unfortunate. We had heard that there were tribal rivalries in the area – depending on who had supported Rome, or not. I had not realised that it went so deep. Do you suppose it was these self-same enemies who killed our messenger and stole your pig? If so, you have only to tell us who they are, and we will see that they are punished – and then, perhaps, we'll put an end to this.'

The elder shook his head. 'That is the problem, citizens. It is impossible to tell you anything. The raiders would rather die than reveal their true identities – obviously, since the price of treason is so high, whether they are acting against the government or simply pursuing ancient feuds. All we know is that new alliances are made and broken all the time, and loyalties are not always what they seem. No one can be absolutely trusted except one's family – and not even them, sometimes. That is why every farmstead tries to arm itself.'

'And why there's such a market in illegal weaponry?' I said, remembering the stalls of armour that I'd seen on Venta's streets.

The old man gave me a startled glance, then made a wry gesture of assent. 'Exactly so.'

Marcus looked startled at this casual evidence of illicit trade and glared at the optio, who said reluctantly, 'We are aware that something of the kind goes on in Venta, secretly.' Not very secretly, I knew, but I said nothing. The poor officer had enough troubles on his mind.

'Not so surprising,' Kiminiros said. 'It's part of the tactics of the rebel tribes. Their raiders make a point of capturing equipment when they can, and harrying the legion's supply lines on the roads. So those who look like allies may be enemies. Not everyone who wears a Roman uniform or throws a Roman lance is necessarily a friend of Rome – as Subulcus discovered yesterday, I hear. Someone told him that I wanted him – a military messenger, he said, but there was no such messenger as far as I can tell. My nephew did not see one, and he was quickly on the scene.' He broke off, frowning. 'Where is he, anyway?' He turned to the young woman who had served the mead. 'Fetch me Thullero. He went to tend the horses in the farthest field, but he should be here by now.'

She dropped a hasty bob. 'At once, Ny— Kiminiros.' She gave him an anxious look and scuttled off.

The exchange had been in Celtic and something in the way she spoke his name reminded me of what I'd suspected at the gate. 'So they call you Nyros, do they, in the family, just as Tholiramanda uses a shortened Latin name? Perhaps you could tell us about the property you own, and which you rent to Lyra in the town? In the street of the oil-lamp sellers, I believe?'

Nyros's face did not alter by a muscle, but even in the firelight I could see his eyes grow cold and glittering. 'By the sun god, pavement-maker, you are astonishingly well informed.'

'And so are you,' I countered. 'When I introduced myself, as I recall, I gave you just my name. But you have called me "pavement-maker" twice. How did you know what my profession was?'

Again that glittering stare bored into me, and then he smiled. 'You have a keen mind, my friend. But there is no mystery. You were on the way to Isca, I believe? One of my family has a contact with the legion there, and it was well known that you and your distinguished patron here were going to visit the garrison – at the invitation of the commanding officer, I hear. And you are to be invited to lay a pavement there. It was quite the talk of Isca for a time. As for the property in Venta, it is mine, as you suggest. It came into my possession when a kinsman died, along with other buildings in the block. It was already let out to the tenant, and since it brings me rent I have continued with the lease. There is nothing particularly unusual in that. But few people outside this household know of it. How did you come to discover it?'

I was about to answer frankly that I'd seen the tax records when the young girl burst into the meeting room again. Her clothes were rumpled and her hair had tumbled from its combs, and she was red-faced and panting as she said, 'Nyros, I am to tell you. I found the land-slave down there on his own. There has been another raid. All the horses have been taken – ridden off or driven into the forest by a group of men. It seems they all had swords.'

He was very still. 'And Thullero?'

'He isn't hurt, just taken by surprise. But – oh, forgive me, Kiminiros – he's gone off after them!'

Chapter Sixteen

For a moment we all remained frozen where we were, startled into immobility by this turn of events. The optio was first to spring to life. He set the remnants of his drink aside and jumped to his feet, suddenly all military efficiency.

'We must alert our escort. We have mounted soldiers with us, after all. They can track these rebellious rascals down – and bring them back to justice. Never fear, Silurian, the thieves will not get far. And we will bring your Thullero back to you.'

The old man had half risen to his feet. 'Subulcus will show you where the horse field is.' He sounded as if he were half dazed with shock.

'Then I will go and see to it at once.' The optio turned to Marcus. 'With your permission, Excellence?' He scarcely waited for my patron to agree before he left the room, and we heard the clatter of his hobnails as he ran towards the gate.

Marcus was muttering vaguely to himself. He was obviously shaken. 'Another raid?' he said aloud. 'Great Minerva! So close! And with all our soldiers in the forest, too. The rebels must have seen us. They were obviously hiding out nearby if they planned to raid this farm. The scoundrels get more daring by the day.' He swallowed what was in his cup – looked pained, as if he had forgotten it was mead – and rose slowly to his feet. He looked at me. 'It's a wonder that they did not ambush us.'

Nyros was still looking very strained but he spoke with a courteous dignity. 'Perhaps it is their intention to do that next. After all, they have more horses now – that will make it easier for them to strike. Of course, you have an escort . . . Why, what is it, child?' This last to the girl who had brought in the message, who had thrown herself down on the bench beside the wall and was now sobbing silently.

She looked up at his words. 'The horses,' she managed, through her tears. 'And Thullero. Will he . . . will he be safe?'

'We will have to pray so,' he returned. 'I shall make a special offering this evening at the sacred—' I was sure that he was going to name the oak, but he recalled himself in time. He glanced at Marcus. '. . . at the scared shrine. As for the horses . . .' He shook his head. 'It will take more than prayers and sacrifice to replace those, I think.'

I looked at him with sudden sympathy. His voice had been a little less than steady as he spoke and it was clear that he was struggling with some deep inner emotion, though he contrived to keep his face expressionless. Obviously the mastery of feelings was a manly virtue here – even the girl had seemed ashamed to weep. Yet this raid would surely be a dreadful loss to them. We Celts have always valued horses above all things, and if I had lost a single one I should have wept. To lose all the animals one had was unimaginable.

The old man sighed. He turned to Marcus. 'If I may make the suggestion, citizens, I know you wish to speak to Thullero, but it might be wiser if you did not wait. Safer for you, if these raiders know you're here, and – forgive me – safer for my household too.'

My patron looked uneasy. 'You may well be right. This is no

place to linger in. And it is getting late. Better if we rejoin our escort and go on, if we propose to get to Isca before dark.'

'That is a long journey. You should eat. Are you sure I can't offer you some venison before you go?' Nyros might be troubled and wish that we would leave, but we were guests beneath his roof and traditional hospitality demanded that he made the offer all the same.

My patron shook his head. I could see him calculating the risk now that some of our escort had been sent off in pursuit of the horse-thieves. 'Safer if we make a move, I think. We do not have our mounted outriders, but the rest of our group will be sufficient guard, and I still have my own mounted bodyguard. Doubtless all our marching troops are down in the valley by the spring, Libertus?' I nodded. They would have been taking advantage of the opportunity to rest, enjoying their bread and water at the well, until this unexpected news broke. 'Tell the optio to bring them up and make them ready to move on again.'

Nyros must have been relieved at this proof that we proposed to leave, though he tried to hide it. 'Don't take unnecessary risks. You, or some member of your retinue, would be a considerable prize, if they could capture you. Or even . . .' Or even kill you, was what he did not say.

I glimpsed the look on Marcus's face and knew that, like me, he had heard the stories of what had happened to the legionary soldiers who had been set upon and killed in these woods on previous occasions: their heads were cut off and stuck triumphantly on poles, for men to scoff at as they passed. That in itself was an unpleasant thought, but I suddenly remembered what Cupidus had said about his ancestors, when they had fallen into the hands of tribesmen hereabouts – something about having your private parts cut off and stuffed into your mouth. I felt myself grow pale. No wonder Nyros spoke about 'atrocities'.

Marcus's voice cut across my thoughts. 'Well, are you going, Libertus?'

'As you command, Excellence,' I blurted, and hurried from the room, blinking in the sudden light as I made my way towards the gate. I had been prepared to go right over to the spring to fetch the troops, but to my surprise I found that the optio had already brought them back and was getting them lined them up outside the palisade. He greeted me with a look of self-satisfaction on his face.

'I thought His Excellence would want us very soon. Half the cavalry have gone with Subulcus – apparently the field where the horses were is some little way away, behind the hill, on the borders of the forest over there.' He gestured vaguely. 'The rebels will have driven the animals into the trees – I think we can certainly assume that.'

I nodded, to show I understood. It seemed a very reasonable deduction to have made. 'They won't want to use the open road where they might be seen, and they've probably got a hide-out in the forest anyway – that seems to be the way they operate.'

It was his turn to nod. 'If we could find that hiding place we would strike a real blow against these ambushes.' He leaned towards me confidentially. 'I've sent five of our horsemen back the way we came, to try to cut the raiders off the other way – or follow them back to their secret camp if possible. I'm hoping they might lead us to the spot.' He gave me a little sidewise smile. 'So you can report back to your patron that we're formed up to leave – and perhaps you'd also tell him what I've done. Put in a word for me? I think I made a bad impression early on.'

'Of course I will,' I said, but when I got back to the roundhouse there was no opportunity. Marcus was already on his feet and waiting impatiently for me.

'Ah, there you are!' he said, as if my whereabouts had been a mystery, and far from being unexpectedly quick about my errand I had been deliberately dallying.

'The optio has drawn up the men, and is waiting for you outside the palisade,' I reported. 'And he has sent the horsemen . . .'

'Never mind all that,' my patron said. 'It's time we made a move. The sun is getting low, and we have many miles to go. There is no time to be lost. It was ill-judged of me to agree to deviate from the path and spend all this time over a foolish servant and some clothes.'

'And a Roman messenger,' I said, trying to mollify his mood.

He tapped his baton on his palm impatiently. 'We should have left that to the mansio, and to the garrison at Isca. We have put ourselves in danger, and we're not yet out of it. You have no notion what these rebels sometimes do to people they capture – especially those they want to make examples of. Nyros has just been telling me. Some of their customs make your blood run cold.'

I glanced at Nyros, who was standing by the fire. One of the women had brought in a length of broad plaid cloth, like a cloak, and he had wrapped himself in it and was permitting the girl to fasten it on one shoulder with a clasp – a lovely thing of silver, shaped like a sinuous dog swallowing its tail. He acknowledged my admiration with a smile.

'I will come with you to the gate. Then I must go out and see the damage for myself.'

I looked at him. A brave man, but – at his age – to walk out to the furthest field alone, when there were hostile raiders in the area? To face his losses, and who knows what dangers too? I said, 'Have you no young men on the farm who could accompany you?' In fact, when I came to think of it, I had not seen a single male, except for Nyros and Subulcus, since I arrived.

The old man man gave a wistful smile. 'Alas, not any more. At one time, this farmstead would have been crowded with masculinity – sons, cousins, nephews, brothers, even grandsons, possibly. Then there were the raids I told you of – we lost the cream of our youth, and since then the others are not anxious to stay here on the farm. Even recently there was a period when I would have had a dozen men at my command to chase and find our horses – now it's only Thullero, and even he is not here all the time.'

'He isn't?' This was new information, and unexpected too.

Nyros shook his head. 'Like the others, he is often in the town, now that travel is so much easier on the roads. That is where trade and money are, he says – but it leaves the farm work to the old, the children and the womenfolk. Obviously we have our land-slaves, too, but we are still vulnerable to our enemies. Thullero calls it progress, but I'm not so sure.' He sighed. 'Modern life is changing everything – not always for the better, it seems to me. Sometimes I think that the old ways were best.'

Marcus had been listening impatiently to all this, tapping that warning baton all the time. 'We thank you, Silurian, for your hospitality, in the name of Jupiter, Best and Brightest, and on behalf of all the Roman state,' he said, hurrying over the formalities and signalling to me with his eyes that it was time to leave. 'Also, we are sorry for your loss, and if you find the culprits we will see that they are punished as severely as the law permits. Now, Libertus, if you'd care to lead the way?'

I glanced at Nyros. For me to do anything of the kind was impolite. He had volunteered to show us out and, since he was a tribal elder, tradition demanded that I should follow him. Fortunately the girl had now stopped fidgeting with his clasp, and he straightened up and strode towards the door, saying as he did so, 'If you take the farm track veering to the right, it will bring you quickly to the military road.' He unlatched the gate for us to pass through, and stopped to watch us go.

The troops fell in around us and we marched away, taking the route which had been pointed out to us. I looked back at Nyros. The last I saw of him, he was standing inside the palisade with one hand raised in a gesture of salute: then, as we turned the corner of the path, he was lost to sight behind the trees and we were in the hostile forest once again.

If it had seemed threatening before, it was now twenty times as bad. The faces of all the men were set and strained and no one said a word. We just marched grimly down the path – Marcus, the optio, Regulus and I right in the centre of the moving guards, for all the world like prisoners in a victory parade. The pace was punishing, and at every rustle in the woods I felt all my few remaining hairs stand upright on my head, knowing that any clump of trees might conceal an ambush and, therefore, that every step might be my last.

Nyros's directions had been accurate. We did soon meet the road, and the lightening of the tension was almost physical. Even the optio visibly relaxed: the cohort spread out a little on the road and the whole company moved more easily, with proper paving stones beneath our feet.

We had not gone very far in this new optimistic mood,

however, before Regulus stopped suddenly and raised a hand. 'Listen!'

The phalanx came to a halt, and we strained our ears. At first, I could hear nothing but the wind among the trees, and then I caught the sound that he had heard. Hoofbeats, faint at first but growing louder all the time.

Regulus was still listening with a furrowed brow. 'Horsemen,' he said briefly. 'Not a chariot or cart. No sound of creaking wheels or harness chains.' He frowned with concentration. 'Four or five horsemen, I should say, at least. Skilful riders, judging from their speed. And coming this way – very quickly too.'

The soldiers knew their business. Almost before I had time to take in what was happening, they had placed themselves in readiness: not the simple fence of shields that we'd seen earlier, but a staggered column bristling with swords, the front men kneeling down behind their shields, ready to thrust up and disembowel any passing horse, while their colleagues stood ready to strike down the riders as they galloped past.

'Get down,' the optio shouted, shooing Marcus and me into the oaks which flanked the road. It was an unceremonious order to a man of rank. Marcus showed signs of protest, but then changed his mind and dived after me into the cover of the trees. This was no time for preserving dignity. The riders were already thundering round the bend.

Chapter Seventeen

There was a moment of complete confusion. We were still sheltering within the woods, and it was difficult for us to see, but we were aware of shouts and oaths and clattering hooves. There was a shrill whinny, the clang of metal sword on shield, a swirl of dust and thuds, and then – as if by magic – all this faded into silence. There was an unearthly calm.

Marcus looked at me, and I at him. He was not at his most imposing, sitting on the ground with bits of fallen oak leaves in his hair, but he was still my patron and it was obvious what he expected me to do.

I ventured out from underneath the overhanging boughs which had provided us with our hiding place and saw that the riders had drawn up short and were dismounting from their animals. Even at first glance I could see that they were in Roman uniform and obviously the optio had called off the defensive manoeuvre. He was striding forward down the path to talk to the newcomers, and our kneeling guards were climbing slowly to their feet again. Regulus was among them, and I caught his eye.

'Some of our own outriders, by the look of it,' he said sheepishly, coming to assist me back onto the road. 'That was almost a catastrophe – they were coming at us very fast. If the optio had not realised who they were and bellowed to them in the nick of time, they would have charged us and

179

we'd have had to cut them down. There would have been
some bloodshed, if we had. There's one cavalryman
wounded, as it is.'

He nodded to the far side of the road, where one rider –
obviously unhorsed – was sitting on the margin of the track,
his head between his knees. His arm-guard was unbuckled
and the sleeve of his tunic rolled back to the neck. He was
bleeding heavily from a sword-thrust in his arm. No one was
paying much attention to his plight, although one of the
junior officers was attempting to round up the horse, which
was sidling down the roadway with its bridle loose and every
evidence of acute alarm.

'Will the rider be all right?' I said. It looked very nasty to
me.

Regulus nodded. 'It's a flesh wound only. You see a lot of
those. He's lost a lot of blood, of course, but nothing vital's
hurt. He is more shaken than anything. See, one of his
comrades has gone to help him now. He should have some
herbs that he can pack it with, and some that he can chew to
dull the pain.'

Sure enough, the rider was sitting up again and his
companion was supporting him, while taking a small packet
of something from a bag round his neck. He shook a little
out, put it in his own mouth and chewed it into a wad before
binding the result against the cut. Only then did he offer the
wounded man a pinch of herbs to chew.

Regulus was watching dispassionately. It was obviously
quite routine to him. 'He should be all right. We'll get him to
a marching-camp and let the army doctor take a look at him,
if necessary. But I expect he'll soon be fit to ride again –
though he may have to work one-handed for a bit.' He was
so matter-of-fact that I was not surprised to hear him add, 'I

am a bit worried about that animal of his – it has had a nasty stumble and a fright, and it's looking very skittish. Someone could easily get hurt. I'll go and lend a hand.' And off he went, to help to catch the horse.

I turned back to Marcus, who was by now emerging from the trees, looking more than a little dishevelled and annoyed. 'Only our own outriders coming back,' I said, as I assisted him across the ditch. 'Just as well the optio was so alert.'

Marcus was wholly unimpressed. 'So you say.' He brushed twigs and dead leaves from his soiled toga as he spoke. 'I do not welcome being forced to cower in a ditch, like some common peasant. It seems particularly unfortunate when there was not even any form of threat.' His voice was dangerously cold and I shuddered for the optio who now came bustling up to us. His chances of promotion were disappearing fast.

'In the name of His Most Imperial Majesty and Divinity the Emperor Commod—'

'Never mind all that. Get on with it,' my patron interrupted. He was seriously angry now. He would not normally treat the Emperor's name with such dangerous disrespect. 'I take it you have something to report. I trust it is sufficiently momentous to account for my having been obliged to scuttle ignominiously beneath a tree? These are our men, I understand, so there was in fact no threat to us at all.'

The optio flushed but he retained his calm and military air. 'I regret to tell you, Excellence, that you are misinformed. There is a very present threat indeed. Not only are there rebels in the wood, from whom it is my clear duty to protect you if I can, but it appears that this encounter was no accident. These are the men that I sent out with Subulcus to the far field where the horses were, to chase the raiders at the farm.'

Marcus's manner did not thaw. 'So? Are you about to tell me that they caught the thieves, discovered where their hideout is, and were riding frantically to tell us so?'

A little pause. 'I fear not, Excellence. But—'

'As I suspected. No success at all. And all this at the expense of much indignity and one rider wounded, I observe. Well, what have you to say that is of such importance?'

The optio kept his face impassive. 'Merely, Excellence, that it appears they met a messenger – a man in imperial uniform – who told them that you had been attacked and ordered them to come to your assistance instantly. That is why they came at such a pace and with their weapons drawn. If I had not recognised the leading man, and managed to shout the password of the day and order him to stop, I believe there might have been a dreadful outcome here. They were all ready to attack our group on sight.'

Marcus looked shaken. He is not a patient man, but he is not wilfully unjust and his manner changed abruptly as he said, 'You think it was a plot, to set our men against each other? And you averted it? I see.' He frowned. 'But who could have sent that message? And who was the messenger?' He looked at me as if I could conjure the answer from the trees. 'Libertus?'

I did my best, and spelt out the obvious. 'I think it was clearly one of the rebels, Excellence, dressed in the uniform of the Isca messenger they caught the other day. I knew there was a danger that they would try something like that – I didn't expect it to be quite so soon, or to be the victim of the ploy ourselves.'

'I'd come to that conclusion too.' Marcus turned towards the optio. 'Did they not challenge him? Require the password, or something of the kind?'

He shook his head. 'It seems not, Excellence. Unfortunately they are not the mansio's men, and they assumed that he was one of ours. Let the leader tell you for himself.'

He signalled to the leading horseman, who approached, though he was clearly terrified. He told his story but had nothing much to add. They had chased the horse-thieves, but found nobody. After a fruitless scramble they gave up the chase and were working their way back towards the place where we had left the vehicles when they were accosted by a Roman messenger, who told them that there had been an ambush further down the road and ordered them to ride down in support. 'We knew that there were rebels in the area, after that problem at the farm, so we set off at once. He had a seal, and uniform and everything,' the hapless rider finished breathlessly. 'We didn't question his authority.'

'You did not stop to ask the password?' Marcus growled.

'We thought you were in danger, Excellence. In any case, he was not from our command. The password is not necessarily the same.'

Marcus harrumphed, but he was clearly mollified by this. 'Very well. In the circumstances I can see that you're not totally to blame. The rebels set a trap and you fell into it. We always knew they were a ruthless group – it appears they are a cunning one as well.'

'And, with respect, Excellence,' I put in nervously, 'we also know that they are still at large, and in the area. It would be prudent not to linger here, perhaps? It makes us an easy target for attack. I think we should be safer on the move, especially now that we have at least some of our mounted outriders again.'

Marcus nodded. 'You may be right, old friend,' he conceded, with an alacrity which indicated how alarmed he was. 'See to it, optio.'

'At once, Excellence,' and he bustled off, happily bristling with responsibility. He was soon back again, however. 'With your permission, Excellence?'

'Well?'

'One of our riders has been hurt, and though it is possible for him to ride, he will delay our progress. However, he is fit enough to march, and he can be supported if necessary. Permission to give his mount to Regulus?'

Marcus looked momentarily vexed, then nodded briefly. 'Very well.'

'Then we are ready to proceed.'

We took our places at the centre of the group, with the wounded horseman in the rank behind, where Regulus had been. There was the usual parting ritual – 'Are you prepared for battle or for death?' 'We are!' – and we were on our way.

It was comforting to have the outriders again, and we marched in silence, as before. In fact we moved so quickly that for me, at least, conversation would have been impossible. My heart pumped and my old legs ached with keeping up, and even Marcus, who exercises regularly at the baths, was beginning to look flushed and out of breath. The foot soldiers, however, marched as though we were on a gentle stroll.

We were still on the alert for ambushes, of course, but if there were still rebels in the woods they did not trouble us. It occurred to me that we were far too strong a force, and that they would not confront us while we outnumbered them. That was a comfort and I moved more easily, and was even able to enjoy the sombre beauty of the place – autumnal leaves that rustled underfoot and patches of feeble sunlight dappling the massive trees.

My private soliloquy was interrupted by a commotion in the ranks behind. The wounded horseman had reeled and fallen to the ground. There was a moment's pause while he was hoisted to his feet and supported by the men on either side, and then the column moved briskly on again. There was no perceptible change in pace at all, though when I glanced behind me I saw that his feet were dragging on the ground and he was being borne along by his companions. They did not even falter in their stride. It was an amazing display of strength and discipline.

There was still no sign of bandits anywhere. We passed another traveller on the road, a fat man with a donkey cart piled high with skins, who moved into the ditch to let us pass. The presence of this simple, unarmed trader put our fears to shame, and I for one felt rather foolish marching by, protected by a fierce contingent, leaving the man to coax his animal back onto the road, and rearrange the dislodged cargo on his cart.

A moment later, though, I had forgotten him. We turned the corner and found ourselves back on a familiar stretch of road, near where we had left the transport, and one of the front outriders was galloping back towards us, visibly distressed.

'Optio, sir, and your mightiness!' It was Regulus, wheeling his borrowed mount beside us and reporting breathlessly. 'There has been a sort of accident ahead. The horses . . .' His voice tailed off. 'Round the corner, sirs. Perhaps you had best come and see for yourselves.' He cantered off.

The phalanx surged forward, almost breaking ranks. There was the clearing and the path, and there was the carriage and the carts, but they were not exactly where we'd left them and it was clear at once that something was amiss. For one thing there were signs that there had been a struggle here. Baskets and belongings from the luggage cart were spread about and lying in the road, and the grass around had been trampled and was dark and stained. A body was stretched out on the verge, a red-headed youth in plaid, but there was no other living thing in sight except ourselves. No slaves, no guards, and – appallingly – no horses, even on the carts. The very harness straps and chains had been removed and the vehicles leaned drunken and useless on their shafts.

'There were men here on guard! Where have they gone?' The optio abandoned all restraint and ran forward, clasping his helmet as he went. After a minute Marcus followed him, and I trailed after them, staring at the scene in disbelief.

This time there were no questions about who might have been responsible. None of us had any doubt at all. The men who had stolen the horses from the farm had clearly stolen ours. It was also evident that Marcus had been right, and that a cunning mind was working here. Turning our own outriders back on us with false rumours of attack had achieved a double purpose. Not only had it caused them to attempt to ride us down, but it had also prevented them from returning here and helping to protect the transport. I looked up and down the track, but there was no sign of any other guards, alive or dead, only the motionless Silurian on the ground.

I knelt beside the dying youth and saw, now that I came close to him, that he had taken a spear-point through his ribs. It had broken at the hilt and he was moaning piteously. I raised his head.

'What happened here?' I whispered, signalling to Regulus to bring a water-skin from the luggage cart. Pouring a few drops of liquid on his tongue was all that I could do. To move the blade would kill him instantly.

For answer the young Silurian turned his head and looked me in the face. His eyes were glazing over. Then, summoning the last remnants of his strength, he spat at me. 'That, for all enemies of Karak . . .' he began, in a voice that cracked and broke, but the effort was too much for him and he slumped back, dead.

I looked at Regulus, who had witnessed all of this, with a questioning lift of my brows. He had come running over straight away, not stopping to search the luggage cart but unfastening his own small water-bottle from his belt. He shook his head. 'Karak? Must be some sort of tribal name. It doesn't mean anything to me.' He knelt down beside me as he spoke and himself held the water to the Silurian's lips, but we both knew that it was far too late. He sighed and rocked back on his heels. 'Now that's a pity. If he'd lived, even for an hour, we might have got something out of him. As it is, he is no use to us at all.' He got back to his feet.

I pulled the young man's cloak round to cover his face and wordlessly, as if with one accord, we lifted the body between us to the ditch where we had found Promptillius earlier. We buried him in the self-same hole, as sketchily as Regulus's party had buried the dead slave the morning before – roughly covered by a mound of leaves. Even then, Marcus was not altogether pleased when we got back to the larger party by the carts.

'Wasting time and ceremony on our enemies,' he grumbled, 'when our horses have been taken and only the gods know what has happened to our men. Serve him right if he was left unburied and forced to walk the earth. There were two slaves with the luggage wagon here – to say nothing of a dozen guards. And how are we to get to Isca now?'

I looked forlornly at the carriage we had travelled in. It did look a sorry sight, bereft of horses and pushed off the road to rest lopsidedly against a fallen tree. Pushed there not long ago, it seemed – it was still rocking slightly on its wheels. I stared at it a moment, before the implication struck me. Rocking?

Regulus was still standing at my side, and it was obvious that the same thought had occurred to him. 'Come on!' I shouted and we set off at a run. He is a younger, fitter man than I am, and he got there first. He pulled aside the leather curtain and flung back the door. A bundled figure fell out at his feet – naked, gagged and trussed up hand and foot, but even before I saw the slave-brand on his back, I knew that it was one of Marcus's slaves.

Regulus drew his dagger and slit through the bonds and the strip of coloured fabric that was serving as a gag. The young man rolled over and sat panting in the dust, flexing his wrists and rubbing at the weals.

'In . . . there . . .' he muttered weakly, flapping at the open carriage door, but Regulus was already there, pulling a second servant from the seat. He had been stripped and tied up in exactly the same way but, being stronger, he had not stopped struggling – it was that which had evidently caused the movement we had seen. He was bruised and knocked about in a way which his companion had escaped and, perhaps because of his continued efforts to free himself, the ropes had bitten more cruelly into him, but once released he was the first to regain coherent power of speech.

'Forgive us, master,' he implored, falling on one knee before Marcus, who had just come up to us, and attempting at the same time to conceal his nakedness. 'It was a trap. The horseman told the guards that there'd been a raid and you'd been taken captive at the farm. Naturally they hastened to rescue you – but that abandoned us. And then the other group attacked. We did our best, but we were hopelessly overpowered.' He glanced around. 'I thought I'd brought down one of them at least but I can't see him now.'

Marcus interrupted. 'Enough!'

He looked thunderous and the terrified man at once abased himself, but my patron's anger was not directed at his slave at all. He gazed into the impenetrable trees and raised his voice. 'Wait till we catch up with you, you shameless scoundrels, you less-than-curs, you treacherous . . .' He was so furious that he was almost lost for words. He turned to me, still muttering, 'These men are not merely enemies of the Empire, they have set out to humiliate and mock. I shall make them wish that they were never born!'

There was no doubt he meant it. It is rare for a high-born Roman to permit himself a personal emotional outburst of that kind. They are expected to exhibit steely self-control while curses and rants are left to the recruits, and there was a slight feeling of embarrassment among the soldiery. Marcus seemed to be aware of this himself, and with almost visible resolve turned his attention to more practical, immediate affairs.

He nodded briskly towards Regulus. 'Very well. Find my poor slaves something to cover themselves with. Give them at least that dignity. There may be something in the luggage wagon still, if those confounded sons of Dis have not stolen everything. Optio, bring your men up front and rear to act as guards, while we decide what's to be done. Cavalry mounts are not the slightest use for this, I suppose? They won't be accustomed to harness.'

'Absolutely, Excellence,' the optio said, with such obvious relief that I realised how much he had dreaded having to explain this very point. 'You are most perceptive. I will send off a group to requisition—' He broke off as Regulus came up and made salute. 'Well, cavalryman? I see that you are in a hurry to report. What is the matter?'

Regulus looked stolidly at nothing, and replied, 'Two matters, optio. First, there is a body in the luggage cart, and second, there are horsemen on the way. I can hear their hoofbeats. As no doubt you can yourself, if you turn your attention that way for a moment.'

We listened, the optio with a look of acute concentration on his face. Sure enough, I could detect it too, now that it had been pointed out to me: a faint, rhythmic thudding noise, right on the edge of audibility. I saw Marcus stiffen as he caught the sound.

Regulus went on reporting, in his official monotone, 'Coming this way through the trees, not moving very fast – scarcely more than walking pace, by the sound of it. There must be quite a little group of them, but they're not even attempting to be quiet. Certainly not threatening another charge or a surprise attack. Probably just travellers or our own men coming back.'

I was impressed, for the second time that day, by how much information an experienced horseman could derive simply from a set of distant sounds. To the optio, however, such skill was clearly commonplace. He listened for an instant more, then nodded briefly. 'I believe you're right. Well, we will soon discover who they are, though it will be some moments before they reach us here. We are prepared to meet them, whoever they might be. We have sentries watching, and mounted men in place. In the meantime, what is this about a body in the cart? Surely we put it there ourselves? The slave belonging to His Excellence?'

Regulus shook his head. 'I fear not, optio. That is still there, if course, but it is not the corpse I was referring to. This is – at least it looks like – the Isca messenger who disappeared the other day. It seems to be the right sort of age and build, as muscular and tanned as you'd expect, and the hands are hard as if from using reins – but of course, I can't be absolutely sure.'

Marcus gave a nod of understanding. 'You didn't personally know the messenger, I suppose?'

Regulus kept his eyes unfocused on some distant spot over my patron's shoulder. 'I crave your pardon, Excellence. But in fact I knew him very well. We have ridden out together many times. As I say, I think that's who it is. Only, without a head, it's difficult to swear to anything.'

Chapter Eighteen

It took a moment for the meaning of this to register with us, and then, as the full horror of the implication struck, we all went running to the cart. Even some of the foot soldiers clustered round with ghoulish curiosity as Marcus gave the word and the cover of the luggage wagon was lifted back across the wooden framework that supported it.

What was revealed inside was not a pretty sight. Promptillius's body still lay, as it had been disinterred, wrapped in what used to be my toga, and that was bad enough. But at his feet was propped another corpse, and that was horrible.

It had been forced into a sort of kneeling posture, and wedged so that the torso was bent forward and the arms outstretched in a ghastly parody of the lament. What made the posture even more obscene was not only that the head had been crudely hewn off at the neck, but that the rest of the body had been stuffed, with deliberate mockery, into a garment that was far too small for it. A pair of hairy buttocks greeted us, under the hem of a short crimson tunic with a gold-embroidered edge – the uniform of Marcus's household slaves. Obviously this one was too small to be any use to them, and they had chosen to mock us in this way.

I had stood back to let my patron pass ahead of me, and now I heard his sharp intake of breath. 'Dear Mercury and all the gods! Wait till the Emperor Commodus learns of this. It is a studied insult to all Roman power.'

And an insult to Marcus in particular, I thought, though of course he didn't mention that. To a patrician Roman magistrate, such as my patron, loss of dignity is almost worse than death. Here, it was outright dangerous, because it undermined his status with the troops. There were already knowing titters in the watching crowd – as the rebels had no doubt intended there should be.

I wondered again at the sharp intelligence which was behind all this. What kind of man had dared to do these things? Someone who was capable of lightning thought: fearless, certainly, and almost contemptuous of Rome, since he visited such indignities on an imperial messenger, stole horses from under the noses of armed troops, and set out to mock and alienate a man of Marcus's influence. I could see how such a person would inspire his men – a bold and reckless leader, harrying what he saw as an occupying power.

Yet there were things about his actions that I didn't understand. Why had he ordered poor Promptillius killed, yet deliberately spared two other slaves today? It couldn't be for fear of witnesses, as I had thought at first – Marcus's servants were quite able to describe the men they'd seen.

Regulus, behind me, had a question too. 'Poor fellow. Why did they cut his head off? Just for spite? It wasn't done to kill him. He was dead already, that's obvious from the wound. You can see that it has hardly bled at all.'

The optio said stiffly, 'I imagine it is intended to make a point to us – to show what they can do. The rebels have tried this sort of thing before.'

Marcus frowned. 'This whole gruesome scene is an atrocity. Well, it won't succeed! Don't look so troubled and upset, Libertus. Do you seriously doubt we'll catch these rogues?'

'Of course not, Excellence,' I murmured. In fact my worried look was caused by something else. I was remembering that oak tree we had seen. Of course there were only harmless statues there, but it proved a point. In this part of the province the old religion was not dead. And if Nyros and his family kept up such a shrine, how much more likely that families which still resisted Rome would maintain the old rites in their purest form – human offerings, blood-sacrifice and all? The whole forest was full of ancient trees.

Somewhere in the area, I was prepared to bet – somewhere far removed from any path, and where only initiates would go – there was a proper old-fashioned Druid grove, its oak trees daubed with blood, where the head of the unfortunate messenger was even now dangling as a gruesome tribute to the gods. And if that was the case, I thought, probably the hide-out of the rebels was not far away. Divine protection is a useful thing.

However, it was not easy to explain all this to Marcus without offending him. If he realised that I'd recognised the signs of forbidden practices and failed to mention them before, I could bring trouble down on more than Nyros and his household. My own deliberate silence contravened the law. I phrased my answer very carefully.

'It is possible, Excellence, that these rebels stick to ancient tribal ways and the head has been taken as a Druid sacrifice . . .' I began, but my concerns were needless. My patron was paying no attention to my words.

He had whirled round to stare at the little knot of horseman on the path who even now were straggling into view, with a rank of marching soldiers at their heels.

My heart lurched for a moment, fearing that these were rebels, but the next glance reassured me. Those were Roman uniforms, and more than that, some of the soldiers had faces I knew. Two of the horsemen I recognised at once as the mounted guards that we had set to watch the carts and carriage, the others were clearly the cavalry the optio had detached from the detail set to chase the rebels through the farm, and sent back the way we had come. All the horsemen seemed to be in total disarray and looked almost comically perplexed. Marching behind them, with an attempt at discipline, were the foot soldiers we had left to guard the carts and the pigs.

The optio was already striding down the path towards the group and starting to harangue one of the mounted guards. The man slid down to stand beside his horse, and there was a brief exchange – a subdued but forceful one, in which the name of Jupiter was several times invoked. Even from where I was standing, that much was audible.

Marcus went down to meet them, and at his approach the optio swung round and raised his voice. 'Exactly the same strategy as the rebels used before,' he said. 'Just as your servants said. A man who claimed to be an army messenger – complete with military uniform and seal – came here and told the guards on duty that we'd been attacked, and that they were to leave the carriages and come.' He looked at Marcus with a gesture of despair. 'They were directed down the other path, where they met our fellows guarding Subulcus's pigs.'

Marcus scowled. 'Let the fellow tell me for himself.' He signalled to the horseman, who took up the tale.

'Your indulgence, Excellence. We did not intend to leave the carts like that – but if you were in danger, what were we to do? We were just discussing where to go from there – whether the rest of the foot guards should give up the pigs and march in our support – when all this other cavalry turned up, riding hell for leather from the other way. They'd been hoping to ambush horse-thieves from the farm, they said, but they hadn't managed to catch anyone. Of course, we thought the thieves had set on you. But then the swineherd came back to his pigs. He told us that he'd seen you to the farm – you were quite safe and had started back to the carts. We realised then it was a false alarm – a trick. We had been drawn away from here deliberately.'

He looked at Marcus and the optio for some sign of understanding, but my patron was tapping his baton on his thigh, his face white and set like the mask of fury at the theatre.

The horseman flung himself at Marcus's feet. 'Your pardon, Excellence.' He gestured at the scene in front of him, and fell down on his knees. 'It wasn't our intention to desert our posts, and leave your horses unattended for the thieves to take.'

Marcus frowned. 'So I should hope, since you were specifically detailed to look after them. We shall deal with you when we get back to camp. And as for your tactics, optio, I am not impressed. It seems that the rebels have achieved a great success. Not only did they seize the messenger's animal and four horses from the escort yesterday, they now have Nyros's and mine as well. They have outwitted you at every point. Look what happened at the farm. It now appears that you sent out two sets of mounted men to try to trap the horse-thieves between them, but both of your pursuit groups were deflected by a trick while the bandits slipped unhampered through the gap, no doubt laughing at me up their sleeves. And then they pulled the same trick here and got away again. That's what you're telling me, I understand?'

The optio flushed. 'I suppose you might describe it in that fashion, Excellence. The raiders have escaped us, certainly.'

'Pausing only to steal my horses and humiliate my slaves?'

This time the optio made no response at all.

'Well,' Marcus went on in his dangerously reasonable tone, 'you are – as you pointed out yourself – the officer in charge. What kind of strategy do you now propose? We are in the forest. There are bandits here and it is getting late. We have three vehicles, two corpses and no carriage-animals – only to be expected, I am sure, since we are protected by only half a hundred men, but posing a little problem all the same. How am I to get to safety for the night? I presume you don't suggest that I should walk? Or, on second thoughts, perhaps you do. I could push one of the carriages, perhaps?' His voice was rising and his colour too.

The optio had turned a dull, embarrassed red and was muttering something wretched to his boots when Regulus stepped forward and put in, 'Permission to volunteer a suggestion, Excellence? I will take two of my colleagues, and we'll ride out to the forest edge and bring back some carriage-horses for you from that staging-post we passed.'

The optio looked more cast down than ever at this but Marcus assented with a nod. 'I suppose you're right. We shall have to send back there, and pay that villain some inflated price for half a dozen of his hopeless nags, at least until we can requisition fresh horses. And this way we don't break up the guard again into foolish little units which are easy to defeat, waylay and misinform. Permission granted. See to it at once.'

The optio snapped to attention. 'Permit me, Excellence.'

He turned to Regulus. 'Tell him the mansio will meet the bill, after we have reached home in safety – not before. That will prevent him hiring us some broken-down old mare so short of wind that it won't get us to Isca. Horse-leasers in the area are famous for that sort of trick.' In other circumstances it might have been comic to see how keen he was to show his grasp of local tradespeople and make some sort of contribution to affairs.

Regulus acknowledged his instructions with a bow, and set off at a run. A moment later he was riding off, together with two of his companions. Marcus watched him go.

'Very well, optio!' The ironic tone had vanished, now that some practical solution was in sight. 'Draw up your men as I proposed before. We are still in danger of attack. I asked for some emergency provisions in the cart. You saw that they were packed, I think?'

'Bread, cheese and fruit as you commanded, Excellence. I doubted you would need such rations on the way, but your foresight has proved valuable.' The optio essayed a fawning little smile, and was severely glared at for his pains.

'Provided that those sons of Pluto have not stolen it, thanks to your failure to mount a proper guard,' Marcus snapped. 'Libertus and I will eat, and my two slaves and those who stopped to guard the pigs can finish anything we don't require. I believe your men were given some refreshment at the spring?'

'That is indeed so, Excellence,' the optio said, clearly understanding the unspoken message here. He and the guards who had failed to watch the carts were to be punished for their part in this affair by being offered nothing. It was not a major matter to the men, perhaps – soldiers carry water with them on the road, and are accustomed to marching long distances with little else to sustain them until the evening meal – but I was very hungry after all the exertions of the day, and even dry bread, strong cheese and withered apple seemed a welcome treat, although I thought again of Nyros's aromatic venison, and sighed.

Marcus, however, dispatched his meagre meal without the least pretence of satisfaction in the task and ordered the remnants of the loaf to be distributed among the designated men. He was so displeased with the events of the day that I feared that at any minute he would instruct the optio to place half a dozen men between the shafts, and drag us back to Venta in that old-fashioned way.

However, that was not necessary. The guards who had been on duty with the pigs were still chewing the final morsels of their crust when Regulus and his companions rode back into view, dragging a string of horses after them. They were, as Marcus had so bitterly foretold, pathetic creatures – mostly skin and bone – and the ride into the forest had already winded them, but at least they were horses of a kind.

Regulus reined in and slid down from his mount. 'Your animals, Excellence,' he said, snapping his heels together and addressing Marcus with a bow. 'The best that I could do. The hirer swears that they are used to pulling carts.'

My patron bestowed a smile on him, turning his back upon the optio, who fumed. 'No trouble with the rebels?' he enquired. 'I feared you might be set on while you were bringing them.'

Regulus was bold enough to laugh. 'We were quite safe, Excellence. Not even the rebels want horses such as these. I never saw such broken-winded nags. All the same, if they are harnessed up, I think they will suffice. They'll get us to the marching-camp, at least, and we can pick up other horses there.'

'Very well.' Marcus nodded to the optio. 'See to it at once.'

The officer looked resentful, but he could not protest. Instead he poured out his irritation on the men, who scurried frantically about in obedience to a barrage of commands. It was effective, though. The animals were strapped and in the shafts faster than I thought possible, and soon the whole procession was on the move again. The pace was a good deal slower now, of course: the men were weary and the hired horses could only plod sluggishly along. We would have made a tempting target for any ambush-group, but we saw no one on the way except the fat man with the cart, who – still cursing – moved his wagon to the ditch to let us through a second time that day, and shouted imprecations at our backs.

Chapter Nineteen

We were glad to reach the safety of the marching-camp, although our arrival there caused quite a stir. The centurion in command had not expected us – only the return of his own troops and animals, and even that not for a day or two after they had delivered us to Isca safe and sound.

The poor man was clearly horrified to find himself suddenly playing host to a man of Marcus's rank, but he did his best, and soon had his soldiers scurrying around preparing food and looking after us. The wounded man was lifted from the cart and treated by the army doctor on the spot, orderlies took our weary horses away to feed and water them, while the corpses were carried off to be given decent burial. There was a fire already lit outside every tent, and soon there was oat-porridge on the boil – not a tasty dish, but welcome all the same, as was the fresh water which was brought so that we could rinse our dusty hands and feet.

Marcus was anxious to get back on the road and wanted new horses and an escort found at once, but though the centurion was only too eager to oblige it was obviously impractical to arrange for that tonight. It was already getting dark, the men were tired, the hired horses were so jaded they could hardly stand upright, and no fresh draught animals could be produced to pull the carts.

'It is most regrettable, Excellence, but earlier today there were reports of rebel movements in the north, and we were required to send cavalry support and a supply-train to provision them. We don't have the animals to spare – we can hardly take those creatures that you hired in exchange for ours. We'll have to send to Venta at first light. Will there be something suitable at the mansio by then?'

He glanced at the optio who was crouching on a stool, finishing his bowl of army gruel. The enquiry was an acknowledgement of his authority at the inn, which usually made him preen with pride. Now though he just looked miserable and shook his head. 'It's possible, though we are not expecting anyone in particular.'

'Then we may have to requisition some. There are pro-Roman farmers round about who will pleased to help. And we'll see that those hired nags of yours are taken back to where they came from, too.'

He had addressed this to the optio again, but Regulus could not resist the opportunity to make it clear whose effort had obtained for us such horses as we had. 'I don't suppose the owner will be very pleased,' he said. 'He obviously makes a living from the staging trade – taking in tired horses from weary travellers, and letting out those broken-winded things. Make sure he gives you the deposit back.'

The optio scowled. Tempers were beginning to fray, and it was clear that we were stuck there for the night. Worse, it was becoming obvious that we would have to return to Venta next day to reprovision and regroup. Marcus himself was clearly furious at this, but he did attempt to hide it: mur-muring rather ungracious thanks to the commanding officer, who gave up his tent and the few luxuries the camp possessed and moved in with his second-in-command so that my patron should have a proper bed. The rest of us were forced to share the draughty leather shelters which always formed the temporary barracks of a marching-camp like this, ready to move off at any time. There were quite a lot of us to house, and the troops that had gone off to join the peace-keeping patrol had taken their tents with them in their packs, so numbers in some of the remaining ones had to be doubled up to make sufficient room.

It was crowded, uncomfortable and cold but I was glad to rest. I must have slept, despite the lumpy straw-packed sack which had been provided as a palliasse, because I was wakened by a trumpet-call at dawn, and the sounds of soldiers tumbling from their beds and struggling with their clanking armour as they dressed. I came out blinking into misty chill, to find Marcus already up, and looking fresh.

He was smiling as he greeted me. 'The commandant has already detailed two lots of volunteers to get fresh horses from the town and take the hired ones back. In the meantime he's invited me to review the troops.'

It was obviously that piece of flattery which had improved his mood, and after a meagre breakfast of grey army bread, washed down by water from a leather flask, I joined him on the parade ground in the enclosure opposite.

The real working business of the camp – the fatigues, patrols and working parties, the duties and the password of the day – had already been decided at the centurion's meeting earlier, but all troops 'fit for duty' were now drawn up on parade. Their officer harangued them and assigned them to their tasks, and led them in the oath of loyalty. Then he stepped back and Marcus's inspection began.

A chilly morning followed. We walked up and down the columns – Marcus imperious in his purple-bordered robes, flanked by the optio and Regulus; I trailing obediently in his wake. A rostrum was produced and Marcus, looking suitably severe, addressed the men. He was always a good speaker and they roared applause. I hoped that this would be the end of it, but our horses had presumably still not arrived, because a display of weapons training was announced, and I stood and froze while soldiers threw heavy wooden javelins, or thrust at wooden stakes with wooden swords.

Marcus had done service with the legions once and was genuinely enthralled, but it was of no real interest to me until I was offered one of their wicker practice shields to try, and found it was very difficult to lift.

That made our centurion laugh aloud. 'The training shields are twice the weight of regulation ones. Makes you strong,' he said, and lifted it to shoulder height.

The optio was not to be outdone. 'I'll show him what's involved. I used to be the champion at this.' Stepping forward, he raised the shield one-handedly and whirled it effortlessly about his head in a series of complex feints and blocking moves which earned him a smattering of surprised applause.

Only Regulus was not impressed. 'Trust him to take an opportunity for showing off,' he grumbled. 'Thank heaven the supply party has returned, or he'd want to prove before His Excellence that he was best at everything.' He nodded towards the tented camp, where indeed a group of men had just galloped in, leading a string of other animals.

The inspection was brought to a hasty close and we returned to find that the men had brought us not only proper horses from the military inn, but also my clean tunic, which had come back from the fuller's by this time. People at the mansio were awaiting our return. The kitchen in particular had been forewarned and was preparing stuffed sow's udder for His Excellence, to make up for the porridge yesterday.

Marcus was suddenly anxious to be gone, and the optio – encouraged by the response to his parade-ground feats – leapt into noisy action once again, ordering his men to get things organised. We did not really need a full escort for the journey back along the open road, but it was provided just the same, and no sooner had I changed my clothes than we were on our way.

Even so, our troubles were not over yet. It was not far to Venta but the biting wind had settled into pouring heavy rain, which made the journey seem far longer than it was. No sooner had we streamed into the mansio, wet, travel-stained and dispirited, than the junior officer who'd been left in temporary command came hurrying from the guard-room area to see the optio.

'Your pardon, sir, but there are people here to see that gentleman.' He kept his voice low, but I heard the words, and saw to my surprise that he was indicating me. 'One of them is a wealthy townsman of some influence. He came here yesterday as well. I told him you were on the way to Isca and I didn't know when you were coming back, but he refused to leave. His family has been humiliated in the courts, he says. Something about a young man being forced to witness on behalf of somebody he didn't know, and without his *paterfamilias* being told.'

The optio looked impatient, but the soldier pressed the point. 'I think it should be dealt with quickly, sir – the complainant in question is a wealthy individual and serves the civitas in several ways – although he's not actually a citizen. You know what these Silurians are like. If he sees this as a personal affront and we don't sort it out he'll get his friends to back him, and before you can say "Mars Lenis" there'll be riots in the street.'

I looked at Marcus and he looked at me, with a scowl that told me that this was all my fault.

'It must be Laxus,' I said stupidly. 'He is the only one who spoke in my defence.' I was surprised. I knew that he'd been carrying an illegal knife, and he knew that I knew. I would not have expected him to raise complaints. He had too much to lose by counterclaims.

'It's not the youth himself,' the soldier said. 'More like his father, by the looks of it.' Of course! It had been idiotic of me to think otherwise. 'Says he has always supported Roman power, but he'd been passed over for appointments several times, and was this all the thanks he's going to get,' the soldier amplified. 'I didn't like to put him off, so I told him he could wait and speak to the senior officer when he got back – I hadn't been expecting to see the pavement-maker and His Excellence again.'

'I wasn't expecting to be here,' Marcus said, 'but since I am, I think I'd better deal with this myself. It was my court, after all. But, Libertus, you can come as well. The wretched boy was called in as a witness on your account. You, optio, can have some towels sent in to us and some refreshments too.' He turned back to our informant. 'Where is the fellow now?'

'I've left him in the commander's anteroom.' The junior officer looked sideways at his optio, but he could not well avoid addressing his answer to Marcus all the same. 'I did take the liberty, Excellence, of offering the man a little something while he waits. I hope I've done the proper thing.'

Marcus beamed at him approvingly, although it is not the custom at a mansio, where those not on official business have to pay their keep, to deal with civilian callers as though they were visitors to a private house. 'In the circumstances, I'm sure you did.'

The optio looked less convinced. Presumably this largesse would be at his expense, while his subordinate got all the praise for it. He managed a tight smile. 'I, personally, will have something sent to you at once,' he said, stressing the 'personally' to show that he had now resumed command. Then, in an obvious effort to ingratiate himself, he added, 'And I'll send a slave in with a towel. Perhaps you'd care to have him to wash your feet as well?'

'No need to delay ourselves with that for now.' Marcus was brisk. 'The sooner we have dealt with this, the sooner we can dry ourselves and dine.' He turned to the junior officer again. 'Lead on, then. Let's see what this angry father wants. He's been a supporter of the Empire, you say. I'll treat him carefully. From what I've experienced of this area, Rome needs to look after all the friends she has. Ah! A towel!' He took the linen napkin from the slave who had run to fetch it and rubbed his head with it. Then he ran a ringed hand through his curly hair, adjusted his spattered toga, squared his shoulders and composed his face into a mask of dignity. 'Come, Libertus!' I trailed damply after him.

As we entered the optio's waiting room, the visitor was already rising to his feet. He was a florid man of middle age, slack-faced and corpulent, but the similarity to Laxus was quite striking all the same. He was dressed in a Grecian-style robe of such a startling white that it made Marcus, in his damp toga, look quite dingy in comparison. An elaborate torc-necklace was round his throat, and on his arms and fingers there were silver bands of beautifully intricate design. His face was flushed with sullen discontent, and he was clearly ready to protest at once.

Marcus walked towards him with both hands outstretched, and a smile of diplomatic welcome on his lips. 'My dear citizen, please accept our most sincere regrets. We had no notion that you were awaiting us. I am Marcus Aurelius Septimus, representative of the outgoing governor. Whom do I have the honour of addressing?' The Latin was punctiliously courteous and correct, and he'd addressed the man as 'citizen'. As a forestalling manoeuvre, it was consummate.

The man before us faltered visibly. He had been expecting a few minutes' interview with the optio, at most, and here was a major dignitary greeting him as though he were a legate, at the least. He hesitated, took the proffered hands, then did as any right-thinking citizen would do and fell on one knee, kissing Marcus's ring. 'They call me Lucidus, Excellence,' he muttered. 'I prefer a Roman name. I am sorry to disturb your mightiness. I was only—'

'It was about your son, I understand?' my patron said. 'He was required in my court yesterday, to bear witness on this citizen's behalf. I summoned him myself, and he was brought, according to the law. You have some complaint about the matter, I believe?' All this was delivered with a smile, but Lucidus was truly flustered now. There were beads of sweat appearing on his brow. He struggled to his feet.

All the swagger had vanished from his frame, and he drooped a little in his finery. He looked like a defeated cockerel as he said, 'I came on my son Laxus's account. His mother asked me to. I have no wish to offend Your Excellence – I only had his version of affairs. He told me he was seized on in the open court and dragged up to testify for some wretch on a murder charge he'd happened to run into in the street.'

Marcus was still smiling as he disengaged his hands and

sat down in the folding chair behind the optio's desk. 'And so he was. The wretch in question was this citizen.' He indicated me. 'A member of my personal retinue, brought to trial on a trumped-up charge. Your son's intervention was of great account in seeing that justice was achieved. I am delighted to have the chance to thank you personally for your family's help.'

'Oh.' Lucidus's righteous outrage was suddenly as deflated as a wine-skin with a leak. 'Honoured to be of service, Excellence.'

My patron glided smoothly on. 'Of course it was a little difficult to perceive my client's status at the time. Unfortunately his slave was murdered – by some rebel, it appears – and his clothes and toga were stolen.' An attendant from the mansio had just appeared, bringing a tray of fruit and dates and wine. Marcus gestured to him to approach, selected a large date from the bowl and bit into it thoughtfully. 'Most unfortunate.'

I was contemplating whether or not I dared to take a plum, so I was only half listening to the man's reply. 'These rebels, Excellence! They are a disgrace to all our peoples. A hundred years now Rome has ruled this area in peace – and brought us prosperity and law. My forefathers knew it and supported them, even in Caractacus's day. This hand,' he held out his right arm dramatically, 'has never faltered in support of Rome.'

I found that I was gazing at it, mesmerised. All his jewellery was decorated with the same device – a convoluted reptile eating its own tail. I realised that I was acting like a snake myself, following the movements of his fingers with my eyes – much as I have seen serpents on the roadside stalls watching the street magician while he plays the flute and begs brass coins from the market crowd. I had to make an effort to tear my gaze away.

Even Marcus noticed. 'What is it now, old friend?' His little success in deflecting Lucidus's complaint had pleased him, patently, and he was in a better humour than I had seen him for some days.

Emboldened by 'old friend', I took a plum and risked a bite of it. I said, 'I was struck by the beauty of the citizen's silver ring. It is a wonderfully delicate design.'

Marcus turned to the Silurian and laughed. 'Trust Libertus to observe a thing like that. He is an artist, of a sort, by trade. But he is right. The work is very fine.'

Lucidus preened, but I saw him register the fact that I was, after all, only a tradesman and of small account. So it was to my patron only that he said, 'A family emblem. And traditional. It belonged to one of my great-great-grandfathers. All his treasures were of this design. See, I have the same pattern on my wrist ornament.' He held it out for the great man to inspect, but Marcus only nodded perfunctorily at it. Now that the complaint had been resolved, his real attention was on the dates and wine.

'This treasure was not used as grave goods, then?' I said. Both men looked at me in surprise and I felt obliged to explain my thoughts. 'It is the Celtic custom, after all, to inter a man's treasures with him when he dies, both as a sign of his importance here, and so that he can have the use of them in the otherworld. Something as valuable and beautiful as that might well have been selected for the afterlife.'

Lucidus looked a little huffy at my intervention, but he answered readily enough. 'It was so valuable and beautiful that when he had it made he decreed that it should not be buried with him, but passed on through the generations as a sign that we are true warriors of the blood. All males are given a piece of it when they come of age, and each will hand it to his heirs in turn. As the first-born of my father, I have the bulk of it. Does that satisfy your curiosity?'

He obviously intended to put me in my place, so I could not resist the temptation to remark, 'It must deplete the treasure quite a bit, if all your eight sons have a piece of it. Apart from Laxus, you have seven others in the legions, I believe?' I took another bite of plum.

He stared at me. 'How do you know that?'

'Something young Aurissimus remarked when he was outside the tavern with your son. Though admittedly he wasn't sober at the time. They were with Cupidus as well and all of them had had far too much to drink. I expect you know the youths I mean?'

Lucidus was already in retreat. He flushed. 'Laxus keeps bad company. I'm sorry, citizen. He is the youngest of the family and his mother spoils him. But you are right. My other boys are in the legions – in defence of Rome. Posted to the Rhineland, and doing very well. Fortunately the hoard was large enough. Each of them inherited a ring.' He gave me a placatory smile. 'I shall leave mine to Laxus when I die, and he will bequeath it to his son, I hope, just as my father passed it on to me. In the meantime, I take care of it.'

I hadn't finished. 'Yet I am sure that I have seen the pattern somewhere else. I am trying to remember where – could it have been on Laxus's dagger-hilt? Or on the sheath, perhaps?' I asked this with affected unconcern, taking another bite of plum meanwhile. Perhaps that was a tactical mistake. The fruit was excellent, but it is difficult to strike a threatening note when one has plum juice dribbling down one's chin.

All the same, my little thrust went home. The punishments for carrying unlawful weapons are severe and Lucidus eyed me anxiously, realising that I knew more about his son than was altogether conducive to his health. I felt a sudden sympathy for him. The unprepossessing Laxus was his mother's pet, and it was at her behest that Lucidus had come here to complain. Given what I'd just revealed about his spotty son, he was obviously wishing that he'd never come. I wondered what would happen to the lad when he got home.

'Perhaps it was his cloak clasp that you saw.' Lucidus ran a tongue round his lips and glanced at Marcus, who – uninterested in Celtic silverwork – was still busying himself with the refreshment tray. 'Laxus was given that when he became a man – the day that he removed the *bulla* from his neck and sacrificed his childhood toga to the gods.' He leaned towards me, dropped his voice, and added urgently – although he clearly did not believe the words himself – 'There is an ancient knife of that design as well, but that's not his at all. I'm sure it's never left the house. We keep it locked up in a chest at home, with all the other things. Of course, citizen, if there is anything that I can do, anything at all that you require . . .'

'Great gods!' I interrupted, with such suddenness that even Marcus looked up from his wine. 'I've suddenly remembered where I've seen this workmanship before! It is a family design, you say? Only a male member of your tribe would wear or carry something of this kind?'

He stared at me as though I were an idiot – but one it was important to appease. 'I believe I have just said so, citizen. The details of the pattern might be copied, I suppose, but even then the silversmith would need a pattern-piece – and I do not see how that could be achieved. No item worked in this design has ever been permitted to leave the family. It is a part of our ancestral heritage.'

Marcus was losing interest in all this. He shrugged. 'Yet Libertus thinks he saw it somewhere else. Perhaps the original craftsman made secret template copies of his own? Such things are not unknown. The design is not to Roman taste, but it is clearly fine. No doubt such things would fetch a splendid price.'

'I do not think so, Excellence.' Lucidus was stung into contradicting him outright – not treatment Marcus was accustomed to. 'My ancestor was a man of culture and though he was a fearsome warrior, he was also an artist in his way. He created the design himself, but it is very intricate and he had no tribesman with the skill to work the silver as he wanted it. The silversmith who did it was captured in the wars, and taken by the family as a slave. This set of pieces was his masterwork. He spent ten years making it, the legend says . . .' He paused.

'So perhaps he made some others afterwards.' Marcus was abrupt.

'Afterwards?' Lucidus shook his head. 'Afterwards my ancestor himself cut off the man's two hands and burned them, together with the bark designs and templates, in front of all the tribe so that the feat could never be repeated.' It was a stark picture and there was a moment's thoughtful silence before he added, 'I do not believe that any man alive could replicate the work, certainly not by eye alone, still less from memory.'

I said softly, 'Then why did I see one like it in the marketplace here, only a day or two ago?'

Chapter Twenty

I had expected some response to what I said: bluster, perhaps, or efforts to explain. In fact what happened was that Lucidus whirled round to stare at me, and said, 'Impossible!'

'Impossible to you, perhaps,' I said, remembering the flattened arm-band that I had noticed on the armour stall. 'But all the same, it's true. I assure you I saw it in this very town, on . . .' I was about to say 'a stall that sells Roman armour', but that was hardly tactful in the mansio, and I amended it, 'on a stall with chiefly Roman things – a sort of trophy by the looks of it. I noticed it particularly, at the time, since it was clearly Celtic workmanship, but I knew there were Silurians who supported Rome and fought alongside the legions during the campaign so I presumed it had belonged to one of them. As I suppose it did? Perhaps one of your forefathers lost it in the struggle, long ago?'

He shook his head. 'That is not possible. The silversmith was captured by your legions in those very wars, and my ancestor was permitted to keep him as a slave, partly as a reward for his support and precisely because it was known that he was seeking such a man. The pattern was not worked till afterwards.' He frowned. 'I am loath to call your word into question, citizen . . .' he was being very careful now to be polite to me, 'but perhaps you are mistaken, after all? There are many very similar designs.'

I took another plum as I considered this. I thought I dared. Marcus is not especially fond of them, and I was very hungry by this time. But I needed to be quick: he had already worked his way absently through all the dates, and was now biting thoughtfully into a peach. Even as he gestured for the page to bring the napkin and the scented-water bowl, so he could rinse his hands and reach for another piece of fruit, he murmured languidly, 'If Libertus says it was the same design, then I expect it was. He's very good at patterns.'

Lucidus was looking unconvinced, but I was absolutely sure of what I'd seen. It troubled me. Marcus was clearly not much interested and I feared that he would soon lose patience with all these questions, but I was very keen to get at the truth. There were too many 'impossibilities' in this town. Though one explanation did occur to me. Was Laxus selling the family treasures on the sly, to pay for his betting on the games? After all, he'd obviously taken the dagger from the chest – somehow he must have got the key.

I thought of giving a detailed description of the design, but since the pattern was in front of me, that hardly proved a thing. Instead I said, 'I'm certain that the decoration was the same as yours. It was an arm-guard. The fineness of the work was unmistakable. I think I could take you to the stall.'

Lucidus was in the process of a dismissive shrug, but suddenly his whole expression changed. 'An arm-piece, did you say? About how long was it?'

I gestured the dimensions with my hands. 'Unusually long.'

'And it was here? For sale? In Venta?' He shook his head. 'I wonder . . . ? It couldn't be! Surely they wouldn't dare!'

Marcus says that I am good with patterns. Perhaps I am. Suddenly something slotted into place, like a tile in a mosaic pavement. 'Wait a moment! Laxus had an uncle, didn't he?

He mentioned him in court. An uncle who "disappeared a moon or two ago". That would be your brother, I presume?'

Lucidus nodded.

'So he would also have inherited an ancestral piece. An arm-band, possibly?'

'You are right, of course.' Lucidus was a different person now. Gone was the lofty townsman of a moment since – I was looking at a fellow Celt, with raw emotions written on his face. His fists were clenched and when he spoke, his voice quivered with baffled grief and rage. 'His name was Claudinus, and he was dear to me. The first of our family to rise to citizen through service to the guard – though I have sons who I believe will one day do the same. I hoped that he was safe somewhere. But it seems that he was ambushed by those confounded bath-siders, after all.' He muttered the last words with such venom, between gritted teeth, that I knew he was swearing vengeance, even then.

'You think the arm-band proves that he is dead?'

'Of course. They murdered him. Or their paid assassins did. Claudinus would never have surrendered that arm-guard to anyone, while he had breath left in his body. Particularly not to our sworn enemies. Ever since he disappeared the family has feared the worst – that something of the kind had happened. But I was not wholly sure.' He glanced around, as if the mansio might even now be concealing spies. 'You see, I knew that he was not simply going off eastward on a trading trip, as everybody thought, to find a good price for our fleeces at the ports.'

'There was more to it than that?'

Lucidus seemed to hesitate again, staring suspiciously at the slave-boy with the bowl.

'This boy is a servant of the commanding officer,' I said.

'I'm sure he has no interest in local politics.' Of course, I had no way of knowing this. I simply breathed a prayer to all the gods that it was true.

Lucidus nodded. 'Very well.' He leaned forward and spoke in a low urgent voice. 'The truth is, citizen, Claudinus was hoping to destroy our rivals, once and for all. He was convinced that he had found out something which would bring them down – something the Emperor himself would want to know.' It was obvious what I was going to ask, and he held up his hand. 'He wouldn't tell me what it was – too dangerous, he said – but he was jubilant. Claimed it would change our family fortunes for all time – honours and distinctions and rewards. He set off, about two moons ago, pretending he was planning to ship our wool to Rome. He wanted to bring the news to someone senior in authority. That's what he was really doing when he disappeared.'

'He set off to the court of Commo— His Most Imperial Divinity, the Emperor himself?' I remembered to add the honorific titles just in time. We were after all in an imperial mansio, and because I was sure that the page was not a spy, it didn't follow that there were no spies at all. Commodus has informers everywhere. 'That was surely very dangerous in itself?'

What I meant, but did not dare to say, was that messengers who brought reports of treason to Rome were more likely than most to disappear. The Emperor almost lost his life once to a palace plot, and since then he has seen conspiracies against him everywhere. Yet perversely, like some generals in the field, he is famed for rewarding the bearers of unwelcome news – however true – by relieving them swiftly of their heads. 'Paying the messenger with steel and not with gold' as the wits in Glevum say.

Lucidus understood exactly what I meant. He shook his head. 'He was going to go directly to someone he knew in Rome, the same man who got my sons commissioned posts in Gaul. Claudinus did not trust anyone round here, especially messengers. Not even Laxus and his friends – he made me swear I would not say a word, and if I was not sure that he was dead, I would not break my oath. He got as far as getting to a port – at least I think he did: I got a message purporting to be from him, sent with an itinerant trader from the east. It said that he'd found one final piece of proof, he hoped to bribe a place aboard an olive-oil boat to Gaul, and he would send word again next day – and that was the last I ever heard of him.'

'So why do you suppose your rivals captured him? Why should you think that, when he was so far from home? He could have fallen prey to bandits – or anything.' Marcus had put down his peach and was suddenly taking an interest in all this, now that affairs of state might be involved.

'I thought so too, at first. All sorts of possibilities occurred to me – that he'd been set upon and robbed, or the captain of the olive boat had cheated him and thrown him in the sea – even that he'd never left the town and the whole message from the trader was a hoax, though it contained the password we'd agreed. There was no way of tracing the itinerant to find out. But I was never sure. Of course, if anything happens to one of us, our first suspicions are always of the bath-side boys. But to be honest, citizen, if they had taken him, I would have expected to receive a sign.'

'What sort of sign?'

He shrugged. 'I don't know. A blood-stained tunic in a parcel, perhaps, turning up outside my door. And a note scrawled on a piece of bark – "This happened to your brother.

Mind your own business or we'll do the same to you."
Something of that kind. But there was nothing. He simply
disappeared.'

I shuddered. 'That was their way of proving they'd captured one of you?' I echoed, still hardly able to believe my
ears.

'Exactly so. If the person is someone of not much account,
they are not above asking for a reward to return the mutilated
corpse, so that we can bury it and give the spirit peace.' He
grimaced. 'The minute we leave the protection of the town
we have to be on our guard. And it's not over yet. Even in my
lifetime I've had body-parts – hands, or ears or fingers –
delivered to my door. Sometimes they wanted money for the
man's return, mostly it was just to prove that he was dead.'

Marcus looked pained. 'And all this under Roman law? I
wonder you didn't call on the authorities for help. Especially
if you suspected that the victims were robbed and murdered
on the road. That is a crucifixion offence and we'd be glad to
help. That sort of thing is very bad for trade.'

'We've never bothered the authorities,' Lucidus said. 'Our
two families were mortal enemies long before you Romans
ever came. Indeed, that's probably why my forefathers
welcomed your legions here in any case – because the other
lot were Caractacus's men. Obviously there was no town of
Venta then, but we were given confiscated property as a
reward for our services, and property in the civitas as soon as
it was built. Of course, our rivals had been largely dis-
possessed, but they hid out in the local caves and woods.
Then, when the fighting had died down, and they were able
to appear respectable, they crept into the cheaper area of
town around the baths. They made those stinking alleyways
their own, and it's been their centre of influence ever since.

Kidnapping, murder, blackmail – anything to harm and harry us. And we've paid them back in kind – great Pluto take them all to Dis!' He seemed to realise that he'd just confessed to criminal intent, and backtracked hastily. 'Of course, there hasn't been a serious instance of this sort of thing for years. But that is what they always used to do – so if our old enemies had captured Claudinus I would have expected to receive a severed hand at least.'

'And if you didn't pay them what they asked, they'd string the victim's body up in mockery, in some very public place, with his private parts cut off and stuffed into his mouth?' I looked round for somewhere to dispose of my plumstones. The slave-boy brought me the water and I washed my hands.

The Silurian was looking at me with renewed respect. 'You have heard about that barbarous little trick? Well, that's true as well – and typical of them, though they swear it was a practice they learned from Rome – it was done to Boudicca's followers, they say. Whatever may be the truth of that, it didn't take them long to copy it. They once used it on a distant relative of mine – admittedly a long, long time ago.'

'And your family has retaliated since? I don't imagine that proud folk like you would take such insults quietly.'

It was a guess, but the dull flush on his cheek showed me that my hunch was justified. 'Once or twice. But only in revenge. How did you learn . . . ?'

'Young Laxus and his friends again,' I said. 'So, your ancient enemies would be only too glad to kill your brother if he fell into their hands. Of course, if he was right in his suspicions, and was about to denounce them in some way, they had a double motive to dispose of him. But you decided that they hadn't, because you had no sign?'

'Yet it looks as if they must have, after all, since you found his arm-band in the marketplace. Not over in the east, where we supposed he was, but here in Venta all the time, which suggests that he was almost home again before they set on him. I'm just amazed they didn't send the arm-band – and probably the forearm wearing it – back to me, with a demand for gold. I'm even more surprised they had the impudence to try to sell it openly in town, where it was possible that I would hear of it. Though it was in the bath-house end of town, I suppose?'

'I suppose it must have been,' I conceded. 'It wasn't in the main forum area.'

He grunted. 'You've heard they have these back-street stalls that sell old Roman armour, and that sort of thing? They claim they find the pieces in the forest area where they were lost in the revolt – though I have my own ideas on that.'

'Probably they'd claim the same for this,' I said. 'I suppose you have absolutely no idea what your brother's suspicions were?'

'Only that it was a matter of enormous consequence. Our enemies would be utterly disgraced and very likely executed too. Claudinus told me he expected to be made a knight, at least, when the Emperor learned the truth.'

I nodded. Elevation to equestrian rank was coveted – a considerable fortune was a requisite and it was the first step to many civic honours and rewards. No wonder Claudinus had hopes of that.

Lucidus was still speaking earnestly. 'That's why I lent him the money for the trip. Our family wouldn't be overlooked for office as it is if we had a few equestrians in our rank.' He glanced at Marcus, who had eaten all his peach and was availing himself of the finger-bowl again. 'Of course, you spoke of services my son had rendered you. If Your Excellence is disposed to think of a reward . . .'

Marcus made a gracious gesture. 'When I return from Isca, I shall look into it,' he said. 'I am sorry to learn of your brother's disappearance, too, especially in the service of the Empire. Do you wish to lay an official charge and try to bring his murderer to court? I would happily preside when I return.'

That was a handsome offer. Cases brought by non-citizens were generally tried by lesser men with less appreciation of the law. However, Lucidus shook his head and turned his eyes away. 'As I say, I have no proof of anything. It is a Caractacus supporter – that is all I know. A member of the family that rules the bath-house end.'

'But who are they? You'll need to name an individual.'

'That is the trouble. No one knows who really has the power. Some shadowy rebel figures who live out in the woods and operate from there. And they act in gangs. There is no one individual that you could bring to court. Even if we knew who was responsible for killing Claudinus, it would be impossible to prove. The family have supporters everywhere, bound to them by blood-ties, or by a mixture of bribery and fear. Most of them look like honest townspeople, but they are liars, butchers, bullies, thieves and cheats. All of them would be prepared to swear in court that black was white, if necessary, in order to provide one of the others with an alibi. They tolerate no disloyalty amongst themselves – there are stories of bodies with their limbs cut off – and anyone from outside the clan who dared to bring any one of them to court could rely on instant retribution from the rest. So no one does, and certainly I am not willing to. Who wants to take a risk like that, when there is no certainty of a result?'

Marcus looked piqued, though if I had been in the Silurian's sandals, I'd have felt the same. Under Roman law a man must not only personally ensure that the accused is brought to court – which might be physically difficult with these vendetta gangs – but also he must stand before the judge and make the charge. From what Lucidus had said, that would be a quick way to ensure that portions of your anatomy would shortly be delivered piecemeal to your relatives.

'In that case . . .' Marcus was rising to his feet. He took the napkin which the pageboy brought and wiped the peach juice fastidiously from his fingertips, then extended a ringed and perfumed hand to show that the interview was at an end, 'I do not think that we can help you much. You might circulate a description of your brother, and we can ask the town guards if they know anything, but otherwise there seems little we can do. Unless you would like Libertus to take you to that stall tomorrow, where the arm-guard was?'

Lucidus turned pale. 'In the back streets at the bath-house end of town? I think not, citizen. I'd never venture there without a guard – since we are not permitted to wear knives in self-defence. Though somebody might make the trip on my behalf, perhaps, and try to purchase the item for me?' He was looking at me meaningfully as he spoke, and it was quite clear which 'somebody' he had in mind. 'At my expense, of course. I will pay whatever price the wretches ask.'

I had no wish to venture to the bath-house end again, after my worrying experience of a day or two before. Of course, in daylight, things were different – clearly the whole town used the public baths – but the stall was down an alley, and I didn't relish the prospect of returning in the least. However, if Marcus ordered it, I would have to go.

I need not have worried. Marcus had a different plan in store for me. He said loftily, 'Perhaps the optio can spare a servant to do the task for you – if you prefer not to send one of your own. Libertus will instruct him where to find the stall. He cannot go himself. We hope to leave for Isca shortly after dawn, as soon as fresh mounts and guards can be arranged.' My face must have betrayed how horrified I felt, because he added with a smile, 'My dear Libertus, don't look so aghast. Of course we must undertake the trip again, otherwise the rebels will have won. We will re-equip the carriage and take a larger force, and this time we will keep up a proper pace – no stopping to investigate the deaths of slaves or interviewing swineherds about herds of wretched pigs.'

This was a rebuke to me, I recognised. Those investigations had been at my behest, and Marcus was making it clear that he held me morally responsible for everything that had delayed us up to now. He was still in this condescending mood as he permitted Lucidus to kiss the ring and take his leave, with many protestations of thanks and loyalty.

When the Silurian had finished bowing himself out, Marcus turned to me. 'Well, I think that was dealt with satisfactorily. He's forgotten that he came here to complain.' He was so pleased with himself that I essayed a smile, but in doing so I clearly over-stepped the mark.

He frowned and formally proffered me the ringed hand in my turn, and I was obliged to make obeisance too. He hadn't demanded that of me for days. 'I will have the optio send your rations to your room,' he said, as I struggled to my knees and bent to press my lips against the ring. 'When I dine tonight I do not think your presence is required.'

He turned and allowed the slave to show him out, leaving

me kneeling rather stiffly on the floor. I smiled a little wryly as I struggled to my feet.

I had not entirely escaped his displeasure, after all.

Chapter Twenty-one

So I was condemned to eat my meal alone, I thought, as I made my way slowly back across the court towards my room. I had taken care to keep my face appropriately chagrined while Marcus was about, but in fact I was secretly relieved. My little punishment was not the deprivation he intended it to be.

For one thing the kitchen at the mansio had been busy half the day preparing a special meal for my patron's sake, and I am not an enthusiast at the best of times for strong-tasting Roman treats. Sow's udders are not my favourite dish, even when exquisitely baked, and kitchen orderlies at a military staging post are not apt to be the most accomplished chefs. Judging by the odours from the kitchen as I passed, tonight's offering would be burnt and tough, and liberally doused with liquamen to disguise the fact -- that revolting fish-paste sauce of which my patron is so fond, and which smells and tastes so powerfully strong that it will mask any shortcomings of the cook. If I was eating on my own, I would be spared all that. I could settle down to honest army stew and even send out for some good old-fashioned mead, instead of being obliged to drink watered Roman wine, of which I have never been particularly fond.

There was no one in the court or corridor to tell me otherwise, so without thinking about it very much I turned towards the sleeping room I'd occupied before. However, it seemed I was mistaken in assuming that it would be mine again. As soon I approached the door I heard the sound of voices from within. There seemed to be some sort of argument going on inside, though from here I could not make out the words.

I paused, surprised. Not so much because the room was occupied – this was after all a military inn, and they had not been anticipating our return. It was entirely to be expected that they would give my room to someone else. But one of the voices sounded like a girl's – and that *was* astonishing.

Mansiones are military establishments, reserved for soldiers on the move, or travellers and messengers on imperial business. Women are not permitted past the gates unless they are accompanying important men – their husbands or their fathers – and rarely even then. I shook my head. There must be some other explanation for the voice. A castratus, or perhaps the youthful favourite of some wealthy man – some rich officials do keep pretty boys as 'pets' until their voices break.

In either case, this was no place for me.

I looked around. There was nobody in sight to ask directions from, and for a moment I stood hesitating, wondering where to go and what to do. Then the door of the room opened and the serving-boy came out – the same slave who had attended us in the office earlier.

He turned to me with an apologetic air. 'I'm sorry, citizen. I went into the room to take your meal and found the lady was already there. I'm very sorry you were not informed. I don't know how she got there, and she's just refused to leave.'

'Lady?' I echoed in astonishment. When we first got back

here to the mansio the officer had spoken of 'people' – in the plural – who had wanted words with me, but I'd forgotten that there might be more than one. And certainly I'd not expected this. 'I don't know any lady in this area, except the Christian widow from the thermopolium, and it seems unlikely she would seek me here.'

He shook his head. 'This is not a widow, citizen, judging by her dress. And not a Christian, as far as I can see.'

I frowned. I could not imagine who it was. Unless . . . That letter I had sent to Glevum! I had asked for Junio. Had Gwellia decided to accompany him? The wax tablet had been carried by the imperial post – the swiftest horse-men in the world. With relays of fresh horses, a message could reach London in a day from anywhere in Britannia, it was said, so mine would have reached my roundhouse at least two days ago. If Gwellia had organised a lift in some light vehicle . . .

I turned to the slave-boy and said, with sudden hope, 'Unless it is my wife?'

He stared thoughtfully at his sandal straps. 'I do not think so, citizen. Not a wife, exactly. Possibly – a friend.' There was a sort of embarrassed knowingness in the way he said this which made it more puzzling than ever.

'A friend? I have no friend in Venta – and certainly no female ones.'

He did not look up. 'She insists that you invited her to come.'

'I've absolutely no idea who it can be,' I said. 'I don't know any women in this town.' And then, of course, I realised that I did. 'It isn't Lyra the brothel-keeper, by any chance?'

The servant was visibly relieved, but he did not meet my eyes. 'I believe that is the name she mentioned, citizen. She said you had been asking for her in the town, and had required her to present herself to you.'

I sighed. 'Well, that's true, up to a point, but not for the reasons that she seems to think. I wanted her brought in for questioning.' Why did I find it necessary to explain myself? 'Well, never mind – I'll go and speak to her. You'd better tell His Excellency she's come.'

He didn't move. 'I shall have to tell the optio as well. My master is particular about these things. It may be that he won't be pleased at all, and . . . well . . .' He tailed off.

'You think he would be angry because she's here without a guard? I suppose it's possible. I wonder that the sentry at the gate admitted her at all, much less permitted her to walk around the mansio unaccompanied in this way. I suppose he gave her directions to wait here in my room because he knew that we were busy interviewing someone else?'

Of course, even as I framed the words, I realised that the sentry had thought nothing of the kind. In the circumstances, what would anybody think? The boy obviously had his own opinions on the matter too, despite my explanations to the contrary. He made no reply but went on carefully scrutinising his feet, as though his toes were of enormous significance all at once.

I was about to protest my lack of interest in Lyra's particular specialties when all at once the door of the sleeping quarters was opened from within and Lyra was standing there herself. She had evidently made an effort for her visit here. The pockmarks on her face were carefully disguised with thick white powdered chalk, and she had taken pains applying lamp-black to her eyes and wine-lees to her lips. Her hennaed hair was piled up in ringlets on her head, though it was clearly visible under the hood of her long green cloak and curls had been coaxed to stray down onto her neck in a way that would make any strict Roman mother blush.

All this titivation had been on my account and it was true that she looked a little more attractive now than I'd remembered her. I would have to disappoint her all the same. With her blackened teeth and exaggerated walk, she was not a type that much appealed to me – especially when that potent smell of cheap scent and onions came wafting from her every time she moved.

She was moving now – towards me, with a smile. 'I hear that you were looking for me, citizen?' she said, making her voice deliberately husky as she spoke. 'I am sorry that I could not come at once, but I was out of town – very important business with a client.' She shook her head free from the hood, and flicked the cloak back with an expert hand so that her inner tunic was revealed.

And not just her tunic, though that was eye-catching enough, being of fine fabric, deep red and richly decorated, but cut short like a man's. I tried not to look at her lower legs – and found myself staring at the low-cut neckline instead. No hint of maidenly modesty about this! I tore my eyes away. 'We had a few questions we wished to ask you,' I said. I was trying to sound brisk and businesslike, but I found my throat was dry. I had not been expecting a reception of this kind, and finding Lyra in one's private room was quite a different matter from encountering the lady in the street.

She smiled again, half closing her eyes into mysterious slits. 'Of course, citizen. Anything you wish. You can ask as many questions as you like.' She succeeded in making it sound as if this was a term agreed between us for improper services. She turned and stepped back inside the room, holding the door invitingly ajar. 'I am at your command. Come in and see.'

It was awkward. The slave-boy was still staring at his feet, no doubt attempting to conceal a smirk. I have never in my life paid a woman for my needs – not even in the dark days when my wife was lost – and though I obviously did not intend to do so now, I still felt ridiculously ill at ease. There was something about the way she held herself, the flaunting walk and the way she leaned against the door-jamb which made me reluctant to be alone with her. Yet if I wanted Marcus and the optio to come – as I most sincerely did – I would obviously have to send the slave away to tell them she was here.

I tried the high-handed and severe approach. 'You know it is against the law to try to ply your trade anywhere except on licensed premises?'

She gave me another smouldering smile. 'Citizen, who said anything about my trade? I came here entirely at your request. I understand you sent a mounted guard to fetch me two days ago. He left instructions that I was to present myself to you for questioning at the earliest opportunity. So of course I came at once, as soon as I learned that you'd come back.' There was nothing but sweet reasonableness in her words, but she allowed her eyes to linger over me and ran her tongue round the inside of her lips in a way which conveyed an altogether different message. She knew that she was creating an uncomfortable effect and she added, in the same honeyed tone, 'As a law-abiding townswoman, what else could I possibly have done?'

I had allowed her to gain the initiative here, and I tried to wrest it back. 'Very well. I will have a stool and water brought for you and you can wait while I eat my meal. Then we will

see about interrogating you. See to it, boy,' I murmured to
the slave. 'And you can make His Excellence aware that she
is here. Ask for his permission to begin the questioning –
perhaps your master could provide us with a room.'

The slave-boy seemed to recognise at last that my inten-
tions towards the lady were after all what I'd declared. He
leapt into obedience, suddenly alert. 'At once, citizen. Allow
me to serve you with your meal.'

I nodded and gestured him to precede me into the sleeping
room, where a small stool and table was awaiting me. On it
was a dish of cooling stew, a hunk of bread, a little end of
cheese and a large metal beaker of red watered wine. At first
I posted Lyra in the corridor to wait but she managed to
look so provocative, leaning there against the wall, that it
embarrassed me. It was obvious that she would flaunt herself
in front of everyone who passed and I would be the gossip of
the mansio; but if I shut the door and simply ate my meal
there was a chance that – being there without a guard – she
would slip away again. Either way I would look an idiot and
Marcus would be seriously displeased. In the end I found a
compromise. I allowed her to come into the room but told
the slave-boy to leave the door ajar.

He nodded and pulled out the stool for me. I looked at my
congealing stew. 'And you can take this plate away,' I said.
'It's cold. Get them to send me down some fresh. In the
meantime, I'll just eat the bread and cheese.' Of course, it
did not really matter to me that the stew was cool. I was
sincerely hungry, by this time, and would have eaten anything, but the cook-house was closer than the optio's offices,
and I hoped that by doing this I could ensure that a slave
from the kitchen would be coming in and out. Lyra's presence
disconcerted me. I would not put it past her to make some

advance and I did not wish to be in the room with her for long without somebody else there.

'And while you are about it,' I went on, 'you can have them send out for some Celtic mead for me. I am not a great enthusiast for wine.' The servant nodded and took away the goblet at my side. I saw his longing gaze, and added with a smile, 'But don't throw that away. It's probably one of the optio's wines – he keeps some first-class ones, I understand. Perhaps you'd better take it back to him – or drink it up yourself.'

'Your pardon, citizen!' Behind me Lyra sounded seriously distressed. 'Surely . . .' I turned round. She was sitting on the palliasse which was provided as a bed and was holding her head in both her hands. 'Forgive me, citizen, but if you do not want that glass yourself, perhaps you'd allow me to have it, instead of that water you were promising? I do not know what has come over me. I am feeling suddenly unwell.'

And indeed she did look extraordinarily pale – even underneath the powder she was chalky white, except for two high spots in her cheeks which were redder than any wine-lees could have rendered them. Her voice, which had been so husky just a moment earlier, was now almost squeaky with distress: there were beads of sweat upon her brow and she was breathing heavily.

I nodded to the servant. 'Let her have the wine.' I wondered for a moment if, given the rivalries that existed in the town, someone had contrived to poison her. But she took the goblet from the boy and raised it to her lips, and immediately I could see the colour flowing back into her cheeks.

'Stupid of me, citizen,' she said, hugging the goblet to her and not moving from the bed. 'Women's problems, possibly. I'm better now. Please, do not let me keep you from your meal.'

I grunted something and sat down to my food, meanwhile sending the slave-boy to fulfil his tasks and hoping that he wouldn't be too long. I was extremely hungry, and even the frugal bread and cheese tasted ambrosial to me. All I needed was a drink to wash it down. I could hear distant footsteps in the corridor, and was beginning to hope that it might be the kitchen-slave when Lyra spoke to me again.

'If you could perhaps assist me, citizen? I am feeling well enough to rise.' She stretched out a hand towards me. 'Better, perhaps, if I am not sitting on your bed when His Excellence and the optio arrive.'

She had a point. I was still apprehensive about touching her, but she had been in distress. I got up, took the proffered arm and raised her to her feet. As I did so she appeared to sway, the goblet which she was still holding tumbled to the floor, spilling its contents everywhere, and she fell against me with a little cry.

Almost instinctively I caught her in my arms to stop her tumbling to the floor. She made no effort to support herself but flopped on me so that I bore all her weight. She was not a large person but she was surprisingly heavy all the same, and I staggered a little as I took the shock.

'Master?' A voice from the open doorway startled me.

I looked over the shoulder of my burden. My apprentice-cum-slave-boy, Junio, was standing in the shadows of the corridor outside. He had obviously arrived from Glevum in answer to my note and was carrying the spare toga I had asked him for. A great feeling of relief swept over me. It had been an extremely awkward moment, having Lyra swooning semi-conscious in my arms, but now I wouldn't have to be alone with her again.

I found myself grinning like an idiot. 'Junio! Thank all the gods you've come! I hope your foot's completely better now?'

He nodded. 'Thank you, master.' But he didn't move.

'Well, in that case,' I said impatiently, 'don't stand there staring at me like that. You can see I've got a problem – come and lend a hand. I'll explain later – it's too complicated now.'

He continued to look hesitant, but he put down his bundle by the door and took an unwilling step into the room.

'Come on,' I said, still struggling with her weight. 'Just help me to lie this woman on the bed. I don't know what's the matter with her all at once – she was perfectly all right a little while ago. I'm afraid it might be something in the wine I gave her.' In which case, I thought suddenly, it was meant for me.

I was about to share this disturbing notion with my serving-boy, when I looked up and realised that he was not alone. As Junio stepped uneasily into the room, I saw who was behind him in the shadowed passageway.

It was my wife Gwellia, and she was very far from pleased.

'Libertus, what exactly is the meaning of this?' She was furiously angry and upset – as I suppose any wife would be who found her husband in a situation of this kind. 'I have travelled non-stop since I got your note, longing to be here at your side, and when I get here, what do I find? You with a painted woman in your arms – and I heard you say you have been plying her with wine.'

I guiltily withdrew my arms from Lyra's waist, where I had reached out instinctively to steady her, but she did not collapse senseless to the floor, as I had half expected that she would when I deprived her of support. Instead she took a step backwards and sank down gracefully onto the mattress. The sudden appearance of my wife seemed to have restored her more or less to health.

She hardly mattered now. I turned towards the woman I loved. All my delight at seeing her had evaporated in embarrassment. 'Gwellia,' I said urgently, 'this isn't what it seems. The lady was brought in to me for questioning – and she was taken suddenly unwell.'

'Lady?' Gwellia is a devoted and loving wife, who is often unwilling to express herself – the long years of servitude after she was wrested from me have cowed her painfully – but she is a woman of some spirit when aroused. She was roused now, and there was such scorn and venom in her

ded. 'I

me at the

ed, but I insisted

y meant. Your business

nd.'

it was nothing of the sort,' I
his woman, Lyra, was summoned to
mansio two days ago to answer some enquiries about her
property. Marcus even sent a messenger to bring her in but
she was not at home, so he left instructions that she was to
report here as soon as possible. Which is exactly what she
did. She was waiting for me here when I returned.'

Gwellia snorted. 'Having somehow talked her way past
the guards and being permitted to wander unescorted to
your room? I wonder how? I had the greatest difficulty getting
in myself, and I had your letter with Marcus's seal on it –
obviously they could not argue with that for very long.
However,' she glanced at Lyra with ill-disguised contempt,
much as I have seen her look at a scrawny chicken in the
marketplace before refusing it, 'doubtless your visitor has
other methods of persuading them, which are not open to a
mere wife.'

'Be silent! I have told you why she's here.' I am by nature
quite a patient man, especially where my beloved Gwellia is
concerned, and I actively encourage her at home to speak
her mind – but there are limits to what any self-respecting
husband can tolerate in a public place. And we had an
audience. The optio's private slave had reappeared – sent in
person from the kitchens, evidently, since he was bearing a
stool for Lyra and a wooden tray on which was a copper
beaker, a jug of what looked and smelled like mead and a

large bowl of freshly steaming stew. It must have been quite heavy, but he stood there holding it. He had been listening, open-mouthed, to every word.

He saw me looking at him and composed his face. 'My master sent me back with this for you. I'm to ask if your visitor wants refreshment too.'

I looked enquiringly at Gwellia, but she shook her head. 'Junio and I brought our own supplies,' she said, with cool disdain. 'We have already eaten on the road. Anyway, how would the optio know that we are here? There was no one but the sentry at the gate. More likely he meant your other visitor.' She went back to glowering at the prostitute, who was still sitting on my bed and appeared to have recovered totally. If anything it was my wife who now looked pale and ill.

'Citizen, what shall I do with this?' The pageboy was still carrying the tray, and I gestured to him to come and put it down.

'My own slave will attend me now,' I said, seating myself at the table while Junio took up his familiar position at my side.

The page nodded. 'And about the . . . uh . . . lady, citizen?' he said.

I saw a way to exculpate myself. 'Are His Excellence and the optio coming here? I presume they will interrogate her later on?' I glanced sideways at Gwellia as I spoke, hoping to prove the point to her, but she refused to meet my eyes.

'They'll send for her when they have finished with their meal,' the boy replied. 'I am to escort her to the guardroom now to wait. His Excellence suggests that, when you've had your food, you should go and start the preliminary questioning. You know what you need to ask, he says.'

241

It should have been the confirmation that I sought, but there was something in his manner which conveyed the opposite. Something was clearly troubling him and though Lyra had risen to her feet and moved obediently to his side, he didn't move. He simply stood there, hovering, and looking so furtive that, far from helping to allay my wife's suspicions, he was making matters worse.

'Very well, then, go!' I urged impatiently. 'Take the woman now, and leave me to my meal.'

'At once, citizen,' but still he did not move. Instead he starting sending signals with his eyes, as though we were partners in some conspiracy.

Gwellia noticed it at once. Before I did, in fact, because I had turned away to eat my stew. 'Husband,' she said, with heavy irony, 'I think the slave has something he wants to say. Something that he would prefer I didn't hear, perhaps.'

'Nonsense,' I protested. 'There is nothing he could have to say to me which I would not be happy for you to overhear. But obviously he can't talk freely with Lyra in the room. There have been investigations into her affairs, and no doubt information about her has come to light.' It was an explanation which had just occurred to me and – judging by the look of horror which crossed Lyra's face – it was at least a reasonable one. Gwellia had the grace to look abashed, and the optio's slave was so visibly relieved that I was persuaded that I'd hit upon the truth. 'Does it concern Lyra?' I enquired.

He nodded passionately.

'In that case, you can tell me when I come to question her. Then it will be fresh in my mind, and there is no chance of her overhearing what you have to say, and changing her testimony to fit.' She was clearly uncomfortable by now, and I thought it would do her good to wait.

It was obviously not the response that the page had hoped to get. He gave me another anguished look. 'But citizen . . .' he began and then, whatever he was going say, abandoned it. 'You know best, citizen. It shall be as you command. Come!' he said to Lyra, and she followed him from the room. She was still looking shaken but she had collected herself a little more by now, and even contrived to sway her hips at me, and give me a would-be-seductive smile as she went.

Gwellia watched all this in stony silence. But after they had gone she sat down on the bed, deliberately avoiding the place where the previous occupant had been, and burst out furiously, 'And you expect me to believe that she's a prisoner in this place, when he lets her walk about without restraint. No chains, no ropes, no guards at all – not even a baton to keep her under check!' She sounded angry, but she was close to tears, and she folded her arms across her chest, tightly, as though to keep her feelings locked inside.

'Gwellia . . .' I said gently.

'Don't try to Gwellia me. Eat your stew before it all goes cold.'

I sighed. It was clear that explanation was no use. However, she was right. I was hungry and my food was getting cold. I offered again to share my meal, but she simply shook her head in an impatient way.

I decided it was best to give her time, and turned my attention to the waiting stew. It was thick and stodgy, full of oatmeal and beans, as tasteless army rations very often are, but it was warm and filling and I ate it gratefully, while Junio stood beside me with the jug of mead. If it was not for my affronted, glowering wife, I could have persuaded myself that I was safe at home and everything was well.

I pushed back my empty plate and smiled up at Junio. He

leaned forward, and refilled my cup with mead, murmuring as he did so, 'With your permission, master, I will find a cloth. I see that there is wine spilt on the floor.'

I stared at him and started to my feet. 'Great gods,' I cried. The appearance of my wife had driven all memory of the spillage from my mind, and all rational thought as well, it seemed. But I now remembered what I'd thought before. 'That wine was meant for me.'

Junio looked at me, aghast. 'You think that there was something wrong with it?'

'I don't know. Lyra was already feeling ill – that's why I gave it her – but once she'd taken just a sip, she half collapsed on me.' I turned to Gwellia. 'That's how you came to find us as you did.'

Gwellia got slowly to her feet. Even as I watched her, I could see the change in her, and the look of real concern that crossed her face. 'You think somebody meant to poison you?'

I shook my head. 'I don't know. I suppose it's possible, but I can't see who it could have been – unless it was the optio himself. He was the one who sent the food for me.' I glanced nervously at my empty plate and at the jug of mead which I had half consumed. 'Yet I've just eaten this, and I am perfectly all right. Perhaps he realised I had witnesses, and changed his mind.'

Gwellia frowned. 'But I still can't work out how he knew that we were here.'

I shrugged. 'He must have done. A message from the sentry, I suppose. After all, he offered you a meal.'

She shook her head. 'We saw no one but the guard on duty at the gate, and there was no way of sending in a messenger. He actually said as much himself. He was grumbling that the mansio was overstretched – there was only a handful of men stationed here, he said, and half of them had been out on escort duty all day, so he was on his own. He didn't even have a message-boy. That's what he said to Junio. I heard.'

Junio nodded. 'He wanted us to wait there in the guard-room at the gate till he could find someone to send to the officer in charge, and get the go-ahead to let us in. He was perfectly polite and apologetic, but he told us he couldn't allow a woman through the gate without personal permission from the optio in command. More than his very skin was worth, he said. It was only the letter with the official seal that changed his mind.'

I glanced at Gwellia. 'So you were right, my dear,' I said. 'Of course you were. I should have paid attention to your words before. You said it was extraordinary that Lyra should come in here and wander round without a proper guard – but it is even more peculiar than I thought. But I think I might know why. Go into the kitchen, Junio – you'll find it on your right as you go out of here – and ask them for a cloth to clean the floor. Try to get chatting to the kitchen-boys. Tell them that Lyra was here with me. See what their reaction is to that. Find out if she's ever been before.'

Junio's face lit up in a delighted grin. He has always loved assisting me in my enquiries and it was clear that he was relishing this opportunity. He asked no further questions, but disappeared at once.

I rose and went over to my wife. She looked up at me, and I saw with distress that there were tears brimming in her eyes. I took her elbows, raised her to her feet, and held her in my arms. 'Gwellia,' I murmured, pressing her against me and fondling her hair, 'did you doubt me so?'

She drew back her head and looked at me. 'What was I to

think? I have been concerned about you ever since you sent asking Junio to go to Plautus's house and try to find out exactly what happened when he died. I know you, Libertus. You have got some theory that you want to prove. Plautus was a wealthy citizen, and owed his rise to Rome. No doubt he made enemies on the way – any man who makes a personal fortune always does. If you suspected that someone murdered him, I didn't know what danger you were in, or what kind of people you were dealing with.'

'So you came to rescue me?'

'I came to keep an eye on you. We two have been parted long enough.' Her voice broke, and she murmured with a sob, 'Libertus, husband, I have missed you so much since you have been gone, and when I saw that woman in your arms I thought . . . I feared . . . perhaps you'd missed me too. That's how these people make their living, after all. Can you forgive me for suspecting you?'

'And can you forgive me for unintentionally causing you such grief?'

She might have answered, but her lips were otherwise engaged.

Chapter Twenty-three

It was some time before I let her go.

When I did, she drew back her head and looked up at me with a quizzical expression in her eyes. 'I should have realised that if you were investigating some affair on Marcus's behalf, you would have time for very little else. So that woman from the wolf-house is connected with this Plautus business, then? What happened? Did he make an enemy of her pimp or patron in some way?' She scanned my face. 'Cross him in business and get murdered for his pains? I hope you're being careful, husband, if that is the case. These brothel-keepers can be very dangerous. But it must be something of the kind. Plautus can't have been a customer of hers; he lived too far away.'

'I'm sure there's some connection, but I don't know what it is. I'm positive she was following him round Venta the first day I arrived.'

'Perhaps . . .' my wife began, and then – as she took in the force of what I'd said – 'Round Venta? What do you mean, "round Venta"? The man's been dead for more than half a moon.'

'Not nearly as dead as you suppose,' I said, and I found myself pouring out the story of all that had occurred. It was the first time that I'd had the chance to tell a wholly sympathetic listener. She didn't pour scorn on anything I said, or interrupt, but heard me out in silence – although, since she looked dismayed to hear of my ordeals, I spared her the worst details of the horrors of yesterday. 'So much has happened in the last few days,' I finished, 'it seems a lifetime since I got here.'

Gwellia was frowning, but the frown was not for me. 'And you saw Gaius Plautus in the street? After that great funeral he had? No wonder you sent Junio to his house.' She gave me a sideways little glance. 'I went up there with him myself, you know. I'd met the widow once or twice before – Sabrina, she's called – and it seemed not unreasonable to call and offer my sympathy on her husband's death. If you were up to something, then I wanted to help. I could talk to her more freely than young Junio could – though he did talk to her about the pavement, as you suggested – and chatted to the servants too.'

My wife is a resourceful woman, but I chided her. 'You might have put yourself in danger, doing things like that.'

'Don't you think I feel the same way about you? Anyway, that's what I did – and she was glad to see me, I believe. Of course she's still in mourning and she has done it properly – torn clothes, scratched cheeks and ashes in her hair – and since the funeral she hasn't left the house. Full of how it's her fault that he met his death. If he's alive, I'm sure she doesn't know.'

'Oh, he's alive, all right,' I said. 'I saw him in Venta with my own two eyes, and he's not a man you'd easily mistake.'

She shook her head. 'That poor woman. I was going to say "his widow" but of course she's not. I don't think she liked her husband much but she seemed genuinely in a state of shock – kept saying that if she had gone out to their country house with him that night, the accident would never have occurred. She's spent a fortune on sacrifices to the gods to make propitiation for her guilt – and all for nothing, if he isn't dead.' Suddenly she paused and looked appalled.

I knew what she was thinking before she spoke the words.

'So who was on that pyre if it wasn't him?' she said, asking the same question I'd asked myself. 'There must have been a corpse. Sabrina was telling me that she'd spent a fortune on embalming oils and herbs, and hiring the best funeral arrangers in town – she was terrified her husband's spirit would return to haunt her if she didn't do it right. Anointing women, professional mourners and musicians, litters, everything: even a priest to see the body was ritually washed and dressed while the whole household kept up the lament. She had them coach her eldest son to lead the eulogies, although he's barely old enough to be a man.' She broke off. 'Oh, I forgot. You know all that, of course. You were at the funeral yourself. You must have seen him. He was laid in state.'

'And what I saw was a dead man decorously draped in linen cloths, because his head was crushed,' I said. 'I assumed that it was Plautus, because they said it was – and so, I suppose, did everybody else. If you attend a funeral, you don't expect the corpse to be a fraud. The funeral arrangers wouldn't know the difference. But you'd think his wife would notice, wouldn't you?'

Gwellia shook her head. 'I'm not so sure she would,' she said. 'If they called me to your workshop in the town one day and the servants brought out a body of your height and build – your age, your colouring and with your clothes and shoes – and said that they had found you crushed to death, I think I would assume that it was you.'

'Even if you didn't recognise my face?'

'Because the skull was crushed to fragments and the features gone?' She had turned comfortingly pale at the very thought of it. 'I wouldn't want to dwell on that for long. I'd look to see the scar of the slave-brand on your back, but apart from that why should I question it? Who could think clearly after they'd had a shock like that? And who would suspect it was a hoax? Or imagine that their husband would connive at it? I'm sure Sabrina didn't. And he didn't have a slave-brand she could know him by. She was shocked. She just went through the motions in a kind of daze.'

I nodded. 'You may be right. Maybe Plautus had no special identifying marks, apart from that scar across his face. No moles on his shoulders or anything like that.'

My wife gave me a little wistful smile. 'Even if he did, I don't believe Sabrina would have known. She told me once their marriage was arranged – as rich girls' matches very often are – but that she'd never liked him very much, and he wasn't really interested in her. He fathered his two sons on her and after that he left her more or less alone – having done his duty by the state. Visited the wolf-houses, perhaps. She wasn't sorry, either, from what she said to me. He was no gentle husband. I doubt if she could identify his moles.'

It was so different from the intimacy of our own marriage bed that I was moved to take her in my arms again, but at that moment Junio came in carrying a wet cloth in his hand. He looked from me to Gwellia and grinned. 'Sorry to interrupt you, master, but I've got the cloth. I couldn't get much information from the kitchen staff, but I promised to play the cook at twelve-stones later on. Perhaps I can learn something from him then.' He winked. 'Do you want me to clean up that wine?'

He did not wait for a reply, but dived under the table

to retrieve the drinking cup, which had rolled there when Lyra let it fall. Gwellia sat down upon the bed to let him pass.

I watched his retreating posterior and smiled. The poor cook had a surprise in store. Junio had been born a slave into a Roman home, where he learned to gamble almost as soon as he could breathe. It was a rare man who could beat him at any game of chance, despite his air of youthful innocence. 'I only hope the cook won't stake more than he can afford to lose,' I teased, as he came back into view. 'What do you propose to do with all your— What is it, Junio?'

He was sitting on his haunches, with the recovered goblet in his hand, and he was looking doubtfully from me to it. All trace of laughter had vanished from his face. 'You did say, master, that the prostitute was ill before she drank the wine you gave to her? You are sure it wasn't that which made her faint?'

'I'm absolutely sure,' I said. 'I did suspect it for a moment, but when I thought it through, I realised she was feeling ill before. Why, what's the matter? Why did you ask that?'

'It is just that when I was wiping the splashes behind the table leg, I found some bits of glass. It looks like part of a little phial to me – the sort they use for poisons – though it is hard to know. It has been broken into tiny fragments, see, as if someone had deliberately crushed it underfoot. The pieces were sticking to my cloth – I almost cut my hand. I've shaken them into the cup, so you can see.'

He held out the goblet in which he had collected the tiny shards of broken coloured glass. The largest of them was no bigger than the nail on my little finger. It was circular, with a small loop attached, and had obviously once contained a cork. Exactly like the neck of a small phial of the kind used for potions and decoctions, just as Junio had said. It was an alarming find.

Most of the contents of these things are curative, of course – or are alleged to be. However, in any street market or town it is possible to find someone skilled with herbs who will supply you with some lethal draught, provided that you pay them handsomely and swear that you intend to poison rats. Just as they will sell you love-philtres, baldness cures and sleeping draughts – though these are less effective on the whole.

From the shattered fragments in the cup it was impossible to tell what this little phial had once contained, or even how long it had been there – the rooms in a busy mansio are not always scrupulously swept. However, it would be foolish to deny the possibility that Junio was right, and that whatever had been in that phial was added to my wine.

I leaned forward gingerly and sniffed at them and then at the water in the washing bowl, in which Junio had been rinsing out the cloth. I fancied I detected a slightly almond scent. It was so faint that I could not be sure at first, and it was in any case obscured by the wine, but all the same I felt my skin go cold. If I was not imagining the smell – and a second sniff persuaded me that I was not – then someone had intended me to die.

It must have been a hefty dose, as well. Lyra had scarcely tasted it, and it had made her faint. Had she taken a little of my wine to dye her lips, while I was talking to the optio's slave outside? Could that be what had made her feel unwell? After all, most drugs take a little while to work. But who would have put it there, and why?

The optio had ordered me the wine, but why should he want to kill me? I had done nothing to offend or startle him.

And anyway why bother with a phial? Why not just put poison in the goblet?

The serving-boy, perhaps? He had the opportunity, but I could think of no motive for the deed – and why bring the poison to the room, instead of adding it before he came? In fact, though I was reluctant to acknowledge it, there was only one candidate that I could see. One person who had been alone in here when the wine was on the tray, and who had the chance to slip in anything she chose.

'Lyra!' I said aloud. It was clear enough when I looked back on it. Lyra, who had panicked when I refused the wine and seemed to be about to send it back – no wonder she suddenly turned pale and asked for it herself. Clearly she had not sipped it, as she'd pretended to – I remembered how she'd hugged it to her chest, and how artistically she'd let it fall and spill by manufacturing a sudden faint. She had feared it would kill the optio or the slave – and then too many questions would be asked. I wondered how she had intended to deal with my own demise: claim that I'd had a seizure of the heart, as a result of my exertions in her arms? She was quite capable of inventing something of the kind: she had shown a remarkable ability for thinking quickly when the need arose. Grudgingly, I had to admire her ingenuity and intelligence.

'But why ever should she want to murder me?' I found that I had spoken the last words aloud. 'Just because I saw her following Plautus in the marketplace? I do have my suspicions about other things, but how could she possibly know about those? I'll try to find out when I question her. What do you think, Gwellia?'

I turned towards my wife, surprised that she'd said nothing on the subject up to now, and saw that she'd rested her head against the wall, and was drifting into sleep.

Chapter Twenty-four

As I spoke she shook herself awake and of course I was instantly contrite. My wife and slave had travelled day and night to come to me, and I had been so exercised about the problems here that I had not even given a thought to how weary they must be. I had a thousand questions still, but they could wait till morning, if necessary.

'You must rest, the pair of you,' I said. 'Junio, go to the kitchens and bring fresh water and another bowl. Your mistress needs to wash her hands and feet. And,' I added, as a plan occurred to me, 'get me another goblet – as like this as you can – and another pitcher of the mansio's wine. Never mind the quality, any wine will do. Then send a message to Marcus and the optio and tell them I am ready to begin. I will arrange another palliasse when I return.'

'No need to tell us anything, old friend. I heard that your wife and slave were here, and thought I'd come to greet them. Gwellia, my dear . . .' Marcus, in his laundered synthesis, had deigned to come in person to my room, and had entered unannounced, with the optio and his servant in his wake. He strode towards us, stretching out both hands to my wife, so that she was obliged to rise and make obeisances.

'I trust the journey was not too severe,' he went on solicitously as she scrambled to her feet. 'Libertus shall have

255

that palliasse he was talking of, and doubtless the mansio could find some stew for you – I would not recommend the sow's udders that we have just been served!'

So the feast had been the disappointment that I had foreseen, and the optio was clearly in disgrace. I saw him skulking at the doorway, looking glum, and I hit on a little strategy.

'It's kind of you to think of it, Excellence,' I said. 'But the optio has already offered our visitor a meal, and it has been declined. Isn't that so, optio?' I saw the look of puzzlement flit across his face, followed by a look of disbelief. The offer had been intended for Lyra, not my wife – that much was now evident – but he could not publicly confess the fact. He was disconcerted and I seized on that. 'Optio, allow me to present my wife.' I waved him forward. 'Gwellia, this is Commander Optimus, who is in charge here at the mansio.'

He gulped, and then recovered visibly. 'Delighted to welcome you, madam citizen. If there is anything at all you want, just let me know.' He smiled, so anxious to pass the moment off that he hadn't seen the trap. Marcus, however, was alert to it.

'Optimus? But isn't that the name . . . ?'

Too late! I saw the optio close his eyes as he recognised the error he had made.

'The name of Lyra's wealthy customer? Exactly so. A nickname gained from prowess on the practice fields, I rather think – as Regulus informed us earlier. The optio was proud to be "the best" at parrying with a shield – though doubtless Lyra would agree that he has other skills as well.' The optio had turned a sullen red, but he said nothing, and I went on cheerfully, 'I realised this morning that we didn't know his name. He never volunteered it anywhere – even when Regulus and others offered theirs – but after what the censor said to us, of course he didn't dare. And since it is courteous to address him by his rank, it did not occur to us to ask for it. But it will be in his records and can easily be checked if he chooses to deny it.'

'All right.' The optio was still burning with embarrassment. 'I'm Optimus. Most of the soldiers know that anyway. And I was Lyra's special customer – I'd rather tell you that myself than have you torture her. I entertain her here from time to time. I know it's counter to the rules – but where's the harm?' He spoke with sudden passion. 'I don't parade it from the rooftops, I keep it to myself. I'm not fiddling the books or trading arms, or neglecting my duties to the state. And I wouldn't be the first. An optio cannot marry till he leaves the force – that's twenty years away – and a man has normal urges, after all. The commanding officer of a mansio can hardly patronise the wolf-house, like the common troops – it's bad for discipline.' He flushed. 'Though it's clear that wretched censor goes from time to time.'

I turned to his slave-boy who was staring at the floor. It seemed to be his habitual response. 'Look at me!' He raised reluctant eyes. 'You knew all this, of course, because you attended them when Lyra came to call. Few men have many secrets from their slaves. You were too loyal – or too scared – to say anything direct, but when you found Lyra in my room tonight you tried to warn me that your master would be jealous and annoyed.'

The lad was more scarlet than his owner by this time, and too afraid to speak, but he nodded nervously and went back to gazing at his feet.

'Lyra visited you in your room?' The optio sounded as if

the words had been forced out of him. 'Here? This afternoon? But she told me . . .' He tailed off.

'What?' Marcus's tone was savage. 'She sent a message to the officer in charge of her arrest?'

'She left a message for me at the gate.' Optimus sounded cowed. 'It was waiting for me in my room when we arrived. She said she would consent to come in for questioning provided that I . . . well . . .' he made a hopeless gesture with his hands, 'protected her. Told her what it was all about. I left a message with the guard to tell her that it was nothing dangerous – simply about who owned her property.' He looked defiant now. 'Well, that was true. She was afraid it was a question about . . . us. It reassured her and she turned up, as you see. Though I don't know why she should come to you,' he added, glowering at me.

'I think there are a good many things about her that you do not know,' I said. 'Do you know, for instance, where she was when we were looking for her the other day?'

'Great Jupiter!' Marcus exclaimed. 'Surely she wasn't here in the mansio with you all the time? They said at the wolf-house that she'd gone to see her special customer.'

The special customer looked wretched. 'She wasn't here,' he said. 'I'd been expecting her the night before, but she didn't come. I was getting worried. I thought that she'd decided not to take the risk – she knew I had important visitors, although I sent word when the invitation came that Your Excellence was going out to a feast, his companion was going shopping and it was safe to come.'

I stared at him. 'And how did you do that? You can hardly send a message to the wolf-house openly?'

'I sent down a member of the guard. It is the safest way. It's a licensed brothel, and the ordinary soldiers call there all the time. That's not against the rules. They have a right to spend their pay and their free time in any way they want. And there is a certain legionnaire who . . . knows.'

'The same one who always let her in?' I asked. 'The one you sent off into town, but put on duty later on, so he didn't know me when I came back to the inn?'

He flushed. 'Well, we weren't expecting you. Your slave brought us the written message . . .' He sighed. 'The sentry insisted on reading it, of course – he thought it was from Lyra, since she hadn't come. It was even written on a tablet-block like hers. But we didn't hear from her at all that night.' He shook his head, as if in disbelief. 'And next day you turned up in jail, there was talk of murder, and your slave had disappeared – and when there was still no sign of her, I began to be seriously disturbed.'

I remembered how agitated he had been that day – I'd put it down to officiousness at the time. He was agitated now, again.

'It isn't what you think,' he blurted. 'She doesn't come for money – or not just for that. We have something real. Oh, it began like that, of course. These things always do. But now it's different. She's half promised that when I get promotion and get posted on . . .' he glanced at Marcus, and amended that, '*if* I get promotion and get posted on, she will give up the business and come after me – live in a *vicus* somewhere – a town outside the camp – and wait for me till I get my discharge.'

'And then she'll marry you?'

'I'm hoping so.' He spoke with dignity. 'So you can imagine how I felt when there was no news of her. I thought . . .' He seemed to consider for a moment, before he burst out again, 'There are people in this town, you know, who bear a grudge against anyone who has anything to do with us. I know her butcher-patron has a stall down at the bath-house end, and that is traditionally a rebel trouble spot. I wondered if somehow he had heard about . . . well . . . our liaison here. He could have whisked her off and beaten her – or killed her even. Some of these extremists can be vicious in that way. It's one reason why she made me swear to secrecy, and insisted that we meet here at the mansio, where nobody could possibly be his spy.'

'That was her idea?'

'It suited me, of course. And she was terrified of him – of what would happen if he ever found out. So when I heard that he was missing too, that day – naturally I began to think the worst. Especially when I heard that she'd been in that part of town – I heard you say so to His Excellence.'

Marcus frowned. 'But the butcher had gone out with his cart that night.'

'So it was rumoured. And it gave me hope. But he doesn't go till dusk. I was imagining all sorts of things. He's a strong man and an expert with a knife. If he'd done anything to her, who would think anything of bloodstains on his clothes, or notice a piece of human bone among that putrid pile of carcasses and skins? And of course I had no proof that he had gone at all. I was relieved when I saw him on the road.'

'You saw him on the road?'

'We saw him twice. You must have noticed him. A fat man with a donkey cart. We forced him into a ditch.'

Of course I'd noticed him. 'That was the butcher? You recognised him, then?'

'I'd seen him once or twice before when he appeared in court on her behalf. I didn't tell him who I was, of course, but obviously I went to hear the proceedings. I introduced her to an advocate in case she needed him – I would have paid the fees – but she didn't in the end. I hear she has since retained him once or twice to represent her girls, but generally it's not a great success. There are always arguments about the cost and I end up squaring the accounts. Not that I blame Lyra. He's a splendid advocate, the best we have, and his fees are consequently high. The poor girl doesn't have that sort of cash.'

'A tall, lean fellow with a learned voice and a skinny slave with acne on his face?'

Optimus looked startled. 'How did you know that?'

'She may have employed him a day or two ago. To represent the soup seller's wife and bring the case against me in the courts.' I exchanged looks with my patron as I spoke. 'I'm very lucky he did not succeed.'

'But why would she do a thing like that?' The optio was appalled. 'Unless the woman came to her for help. Lyra is soft-hearted when it comes to things like that.'

'Well, here is Junio with the tray,' I said. 'Let's ask her. She can answer that herself.'

'But surely, now that I've explained, you won't need to question her again?' He was almost pathetic in his anxiety for her.

'There is still the question of the property.'

His face cleared. 'Oh, of course. But we have found out now who Nyros is. Is it necessary to ask her any more?'

Marcus placed a hand upon his arm. 'Libertus clearly thinks so. And I for one would like to know where she'd disappeared to when we wanted her.'

'And what she knows of Gaius Plautus,' Gwellia said. She had been standing by discreetly, as becomes a wife, but she had been listening and now she intervened.

'Gaius Plautus?' Optimus sounded as astonished as he looked. 'The man from Glevum you thought you saw in town the other day? How could she know anything of him?'

'That is exactly what I'm hoping to find out,' I said.

Chapter Twenty-five

Lyra was to be questioned in the optio's rooms, where we had spoken with Lucidus earlier. Optimus dispatched his slave to have her fetched down, under guard, and he and Marcus went to wait for her.

I lingered for a moment, under the pretence of saying goodnight to my weary wife. I got Junio to assist her with her shoes and help her settle on the bed, while I relieved him of the tray. I put it on the table and poured a little of the wine into the cup he'd brought. 'Do you think she'll marry him?' I asked my wife.

'That woman who was here before? Of course she won't. She sees him as an easy target for her wiles – no doubt he pays her handsomely enough.' She pulled the cover over her and laughed. 'He may be an expert with a parry-shield, but he's no match for her. She got under his defences easily enough.'

I went to her and kissed her. 'Just as you got under mine,' I said. 'Now go to sleep. We're due to go to Isca at first light – though much depends on what we learn from Lyra. I'll see you later, when I come to bed. Are you content to stay here on your own, or shall I leave Junio with you?'

I asked because the boy was at the door, obviously anxious to accompany me. She smiled. 'If it's not safe here, in a mansio, it's not safe anywhere. There are soldiers here to guard me as I sleep. You take the boy. It's clear he wants to go.'

I nodded, and picked up the taper from the bench, leaving Gwellia only the torchlight from the hall. It was quite dark now, and we would be glad of the glow to show our way. Junio picked up the tray again, and we tiptoed out, but Gwellia was asleep before we reached the door.

'Master,' Junio whispered as we crossed the court. 'You have put very little wine into that cup. It is half full, if that. Do you want me to go back for the jug?'

'I only want a little,' I explained. 'I hope it is enough. You'll see why in a minute. Tell me, though, while we have a chance to talk alone. Gwellia says you went to Plautus's house. Did you learn anything useful from his slaves?'

He gave a rueful sigh and shook his head. 'Not very much. I'm sorry, master, but it didn't happen there. It happened at his country villa, it appears – and none of the household staff were there.'

'What exactly happened?' We had halted in the shadows of the court.

'Why, the accident.' He stared at me. I'd forgotten that he didn't know the truth.

'Only there wasn't one,' I muttered hastily. 'The man is still alive – I've seen him recently.'

'No accident?' he repeated, stupefied.

'There might have been,' I said. 'Only it wasn't Plautus who was crushed. Now, quickly, because we don't have much time. Do you have any notion what led up to it?' I held the taper up to see his face.

He shrugged. 'It's all a trifle hazy, I'm afraid. Plautus went out on business as usual that afternoon, it seems – some wealthy Roman who turned up at the house and insisted that he had to talk to him – something about shipping olive oil, I think. Gaius Plautus had a ship in port, and he volunteered to take the man to see.' He paused. 'Is this the sort of thing you want to know?'

I nodded. 'Go on. Everything you know.'

'It must have been a profitable deal, because a little afterwards he came back home, and said that he and his ship-master were going out to dine to celebrate, and then he planned to take him out to see their country house and show off the extension he was having built. He could afford a finer building now, he said, and he wanted to look at it tonight so he could discuss the changes that he had in mind with his master architect before the men came in and started work next day. He was obviously excited, or a little drunk, they said. His wife was unwilling to agree to it – it was far too late to ride out there, she said, even with a hired vehicle – but he was adamant. You couldn't argue with him when he got like that.'

'And?' I prompted.

'It seems they went – there are lots of witnesses to that. The two men dined together at the oil-guild club and then they hired a cart. They took some pottery with them that they'd shipped in from Gaul, and got the driver to assist them to put it in the house. Plautus had a page with him, but he was very young and not especially strong, so they left him to watch the horse and the cart. They went out in the garden – all three of them. The driver was asked to bring his brand to light the way, and Plautus lit a travelling oil lamp from the flame. There was a new wall there, apparently, and a pile of stones – Plautus commented that it was dangerous. They went back to the carriage, but he changed his mind and went back alone with the lamp to have another look. He was gone for simply ages – so the driver said – and in the end they went to have a look. They found his corpse – or somebody's – right underneath the wall, as if the stones had all collapsed on it. The boat-master sent the others off for help, and that is all I know. They pressed the page-boy and the driver afterwards – literally pressed them, with stones on the chest – but all the stories tallied perfectly.'

'So if some enemy had been waiting in the house,' I said, 'Plautus might have killed him and had time to disappear.'

Junio looked doubtful. 'I suppose so. I hadn't thought of that. What makes you think that might have been the case?'

'I think he might have got himself mixed up in something dangerous,' I said. 'Plautus was not the only Silurian Roman citizen to disappear at that time. There was a man called Claudinus as well, who went to Glevum round about then and has not been heard of since. It is known that he was seeking to take a ship to Gaul – an olive-oil ship was mentioned, I understand. He had vital information about the rebels here – something that would crush them utterly – and I believe that they were on his track. Suppose he was Plautus's visitor? It would make a kind of sense. Plautus could help him to get passage on the ship – he may have been offered a handsome bribe, which would explain the unexpected wealth – but Claudinus was being followed, I am sure of that. Once Plautus was involved with him, he was in danger too – and if he talked publicly of going out to his country house that night, it would not be difficult to lie in wait.'

'So Plautus killed his would-be murderer and pulled the wall on him – crushing the body to disguise the face? I suppose that might be possible, though he wouldn't have much time. The others were still waiting in the cart.'

I'd thought of that. 'They were all his servants, weren't they, in some capacity? They wouldn't dare to come till they were called, or at least till they were seriously alarmed.'

'But why do it anyway? Why not go back to them and say he'd been attacked?'

I shook my head. 'Some of these local feuds go back a long, long way,' I said. 'I think the hit-man was from Venta, and Plautus knew he was. I suspect he came back here to seek revenge. It's probable Claudinus was murdered before he sailed. Perhaps he really got away to Gaul and has not yet reached the Emperor with his news. More likely he is dead. His arm-guard was seen in Venta on a market stall. If so, that threat has been removed. But if Plautus knew his secret, or the rebels even thought he did, he would be hunted down. Nobody could rest till he was dead.'

Junio nodded with such vigour that he nearly spilt the wine. 'But if he staged his death . . .'

'Exactly. And if he knew where to find the evidence Claudinus found and could get it safely to the Emperor – in one of his oil boats perhaps – then later he could safely reappear, and expect rewards and honours from the Emperor, while all his enemies expired in jail. In his place I might have done the same.'

'And what has Lyra got to do with it?'

'I think she's got everything to do with it. I think the lady plays a double game and, what's more, I think that Plautus knows. That may have been the secret that Claudinus knew – and why he didn't report it to the garrison here. I knew long ago that she had links with both factions in the town, but at the time I didn't see the half of it. She hires premises on this side of town, respectable, prosperous and well disposed to Rome; but her legal patron is a butcher from the bath-house end, where the sympathies are on the rebel side. In fact, she owns his building, I have since found out – which suggests that he is in her pay, rather than the other way about.'

Junio was nodding, to show he understood.

'This butcher goes into the countryside once or twice each moon. Nobody thinks anything of that. But suppose he is a channel to the rebel hide-outs there? I've learned tonight that he was in the forest yesterday. There are few farms out there.'

'You think he's in communication with the rebels, then? He takes them food, perhaps?'

'And information too – about the movements of supply-trains and when small parties of Roman troops and horses are likely to be moving on the roads. And where does the information come from? Some from the soldiers who visit the wolf-house every day. But most of all, from the optio himself, whispering sweet nothings into Lyra's ear. She even persuaded him to bring her here, so she knows everything that goes on in the mansio, and where the messengers are going and why. And the poor fool supposes that she comes for love of him.'

Junio gave a low whistle. 'It's a clever system – he has to keep it secret on his own account.'

'She's a clever girl. Quick-thinking and intelligent. She's proved that all along. It won't be easy to persuade her to betray herself, but that's what I'll have to do. I've not a shred of evidence for this – Marcus won't move on hypothesis alone. The optio will release her if he can, but once she knows that I suspect her she will raise the alarm, and then the gang will melt away and none of them will ever be caught.'

'And Plautus?'

'He may be in mortal danger as we speak. I think he's sought asylum with the Silurian chief who owns the land where Lyra's brothel is. Of course, once she knows that he is there she will be on his trail. That butcher friend of hers is in the area, I know – and as the optio said, who'd notice a few more bloodstains on his clothes? Let's hope we're not too late. But here she comes. And not very happy, by the look of it.'

She was more than unhappy, she was furious. Gone was the elaborate and exotic face-paint which she'd flaunted earlier. Her face was streaked and swollen, as if there had been tears, and her hair and clothes suggested that she'd been struggling very hard. And shouting, possibly, because someone had forced a rag into her mouth to gag her, and she was being marched along with her two hands bound in front of her. The burly soldier on one side of her tugged at that rope-end, while the other held the noose round her neck.

Even then, she was protesting, lashing at them with her elbows when she could. Despite myself I felt a kind of admiration for her spirit. She saw us in the shadows and her manner changed at once. She drew herself upright, as much as her plight permitted her to do, and she walked with her head held in the air. She looked deliberately towards me and met my eyes.

The soldier with the noose released the rope, strode over and knocked twice on the optio's door. It opened instantly. She looked at me again, and as she was led past us into the lighted room, I swear she actually contrived to sway her hips.

I gave a sign to Junio and we walked in after her.

Chapter Twenty-six

Marcus was sitting formally behind the desk – not reclining, but sitting upright on a folding chair – a sure sign that he was in official mode. He glanced at Junio and me as we came in, but his attention was on Lyra most of all.

'Untie her, guards,' he ordered, and as I took my place beside him on a stool the soldiers set her free. But Lyra was no model prisoner. No sooner was the gag removed than she began to storm and rage.

'What is the meaning of this outrage, gentlemen? I came here freely, under no duress, exactly as I was requested to. Others who were also asked to come were questioned for a little while and then released. Why have I been tied up and dragged here like a dog?'

Marcus looked enquiringly at her escort. 'It's a surprise to me. I understood she had the freedom of the mansio, more or less.'

'I don't know anything about that,' the larger soldier said. 'I've never set eyes on her before – not in the mansio anyway.' He was a stolid sort of man, and not even the optio's glowerings made him flinch. 'I just follow orders. I was told to fetch her and that's what I did. I found her in the guardhouse where she'd been put to wait. Asked her politely first. She didn't want to come. Offered me money to get her smuggled out through the gate, or take a note to someone else who would, but I wasn't having that. So it was tears and sobbing for a while. No use. That really set her off. Struggled and fought and carried on.' He exhibited a bite mark on his arm. 'I sent for reinforcements in the end, and even then we had to tie her up. But here she is, as ordered.' He snapped to a salute.

I looked at Lyra, wondering why she had attempted to escape. Perhaps she had never intended to stay for questioning – simply to poison me and get away. Certainly it wasn't fear that prompted her. Her eyes were flashing and her face was furious and defiant even now – if I were in her place, I thought, I should not be so brave.

She tossed her head and looked around the room. 'Who is the commanding officer? You?' She lighted on the optio. 'Then it is to you that I must presumably complain. This is preposterous. I fought because your soldier here assaulted me – because I am a prostitute, perhaps, he thinks that he can treat me as he likes. But I am here at this gentleman's request' – she indicated me – 'and as his guest I expect to be treated with respect. As officer-in-charge you are responsible. I shall write to military headquarters and complain. And don't suppose I can't defend myself in law. I have a patron and an advocate.'

The optio said, 'Lyra!' but it did no good.

'That is indeed my name, as you are obviously aware. Perhaps you would be good enough to give me yours – so I know who is to blame for this affair.'

'Lyra,' the optio said again. 'It is no use to talk like that. I've told them everything.'

Her expression flickered, but she held her ground. 'I can't imagine what there is to tell. I came here to answer questions about my premises, and I am ready to do that at any time.

Come and examine the establishment yourselves; there's nothing to hide. I have a proper licence and my girls are clean. If we charge a little more than other brothels in the town, it's because we offer better services.'

It was almost convincing, even now.

The optio said gently, 'I've told them about us. That you come here to visit me, and that I instruct the guard to let you in and out. It's no good pretending that you don't know who I am.'

A pause, and then she allowed her face to fall into dismay. 'In that case I am sorry for the embarrassment. And I withdraw everything I said about this soldier here. If he heard that I was working in the place, his behaviour is entirely understandable. Obviously he thought I was for hire.' She flashed the guard in question another of her smiles, and he was sufficiently bemused to look relieved. 'I'll see he gets a special rate, next time he comes to see my girls.' She turned reproachful eyes towards the optio. 'I thought I was protecting your career, and now it seems you have got me into trouble with your authorities.'

'Lyra,' the optio said plaintively, 'that doesn't matter now. They'll discipline me, probably, but that's not why they're here. They want to question you about your property. Just tell them what they want to know, and they will let you go.'

'Very well.' She turned to Marcus. 'I hire a building from a landlord, and run it as a licensed brothel. He knows the use I put it to, and doesn't care. He's only interested in the rent. Is that in contravention of the law?'

Marcus and the optio looked at me. After all, this interview was my idea. 'But you own a property yourself?' I said. 'Over on the bath-house side of town. Close to where I spoke to you the other day.'

That startled her, but she recovered well. She smiled. 'It isn't suitable for what I want,' she said. 'Our customers don't like that area. But I still have relatives who live nearby, and I often visit them.'

'Including the butcher who's your patron? I hear you own his shop.'

'He's a sort of relative,' she said. 'I don't want to use the place myself, but he has children and is glad of it. I charge him very little rent, and in return he looks after me – speaks up for me in court, gets rid of undesirable customers, and all that sort of thing.'

'And does he visit Nyros, who's your landlord, too? Is that what he was doing on the forest road?'

She stiffened. 'I don't know what you mean. I can't help who my relations are. Optimus, why are you letting him talk to me like this? You know what my brother's like. I can't ask him questions about where he goes and why. I suppose he goes there to deliver meat.'

So the butcher was her brother! I had rattled her this time. She clearly hadn't meant to tell us that. I could see that Optimus was about to intervene, and I quickly slipped another question in. 'Does he deliver information, too, perhaps? About the fact that Gaius Plautus is with Nyros now, for instance? I'm sure the rebels in the forest would be glad to know.'

She had turned deathly pale. 'Optimus! Protect me! I don't know what he means. What is he alleging that I've done?'

He had half risen to his feet in his concern for her. 'There's nothing to be afraid of. This is not to do with you. It's about some man from Glevum who has disappeared. They were looking through the tax records in case they found his name,

274

and they discovered that Nyros owned your property, that's all.' He glared at me. 'Though I don't know exactly what he hopes to gain by this. Are all these questions really necessary? I'm sure Lyra has told us everything she knows.'

It was the other way round, I thought. He had told her everything he knew. And now she would be truly on her guard. I was proving nothing and if I was not careful Marcus would decide to call a halt. It was time to try my other strategy.

'You're right,' I said, more gently. 'The lady is distressed. She has had a shock this evening. Junio, fetch a stool for her and let her have a little of that wine.'

Her head went up suspiciously. 'Wine? What wine?'

'A little of the wine you had before,' I said. 'You were feeling quite ill until you had a sip, and though you were a little faint at first, you were entirely recovered shortly afterwards. Luckily, when you dropped the cup, it lodged against the wall so not all of it was spilt. Do have a little more.'

Junio had seen what I was up to, and he brought the cup and offered it to Lyra with a smile.

'I don't require any wine,' she said. She was breathing heavily and refused to take the goblet from his hand.

'Do have some, Lyra,' the optio urged. 'It will do you good. It is the very wine you particularly like. I sent it for the citizen myself.'

She looked desperately from me to him. 'This is some kind of trap.'

'Trap?' I repeated. 'How can it be a trap? Unless you know something about the wine that we do not. Soldier,' I added, to the larger guard, who was still standing to attention by the door. 'Assist the lady to refresh herself.'

The optio was standing up by now, and would have moved to interrupt, but Marcus put out a restraining hand. 'I am interested in this,' he said. 'I wonder why she's so reluctant to comply?' He nodded to the soldier. 'Do as the citizen suggests.'

The soldier took the wine from Junio. He seized Lyra, imprisoning her arms, and forced the cup against her lips. She twisted violently and turned her head away. The man did not release his grip, but turned towards me enquiringly.

'Very well,' I said to her. 'We'll have some answers now. If I am not satisfied with what you say, I'll give the word, and you can drink the poison that you meant for me.'

The optio sat down heavily. 'Poison?' he repeated stupidly. 'What is this? Lyra? What does it mean?'

'It means that she has played you for a fool,' I said. 'She flatters you with blandishments and all the time she is betraying your secrets to the rebel groups marauding in the woods. She gets the information to the butcher – who she admits now is her brother, not some distant relative – and he passes the messages to them when he goes out with his cart. And disposes of grisly evidence, I suspect – you told me yourself how easy it would be and how a butcher's clothes are always splashed with blood. And did you not say to me that attacks on goods and soldiers had increased again recently, as if the rebels were in touch with your every move?'

The optio had turned the colour of bad milk. 'It isn't true. Lyra, tell me that it isn't true.'

'You can prove nothing,' she said defiantly. I signalled to the guard. He forced the cup towards her face again. 'All right!' she cried suddenly. 'It's true! What difference does it make? You'll kill me anyway.' She looked at the optio and sneered. 'What makes you suppose I'd care anything for you?

276

Your vanity, perhaps! Pompous little self-important idiot. Well, I tricked you, and I'm glad I did. I hope they send you to the Wall and keep you there for life – or better still, condemn you to the mines. With any luck they will, when they find out what you've done. All those details about troops and funds, and what a trial it was to deal with messengers.' She was mocking now. ' "Poor dear Optimus," I'd murmur – and I'd stroke your hair, and off you'd go again. Well, you can spend what time remains to you reflecting on the damage you have done, and how many men and horses you've betrayed to us.'

The optio was hardly listening any more. His mouth was working, but no sound was coming out, and he was staring fixedly at her in disbelief.

She twisted her head savagely to look at me. 'Well, it's over now. This is your doing, pavement-maker. They warned me you were trouble – that's why you had to die. I thought I'd managed it, but you refused the wine. It would have done the trick – even a mouthful is enough to kill, and that would have stopped your meddling once and for all. And as for you,' she turned on Marcus now, 'you are the worst of all. A proper Roman, purple stripes and all.' She spat deliberately at him. 'Pig! I wish I'd let them kill you yesterday at the farm.'

Marcus had turned pale with rage, and his voice was dangerously controlled. 'Be very careful what you say. I could have you tortured for a week, after what you've admitted here tonight, till you were begging them to let you die.'

She looked at him, exultant. 'I know you could. But you won't get the chance. And don't think you'll round up my family, either, when I'm gone. My brother's boys are watching at the gate. They always do. They know I'm here for questioning. They're all prepared. When I don't get home again tonight, they'll know that something dreadful's happened here and disappear into the forest and the caves. The lot of them. There are still scores of us, you know. And we have hideaways that no one's found – not since the legions occupied the place. But I've said too much. You'll get no more from me. I'm a daughter of Caractacus – I'm not afraid to die. I only wish that I could take you with me as I go.' She seized the goblet in her own two hands and drained it at a gulp.

Chapter Twenty-seven

Nothing happened. It wasn't likely to, since there was nothing in the goblet except wine – though no one knew that except Junio and me. There was a dreadful stillness in the room. Lyra waited, wild-eyed and tense, for the poison to stream into her veins. And still nothing happened.

It must be difficult to find that your heroic gesture of self-sacrifice has failed. Lyra thought so, certainly. She paled and shook, and for a moment I thought she would collapse. For the first time since she had come into the room, she looked wholly at a loss.

At last she raised her eyes to look at me and they were full of hatred and contempt. 'You tricked me,' she whispered hoarsely. 'But it won't do you any good. My nephews will already be raising the alarm. They'll all be gone before you get to them. And whatever happens, you can't force information out of me. I can't tell you anything. I don't know where the hide-outs are myself.'

'You've already told me something,' I said evenly. 'Your actions show you tried to kill me. Why?'

'Surely that must be obvious! Because you knew what she was up to!' Marcus was surprised.

'But I didn't know it when she came here, and she came prepared. There is only one reason for it that I can understand – because I saw her following Gaius Plautus in the street. See – she tries to hide it, but she looks uncomfortable at the very mention of his name. I knew who he was and I'm sure that is the key. And if she wants to silence me, then the chances are that he is still alive, and it is not too late for us to rescue him.'

I was proud of my deduction, and I looked at her, waiting for her reaction to my words.

It came. Defiant words. 'I told you, citizen, I don't know anyone called Gaius Plautus. The only Gaius Plautus I ever met was an auxiliary bowman from Jerusalem who used to visit the wolf-house years ago – and he was killed in border skirmishes.'

And then, at last, I saw. Saw with such clarity that I leaned forward on the desk and buried my face in both my hands. I think I may possibly have moaned.

'What is it, Libertus?' Marcus was all concern.

I raised my head and looked at him. 'Excellence, I am an idiot,' I said. 'I had the answer to this puzzle long ago.'

He was still looking startled.

'Patron,' I said. 'You know me very well. Better than almost anyone, in fact, apart from Gwellia and Junio. Agreed?' He nodded. 'In that case, remind me, what's my name?'

He goggled at me in disbelief. 'Longinus Flavius Libertus, I believe.'

'Exactly so. And is that the name my mother gave to me?'

He frowned. 'Well, I don't imagine so. But it's become your name. Even your wife and servants call you that.'

'Precisely. It became my name when I became a citizen of Rome. I adopted it, to mark my change of role. Just as Gaius Plautus of Jerusalem did – though, being an auxiliary, he could not be a proper citizen till he retired. And Gaius of Glevum did the same, of course. People all over the Empire do. It is different for you and Junio. You got your Roman names when you were born.'

Marcus was looking at me with interest. 'So?'

'You remember when we were looking in the tax-rolls for Gaius Plautus and I pointed out that his family might not be Flaminians themselves?' I shook my head. 'Of course they're not. Plautus is a Roman citizen, but he was Silurian by birth. He isn't hiding from the rebels, he is one of them. He's been doing the same thing that Lyra did, but in a different way. He mixed with all the most important men, and knew of all the most important deals. If anything of value came to Glevum, he would know of it – and see that his kinsmen knew as well so they knew when to plan their raids. He bought his way to Roman status and he did it on purpose to work against the Empire from within. Even the name – it wouldn't surprise me if he chose it as a kind of joke because he killed the auxiliary from Jerusalem himself. The soldier used the wolf-house, so doubtless Lyra betrayed him as well.'

It was fortunate that Lyra was heavily restrained, otherwise she would have flown at me. 'You can't prove anything!' She almost spat the words.

Marcus ignored her. 'So where is Plautus now?'

'Exactly where I thought he was, at Nyros's farmstead.'

'But I thought Nyros sympathised with Rome.'

'So did I. It was Lyra who showed me I was wrong. She called herself a daughter of Caractacus – and you know the story there. The Romans were so impressed with his dignity and bearing in defeat that they didn't kill him after all – they simply stripped him of everything he had. Exactly the story Nyros told us of his ancestor.'

Marcus was struggling to come to terms with this. 'Plautus boasted of the wealthy uncle who'd adopted him, and given him a proper start in life. It was Nyros? When he came here, he was coming home?'

'It looks that way. Nyros told us himself that his nephew was at home. The famous Thullero – the man we never saw. Nyros is impressive. He's a clever man. He even staged that imitation raid, to help persuade us of his innocence and give Thullero the opportunity to hide. It meant we didn't see the horses either – which was clever too, since he'd almost certainly stolen them from the Iscan cavalry. Regulus, for instance, would have known them instantly.'

'So when Regulus saw Plautus with the pigs . . . ?'

'He was on his own domain. Plautus was the "young master" that Subulcus talked about. Admittedly, Plautus is hardly in the flush of youth, but he is Nyros's heir, of course, and young by comparison with him. He must have gone from Venta in a cart – it's the only way he could have got there in the time – and arrived to find the raid on Regulus's force was taking place. It was obviously planned that they should all be killed and one of the rebels sent here in their stead, wearing the dead messenger's livery, and with the sealed letter telling us the mounted escort was on its way. You can imagine who the escort would have been, if they had captured all those uniforms.'

I looked at Lyra but she wouldn't look at me. Marcus said, 'Of course! But Regulus and his comrades were too good for them. They lost their horses but they won the fight, and forced the rebels off.'

'Worse than that, they started following the tracks which might have led them directly to the farm. Plautus – or Thullero as we should call him now – met up with his comrades and devised a plan. He got the man dressed as a messenger to get rid of Subulcus. That was a necessary start, because poor Subulcus was too stupidly honest to do anything but tell the truth and give the game away.'

'But wasn't that a risk?' the optio said. 'If it was someone from the tribe? Subulcus might have recognised him.'

I shook my head. 'The pigman is a simple soul. They knew he wouldn't question a Roman uniform. The helmet and cheek-pieces would largely hide the face and no doubt the man on horseback changed his voice, as well. And of course, it worked. Once Subulcus was safely gone, the others planned to drive the pigs into the woods to interrupt the hoof-tracks, and Plautus – who wasn't wearing plaid like the other tribespeople – would waylay the Romans if he could, claiming that he'd been the victim of a raid. Unfortunately the swineherd came back again too soon, to see the men on horses driving his pigs into the wood and riding off with one – the story that he told us later on. Plautus, the "young master" had to send him off again, so that he could be there himself to deal with the tracking party. If he'd been hiding in the butcher's cart – as I suspect – he would smell like a pigman anyway. No wonder they offered him my tunic! Of course he didn't want it, so he passed it on to Subulcus when he returned.'

'Why hide in the butcher's cart? It sounds an awful way to travel.'

'He had to get out to the farm, and quickly too. I'd seen him in the town, and the cart enabled him to leave the city after dark without being noticed at the gates. The butcher picks the wagon up at dusk, but he obviously brings it into town first to pile it up with skins and carcasses – he's not allowed to do that during daylight hours. It's the obvious way to get out past the guards – no one was going to search that vehicle. In fact, I rather think I might have seen the cart myself – probably as Plautus first met up with it. It was blocking my way as I tried to get back to the inn, after I'd left the thermopolium. I heard footsteps behind me, which then mysteriously disappeared – presumably when Plautus got into the cart. The butcher saw me, but he had no idea then who I was. Otherwise I might not have lived to tell the tale.'

'The thermopolium where the man was killed? You think one of them did that?'

'I'm convinced of it. Probably Plautus – Thullero – himself, since he was on my heels – but if not him, another of the gang. When Lyra's little spy went back that night and told them where I was, they came out looking to get rid of me. They missed me – not by very long – but by that time Lupus was a danger too. I might have told him what I'd seen – and that was dangerous. I imagine they were on the look-out for me all night after that – but they could hardly jump on me when I was on the Roman side of town, especially when I had companions, as I did. When I got arrested, the family must have been appalled. I was safe from their clutches absolutely, then. So they did the next best thing – tried to get me executed or exiled for the crime, using the best advocate in town – the one the optio had introduced them to. Of course Lyra couldn't turn up at the court herself, but she sent her girls along. Lupus's widow must have been delighted with her luck – probably saw it as an answer to her prayers. Of course if you find that treasure chest somewhere, either at the butcher's shop or at the farm, you will have proof of this.'

'And you would make a formal accusation in the court?' Marcus asked.

'If necessary,' I said. 'And if I don't I know somebody who would. Lucidus would only be too pleased to bring a charge against his enemies – and since Laxus was called in to testify for me, he already has an interest in the case.'

Marcus was getting to his feet. 'Then I think we should go and round these rebels up. You'll have night riders, won't you, optio? Get them to Nyros's farm and the butcher's shop. We'll take them by surprise. And when we've got them, I'm sure we'll find some method of making them confess. In the meantime, lock this woman up and lose the key.'

'I still cannot believe this, Lyra,' Optimus was saying, rather desperately. 'Is it true? Your whole family has been conspiring against us all this time?'

'Why should I tell you anything?' she said. The guard was holding her, but she was fighting still. 'Go on then. Do your worst. Go out and arrest them, if you can. I told you, by the time your soldiers reach them, it will be too late. You can get rid of me, but they will live to fight another day.'

'She's right,' I said. 'For one thing, we don't know who they are. The butcher is obviously not the only one. We know that when he's out of town, he leaves his brother managing his shop. So that's Lyra's brother too, of course.' I stopped. 'In fact, I have just realised who it is. I knew I recognised the man when he was here. He keeps the armour stall. The one where Claudinus's arm-guard was displayed.'

'You're going to tell me they killed Claudinus as well?'

'Who did we bury at the funeral? Obviously not anyone sent to murder Plautus, as I thought earlier. It must have been Claudinus,' I said wearily. 'I don't know why I didn't realise before. I have been looking for an extra man, and it made me overlook the obvious. He went to Glevum with a secret, dangerous to the rebels, and was never seen again. Of course it was his corpse beneath the stones – he was about the same age and height as Plautus, he had Silurian red hair, and once the face was crushed, it was not difficult to change the clothes. He was a citizen. He did not have work-hardened hands or sunburned legs. A toga would sit easily on him.'

'So Plautus somehow lured him to the villa after dark?'

I shook my head. 'I think he was dead already and was taken in a box – it was supposed to contain imported pottery and it needed three men to carry it. I'd like to know what happened to that box, and whether any pottery was ever on the ship at all. I dare say those things could be checked.'

'A ship?' Marcus was perplexed.

'You remember that Claudinus hoped to get to Gaul and bribed his way aboard an olive-oil boat? Well, that was Plautus's, of course. He made his fortune out of olive oil – that was another link we should have seen. Nyros owned a block of buildings where the wolf-house is – in the street of the oil-lamp sellers. Plautus presumably provided all the fuel. Claudinus obviously didn't make the connection. He knew the wolf-house was a centre for intelligence, but he thought Plautus – a Roman citizen – was an ally and he went to him for help. Probably the rebels helped to lure him there – he talked of finding one more link to prove his case. Once he was on the ship, of course, there were no other witnesses except the ship-master, who was one of Plautus's men. It would be fairly easy there to cut his throat or slip him poisoned wine and stuff him in the box. Plautus had to take the arm-guard off, of course.'

'Rather dangerous to bring it back here where it might be recognised,' Marcus observed.

'What else was he to do with it? He couldn't leave it there. And if it ever was discovered on the Venta stall, it would be taken – as it was, in fact – as evidence that Claudinus was dead, and murdered by the rebels. They couldn't send body-bits back to Lucidus, this time, as they might otherwise have done. The corpse was needed for the funeral.'

'So that's another murder we could charge them with. And of a very wealthy man. Probably enough to sentence them to death, even if we never find their hideaway and prove they were responsible for the raids, and all the deaths and robberies which they entailed. I presume it was Plautus who dressed up as a messenger and sent our men on fruitless marches in defence of us – leaving the carts unguarded and open to attack?'

'Not Plautus himself on that occasion, I don't think – he knew we might be there, but certainly he'd hope to do it, if they used the plot elsewhere. He spoke perfect Latin and could write it too, which might be needed for a messenger. Interesting that they only killed the Romans, by and large, and left the slaves alone – part of the vendetta, I suppose.'

'They killed my poor Promptillius,' Marcus said. 'Why make an exception out of him?'

'That was Lyra's doing. The sentry recognised her writing block – he told the optio so. And Promptillius posed a different sort of danger to the group. If I had disappeared that night – been killed as they intended that I should – even Promptillius would have come back in the end, and raised a search for me. Lyra pre-empted that. She sent her nephew with a message, so Promptillius came back for my clothes – which meant that no one at the mansio would look for me. When he turned up at the address she gave, they murdered him and took him to the place where he was found. No doubt he travelled on the butcher's cart as well. Is that right, Lyra?'

Lyra looked maliciously at me. 'Prove it!' she challenged.

'I think I almost could. Whoever sent that message knew

where Marcus was, and that he'd been invited to stay overnight. Who knew that, outside the mansio, except the man himself? It was a late invitation. Only you, Lyra, because the optio sent a messenger to tell you so – and let you know the coast was clear to come. And who knew I was out shopping near the forum with a slave? Only you again. Not even Marcus knew.'

She twisted in the soldier's arms and tried to spit at me. 'I'm admitting nothing, do you hear!'

Her courage was amazing. She must know what lay in wait for her. Marcus had the clearest notions where his duties lay where state security was concerned, and nothing I could say would change his mind. There was no way she could avoid the torturers after this.

I pulled myself up short. Of course there was. I should have guessed that clever Lyra would have something up her sleeve.

'Search her, guards!' I ordered, and though she wriggled like a demon, they did as I had said.

They were only just in time. In the split second that they hesitated, waiting for Marcus to nod and authorise the search, she had wrested one hand free, lifted her skirt, found the little bottle and raised it to her lips.

It had not been literally up her sleeve, of course. It was hanging on an inner belt round her waist, suspended by a little loop of cord – a small round-necked phial, made of coloured glass, exactly like the pieces I had seen. She had already pulled the cork out with her teeth and if the soldiers had not forced her hands away she would have drunk the poison at a draught. She wriggled like a demon, fought and bit, but they prised her fingers from the glass and took the phial away.

Almost at once, her whole demeanour changed. She was a prisoner of the Romans now, with no means of merciful escape. The fight went out of her and she stopped struggling at once, though she still glowered resentfully at me.

'How did you know I had another phial?'

'I guessed you must have something of the kind. You came in here to poison me, and it was always possible that you'd be caught. Even the optio's servant knew you were in my room. You might have bluffed your way out of it – I can think of several things you might have tried – but if you failed it was important you should have a quick way out, so that you could not be made to talk.'

I could see the sweat-beads forming in her hair. She was terrified, and with good reason too. 'Are you going to torture me?' she said, and her voice was not as steady as it had been before. 'It won't do you any good. I've told you, I know nothing. And if I don't reappear they'll melt into the hills – and then you'll never find them. That's what will happen if you don't let me go.'

'We'll pick up those nephews of yours outside the gates. They're young; it won't be difficult to make them talk.'

'If you can catch them,' she replied. 'They know drains and culverts that you don't know exist. And somebody would see you if you did. We have networks of watchers at a time like this. Our people would be in the caves in hours.'

'We can go down to the bath-house end of town,' Marcus said grimly, 'turn out every building and set fire to it, if that's what we have to do. We'll flush your friends out somehow.'

'But as the pavement-maker says, you don't know who they are. You don't even know how many. So how can you round them up?' She was white and shaken but she still had Celtic pluck. 'And it's no good attempting to force it out of

289

me – I'll only tell you lies to make you stop. I don't know who the others are, so I can't tell you. They deliberately manage things that way.'

'We can pick up the butcher, anyway. And the armourer. And Nyros too, if we act tonight.'

'Not necessarily,' I said. 'They're poised for flight. The first sight of soldiers and they'll disappear. They have sympathisers through the area – women; children too. We can't put the whole population to the sword – we'd have riots on our hands, and hundreds more would join the rebels in support. Besides, we might pick up a messenger or two but the real raiders would still be out in the caves. Better if we catch them unawares. I have a better plan. Lyra will write a letter to her brothers, telling them there's been a change of plan. Her liaison with the optio is about to revealed, and rather than face demotion and disgrace, he is offering to elope with her. He would be a valuable captive: he has a lot of useful information and could be ransomed too, so instead of leaving him she will deliver him into rebel hands tomorrow with as many goods and horses as she can contrive. He plans to go to Isca where they can cross the frontier and escape, but she will ensure that on the way they call in at the roundhouse, where Nyros and his men can deal with him.'

'And what is the use of—' the optio began, but Lyra was too quick for him.

'I refuse to write anything of the kind!'

'My dear lady, it doesn't matter if you write the note or not. On a rough wax tablet it is impossible to say who scratched the words. The thing is, it will appear to come from you. Your two nephews will be satisfied, and – when you go out to the forest at first light – I think we can be sure your party will not be set upon by ambushes. Though I'm sure that they'll be watching for you on the road – so we had better make sure that you are there.' I turned to Marcus. 'You'll have to set off with your escort, too, as though everything was just as usual, though you won't go further than the marching-camp. Meantime, Regulus, with all the fast men and horses, he can get, will gallop round the back route to the farm, come in across the fields and break in upon the party from the rear. That way, with any luck, we'll catch them in the act. He'll still have to broach the defensive palisades and take the place by force, but with sufficient numbers they should manage that, and most of the rebels' attention will be occupied elsewhere. If this succeeds we can arrest them all – and have the evidence against them too. We'll have to send a warning to the marching-camp tonight – after Lyra's little messengers have gone.'

'They won't go anywhere. They know better than to trust a Roman trick. They won't believe that such a letter is from me. Not even if it's handed to them by the sentry they know. They would have to see me with their own eyes, and have my signal that it was all right. And I refuse to do it.'

'You won't say that when you have a dagger in your ribs.' Marcus had said little up to now, but I realised now that he was going to implement my plan.

'Oh, you could force me out at sword-point, but what's the use of that? Or having one of your great guardsmen pretending to be me? That will hardly convince the boys that the note is genuine. And I won't go to Nyros either, and betray my friends.'

'As to travelling tomorrow, madam, you may have no choice,' I said. 'But if you will not go out to the gate and persuade your nephews to accept the note, there is another lady in the mansio who will.'

Chapter Twenty-eight

It was a desperate expedient, but we were working against time, and the plan worked better than I feared it might. Lyra, realising at last that she was under real duress, was forced to scratch the letter in the wax herself, and if the letters occasionally wavered – the result of a warning knifepoint at her back – it was no more than could have been expected from a scribbled note.

I was wary of attempts to send coded messages, so I insisted on dictating exactly what she wrote. I kept it simple, and she wrote it slowly, but clearly and with no mistakes. She was more literate than I would have guessed, and I remembered what Nyros had said about educating his whole family. When she had finished, I sealed the tablet up, and took it in to Gwellia, who had been most unkindly roused from sleep to help.

She did it splendidly. I would never have believed that my respectable wife could have echoed that swaying walk with such success. Gwellia was almost forty and her hair was turning grey, but under Lyra's hooded cloak it was impossible to tell, and as she flaunted her way to the gate even the optio was gazing goggle-eyed.

She didn't hurry, that was the clever thing. She stood and whispered to the sentry on duty – who had already been forewarned of what to do – then drew his attention to something imaginary in the tall trees opposite, and he brought his beacon out to have a look. While he was gazing heavenwards, she beckoned with her hand. From where I was watching in the shadowed court, I saw two figures flit across the street. Paulinus and Rufinus, I'd stake my life on it.

She put a finger to her lips, put down the tablet by the wall, and walked back to the gatehouse once again, still remembering to sway her hips and toss her head. She'd kept her distance, it was dark and she was hidden by the cloak, but I was still afraid they might have seen her face. It didn't seem so, though.

It was some minutes before the children made a move, but then – when the sentry's attention was elsewhere – the smaller figure came and seized the tablet-case. It was so quick, scarcely a flicker in the shadows and he was gone again, but the message was safely on its way. Now all we could do was wait till morning, and hope that the ruse had worked.

Lyra had been dragged off to the cells by now, without her cloak and abbreviated gold-trimmed shift and only my travel-stained old tunic to cover her somewhat raddled charms. She had gone from furious struggling to dumb obedience, and I wondered if she had some counter-plan in mind, but she went with little ado, and we heard no more at all from her that night. Marcus sent a messenger to warn the marching-camp to be prepared to give us full support – and then we, too, retired for the night. The extra palliasse had been brought into my room and put down on the floor, but we were all three so weary that we could have slept on the bare flags and never stirred.

All the same we were roused before the sun. The optio,

who had been so stunned the night before that he had said and done almost nothing, was now anxious to atone. He had personally risen to make sure that suitable horses were available, a gig and a cart prepared, and that a spendid breakfast was prepared for us – fresh bread, lentil porridge, watered wine and cheese – though he hardly managed to force down a crumb himself.

The idea that he had managed to betray his men, and caused such loss and devastation to the state, was obviously weighing hard on him, and Lyra's personal repudiation had hurt his self-esteem as much as his heart. When they brought her from the cells a little later he could hardly bring himself to look at her.

I had expected her to struggle, and at first she did, although they'd bound her hand and foot beneath her cloak. But when they threatened to throw her bodily into the cart, she stopped resisting, and submitted to being lifted up into the gig and propped beside the optio, who was driving, in the front. I sat alongside Junio in the back, both of us dressed in servant's tunics, while the optio's real servant followed in the cart, with a hastily assembled pile of his personal effects. Marcus had been anxious to come with us at first, but it was self-evidently a tight squeeze as it was, and the presence of that broad-striped toga in our midst would have attracted the attention of the merest passer-by, let alone a watching rebel band. Unless he would consent to our disguise?

That persuaded him, as I was sure it would, and he agreed to go as I'd suggested to the marching-camp, and ride out with the second group from there. The commandant had sent a message back, putting his entire force at our command. A swift group of cavalry to make the first attack, and the rest of his contingent in two groups – one to follow up the rear assault, the rest – quite openly – as protection for Marcus and his vehicles on the public road.

Marcus's carriage and carts were brought round to the front, and, surrounded by his own escort and a handful of bewildered soldiers from the mansio, they set off as before. We watched them jolt out of the court and through the gate in the first light of dawn. It all looked convincingly normal, and with the leather curtains of the carriage closed I hoped that my absence would never be noticed. When they had gone, the place seemed very still.

We let them get perhaps half an hour ahead, and when we dared not leave it any longer we went out ourselves. The gig was light and fast, and without the company of marching men we made much swifter time. I was afraid that we would overtake them on the road, and arrive at the roundhouse far too long before our horsemen did, but there was no sign of anyone and I breathed again.

It was a jolting journey. I had to hold on with my hands to save my bottom from a battering. Lyra could do nothing to protect herself, and several times I heard her squeal aloud. The roads were drier now and our wheels and horses raised a cloud of dust, till I'm sure the servant in the cart behind could hardly see the country as we passed. I realised again how vulnerable a traveller could be, in these empty wastes, and hoped that our rebels were the only thieves and raiders on the road.

We slowed when we reached the shelter of the trees. It was a necessary act – the road was rutted here and slippery with leaves – but it also bought us time. The optio would have sold himself into slavery now, if he thought that it would help, and he was doing his very best for us. I recognised the clearing where we'd stopped before, and shortly afterwards the track that led to Nyro's homestead and the farm. I saw the optio take his dagger in one hand, and hold it fiercely against Lyra's side. 'One trick from you, and you will find this between your ribs,' I heard him say.

It was no more than a forest lane, and we swayed along it like a ship at sea, bumping over branches, roots and stones. At each jolt I saw Lyra flinch against the knife, but she dared not draw away. We had slowed to the merest crawl by now, and in the silence of the trees I felt my heartbeat thud. I missed the reassurance of armed soldiers at our side. We passed the sacred oak – this time, somehow, I couldn't look at it – and went on up the winding lane until we turned the corner and saw the palisades of Nyros's farm.

They were waiting for us. All of them. Nyros, with Plautus at his side, and a score of men I'd never seen before – all with the same crop of sandy hair, and most dressed in the same plaid that Nyros wore. I saw the tunicked figures of the butcher and his boys among them too – they must have come down in the cart last night. Nyros was opening the gate, and coming towards us with his arms outstretched. Obviously the intention was to lure us in, take possession of our goods, and deal with us at leisure once we were secured.

'Lyra, be welcome to my house,' he cried – in Latin, for the optio's benefit. And then, in Celtic, 'Get him in the great-house. We'll deal with him in there.' The smile of welcome never faltered from his face.

Suddenly Lyra twisted in her seat. 'Be careful, Nyros, it's a tra—' She began to shout the warning, but she never finished it. The optio had already run her through.

There was chaos then, of course. Most of the men were still inside the gates, and all were conspiciously unarmed, which is why I have lived to tell the tale. Some of them rushed back towards the roundhouses and came back with weapons in their hands, others surged forward and tried to get at us.

Nyros was already at the gig and had stretched out a hand to take the horse. The optio flicked the reins and made it rear, which upended Junio and me and we both landed heavily on the ground. Lyra's body also tumbled lifeless from the driver's seat and crashed at Nyros's feet. He started backwards, and at that moment the optio urged the gig forward, into the group of men that had now worked their way through the triple gate and were coming for us down the path. They scattered. At the last instant the optio jumped clear, and ran back towards us, leaving the horse to career on into them. Behind us, the slave had unhitched the other horses, and regardless of the goods piled up on it, was pushing the cart over on its side to act as a kind of barricade across the path. I saw his plan. The path was narrow between thorny thickets here, and the cart would completely block the way.

Junio helped me to my feet and then ran to help him in his task. I panted after him and just reached the other side before the cart went over, depositing the cups and furniture and clothes in a tumbling heap across the track. The optio reached it even as it fell. He was nimble and he vaulted over the wooden chest that clattered at his feet, but it slowed his progress and the men were at his heels. He turned and drew his sword, and picking up a little table in his other hand he stood tall to face them.

They were more interested in him than us, and they wanted him alive if possible. Alive but not necessarily intact. They formed a semicircle round him, where he stood precariously on the pile, and very slowly they advanced on him.

Not for nothing was he a champion with the shield. The table flashed from left to right, parrying the stones they hurled at him, and he kept them at a distance with his sword. But it could not last. The men who had gone for weapons had by now arrived, and they were many, whereas he was one. He fought them bravely, step by step, until he was backed atop the heap against the cart, and even then he tried to vault over and escape, but they were too quick for him and a sword-thrust caught him through the leg. He stumbled, and they stabbed him through the arm. It was all over then. Two of the attackers tore the sword and the makeshift shield from him and began to drag him, bleeding, back up towards the gate.

Then the rest turned their attention towards us. I peeped out from my hiding place and saw Plautus scrabbling the objects from the path, ready to pull the cart away. As I looked at him he looked at me. I saw the recognition dawn.

'Look out!' he cried. 'There may be others on the way! I know that man. He's not a slave at all. There's something else afoot, otherwise he would not be here. You, you, and you – get down towards the road and watch out for reinforcements on the way. The rest of you, get back behind the barricades – we'll take this wretch in and force the truth from him.'

A dozen hands were helping him by now, and swords were slashing at the thorns beside the path. Others had found a way of skirting round, and soon heavy hands were pulling us upright from where we were cowering between the wheels. I found myself yanked along the track towards the largest house, where the optio was already being bundled through the door. For a moment I thought that everything was lost.

And then I heard them. Not from the direction where the lookouts had been sent, but from the farm itself. Shouts, whoops and galloping hooves. I looked up and saw the shapes of swords and helmets on the skyline swooping down on us.

It was all over fairly quickly after that. The rebels were good fighters, but they were not prepared, and scattered men on foot are no match for cavalry. They did try to push us captives into a hut and set fire to us, but a hail of javelins put a stop to that. There was a brief, brave skirmish, and there were several Silurian bodies on the ground before Nyros reluctantly laid down his sword – he had wounded several of his enemies, despite his age – and knelt at the feet of Regulus, who had led the charge. His remaining followers did the same. By the time the lookouts came running back to say that Marcus and his marching troops were on their way, the whole tribe had been rounded up and imprisoned in the largest roundhouse – all the women and the children as well. The scouts quickly found themselves prisoners too.

No attempt was made to question anyone till Marcus arrived, and when he did he took control at once. He had the optio, who was weak with loss of blood, taken to his carriage by his men, and gave orders that his wounds were to be cleaned and dressed. Then he installed himself in Nyros's chair and demanded that the old man be brought to kneel in front of him.

'So!' he thundered. 'We see you now for what you really are. A rebel and a traitor and a thief. You will soon learn the penalty for defying Rome.'

Even now, Nyros behaved with dignity. I could see why his distinguished ancestor had gained the admiration of his captors as he had. 'I am no traitor, Roman. I am a patriot. This land was mine before you ever came, and I defend it

and my people – that is all. I told you that your supporters
had attacked my tribe – look at my nephews there.' He
indicated Subulcus and Plautus, who were tied up, side by
side. 'One slashed across the face so that he almost died, the
other made an idiot for life. And these were children – babies
– at the time. What those men did to the women, I'll not
sully my tongue with, nor how they treated the young men
they captured. My brothers, my father – my wife and mother
too. They burned our houses, killed our cows and left us all
to die. I was not there – I was away from the roundhouse at
the time – but when I returned and found what they had
done I swore I would take revenge. I have done it, and I have
no regrets. My own two infant sons were dead, but I raised
my brothers' children in the same desire, and they have
followed me in every way they can. They demeaned themselves, as common butchers, market stall-keepers, prostitutes
– even consented to be Roman citizens – so we could work
against the oppressors and their ways.'

There was a little silence before Marcus said, 'Well, it's
over now.'

Nyros looked at him. 'I know. We expect no mercy from
our conquerors.'

'You will be given none.'

Nyros was still kneeling at his feet. 'There is one favour,
though, that I would ask of you. You are a fair man, I believe,
and not wholly ignorant of Celtic ways. You have a close
companion of our race. I ask you, then, before you take us
off to meet our fate, to permit us to make a final sacrifice, a
tribute to our great ancestor in whose service and memory
we fought. A ritual feast of sacred venison to venerate the
gods – we prepared some in your honour a day or two ago, so
it will not take long – and with the remnants of the cooking-

fire we'll set light to the huts so that they cannot be desecrated when we've gone. That is the only boon we ask.'

Marcus looked doubtfully at me.

'Why not?' I said. 'It seems not much to ask, and in a little while the soldiers of the rearguard will arrive and they can help us to march our prisoners back to town.'

Marcus nodded briefly. 'Very well.'

'Then, in my way, I bless you,' Nyros said. He rose to his feet and clapped his hands. 'The venison,' he said, in Celtic, to the tribe. He turned to Marcus. 'Some of the women will have to be released to heat and serve it to us.'

Marcus gave the word. 'But not the men,' he said. He saw that I was ready to protest. 'They do not need to free their hands to eat. I do not trust these rebels. I would not be surprised if they still tried some other trick.'

He watched suspiciously as the bowls were brought, and the great pot was carried to the fire. However, all was reverence as the women worked. They stirred the pot in silence till slowly the warm smell of stew came floating through the hut and they poured a little of the liquid on the flames. Nyros muttered an incantation and a prayer. Only then did they take ladles and begin to serve it out. The men first, beginning with the old man himself – lifting the liquid in ladles to their lips, and allowing them to drink. Then the children and the women took their turn.

'Would you care to join us? After all, we prepared the stew for you.' It was only as Nyros turned his head that I remembered the old stories. I saw the touch of foam upon his lips. 'Caractacus!' he cried triumphantly, and I knew what they had done. I saw his eyes film and he slumped sideways to the floor.

It was not a wholly painless passing, even then, but only

Subulcus made any murmur as he died. 'I hope somebody takes care of the pigs,' he whispered, and then he, too, was gone.

They had escaped our justice and preferred their own, and I was glad they had. They were both brave and foolish, but the future was not theirs.

Chapter Twenty-nine

It was several days later – the moon was full again – and we were in Isca, following a feast: Marcus, myself, my wife and Junio. We had gone back to Venta following the raid, of course, to report our success and round up the armourer, and the fuller-dyer too – Lyra had admitted that he too was a relative. I wondered who would clean the togas now.

We had made our long-delayed journey here the day after. No need for elaborate escorts now – just the usual outriders to protect against thieves – and we were given the freedom of the fort. The commander of the garrison was an important man, the head of all the forces in this area, and for days had made an enormous fuss of us – games in our honour, races and parades. Even the myrmillo was in action with his partner once again – and I had to agree with what Big-ears had said to Cupidus. It was patently a fix.

Marcus was guest of honour in all this, naturally, but I had been treated like an emperor as well. Even Gwellia was a beneficiary. Someone had mentioned to the commander that I'd been looking for a silver dress-clasp for my wife, and she had been given the finest one that I had ever seen, together with a bracelet and a fine comb for her hair.

She and I walked back together in the moonlight from the banquet hall. It had been a military affair, but it was our last evening in the fort, so Gwellia had for once accompanied me. She had been entertained most other evenings by the auxiliary commander's lady, who had a pleasant home and kitchen slaves famous for their food. This lady was not, of course, the commander's wife – like the optio he was not permitted one – but his consort from the vicus, the town of camp-followers and craftsmen which had grown up nearby. She was a wealthy woman, of some delicacy and taste, and they had several children. The centurion hoped to marry her when he retired, and make proper Roman citizens of them all.

Gwellia had become fond of her, and of the children in particular, and tonight she was in slightly wistful mood.

'I can't help feeling sorry for the optio,' she said, as we paused in the moonlight to look out at the view through one of the loopholes in the wall. The woods and fields were white and silent, the military road an empty stretch of greyness in the dark. It was hard to imagine any threat. 'If he'd chosen a different woman, or had been posted to a different garrison, he could have had a family just like that.'

I reached out for her hand. 'He was lucky only to be dismissed and sentenced to the mines. He could have been executed for the secrets he betrayed.' I knew what she was really thinking, though. It had been a sadness to me too, that now we were reunited it was too late to have a family of our own.

Her next words proved me right. 'I'd like to send a present for those children, when we get home again,' she said. 'A wooden toy perhaps. Could you devise one? Or a cup and ball, like the one the butcher's children had?'

The memory of the two boys saddened me, though they had drunk their poison defiantly enough. 'Or course we can,' I said. 'We can certainly afford it now. The money I have earned from this will more than compensate for the loss of the commission for that memorial pavement.' For my part in uncovering a conspiracy against the state I could expect a share of Nyros's estate, which would be forfeit to the Emperor and sold. And Plautus's as well, perhaps, if his widow's family could not plead her cause eloquently enough, and prove that the property had already been given to her sons, and was therefore not subject to seizure by the state.

She nodded, and we spoke no more of it until much later when we had retired for the night. We were lying side by side on the finest bed the fort could boast, with soft pillows underneath our heads and fine woven blankets over us, while Junio slept on a mattress at our feet. Many patricians cannot boast such comforts.

I was luxuriating in all this when suddenly I felt a little sob go through my wife. I turned to her, surprised. 'What is it, Gwellia?'

A pause. Then, 'Only that I longed to have a family of our own.'

I leaned up on one elbow and tried to see her face in the light of the small oil light by the bed. 'I understand,' I whispered. 'I wish the same myself.'

She turned her head away from me and said, in a small voice, 'You know, there might have been a child.'

'Of course there might.' I sought to comfort her. 'If you and I had not been torn apart . . .'

She turned her face to me and I could see the tears. 'Better, perhaps, that things are as they are. When I think of what might have happened to a child, if it had been taken into slavery as well . . . But now I grieve that we have lost our chance. Of course, we are too old, in any case, but still, it would have been nice to have an heir. And now we never shall.'

I twined her fingers into mine, and gently voiced a thought I'd had before. 'Unless we were to adopt one, possibly?'

I saw her glance at Junio's sleeping form, and the ghost of a dawning smile lit up her face. 'Perhaps,' she murmured. She raised my fingers to her lips. 'We'll speak of this again.' But the shadow had departed and she snuggled close to me. 'In the meantime, husband,' she kissed my hand again, 'we may be far too old to make an heir, but surely we are not too old to try?'

I laughed softly, blew out the light and took her in my arms.